THE DISGRACED DEBUTANTE

The Notorious Nightingales Series

WENDY VELLA

The Disgraced Debutante is published by Wendy Vella

Sign up for my newsletter at www.wendyvella.com

Wendy's Books

The Raven & Sinclair Series
Sensing Danger
Seeing Danger
Touched By Danger
Scent Of Danger
Vision Of Danger
Tempting Danger
Seductive Danger
Guarding Danger
Courting Danger
Defending Danger
Detecting Danger

The Deville Brothers Series
Seduced By A Devil
Rescued By A Devil
Protected By A Devil
Surrender To A Devil
Unmasked By A Devil

The Langley Sisters Series
Lady In Disguise
Lady In Demand
Lady In Distress

The Lady Plays Her Ace

The Lady Seals Her Fate

The Lady's Dangerous Love

The Lady's Forbidden Love

Regency Rakes Series

Duchess By Chance

Rescued By A Viscount

Tempting Miss Allender

The Lords Of Night Street Series

Lord Gallant

Lord Valiant

Lord Valorous

Lord Noble

Stand-Alone Titles

The Reluctant Countess

Christmas Wishes

Mistletoe And The Marquess

Rescued By A Rake

The Notorious Nightingales

The Disgraced Debutante

This year we lost another loved one.
This book is for Cheryl, my mother-in-law,
and these are the words she left us with.

One day, my heart will cease to beat.
My life, once lived, will be complete.
I hope I've danced, I hope I've sung.
I hope I lived like I was young.
For those whose lives I got to know.
I hope they'll miss me with I go.

Chapter 1

Outside the carriage window, Ellen Nightingale saw London was now cloaked in fog as darkness slowly settled over the city. Night suited her. She liked to be concealed from the eyes of society. Not that she walked in their exalted ranks anymore and hoped never to again. Which was ironic, really, considering she lived not that far from the world she'd been raised in and yet it could be an entire continent away.

Opening the door above her head, she spoke to the driver.

"Are we near to home, Mungo?"

"Approaching the shops on the corner of Crabbett Close, Miss Ellen."

"Halt then, please."

The carriage rolled to a stop. Stepping down, Ellen looked up at the large man who sat on the driver's seat.

"Go home, Mungo. I shall walk the remaining distance."

"You'll not in this fog!" he barked back at her.

"It is a matter of a few feet. I wish to return my book

to Mr. Nicholson, as I promised him I would do so today." Ellen stared up at her family's driver, footman, and whatever else he was on any given day.

"I'll wait."

"I am unsure how long I will be. The horses will get cold if you wait. Besides, I have my umbrella."

She felt the weight of his gaze, even though she saw only his large outline through the fog.

"I'll return on foot to collect you, then. Stay in the shop until I arrive," he said in his broad Scottish brogue. "Your uncle would have my head were I to allow you to stroll about London at such a time and with the fog thick as it is tonight."

Ellen sometimes wondered who was the servant and who was the master in their relationship. In fact, he was this way with all their family, even Uncle Bram, his friend and employer.

"Oh, very well." She knew better than to argue with a man who was as malleable as English Oak. Of course, she did not utter those words, as the insult would be extreme due to his birthplace.

"Not one foot, Miss Ellen."

"For heaven's sake, Mungo, I have agreed to not leave the bookshop."

"You'll pardon me for wanting the reassurance, but considering your reckless need to charge into danger, I would like it."

"I am not reckless, and the single occasion you recount constantly was an accident."

"How is it an accident when you run from your family and into a melee, where a stray punch then knocked you to the ground before we could aid you?"

Ellen hissed out a breath. "I felt the need, as clearly that woman was in trouble." She raised a hand that he probably couldn't see and continued. "Before you resume your lecture, the bookshop is but a few feet."

"I will stay here until you reach your destination," Mungo said.

Ellen fought back the sigh and walked away. Thick fog wrapped its eery fingers around her as she made her way to Nicholson's Book Store. The tap of the heels of her sensible leather ankle boots were the only sounds in the air.

She knew to her right was the sign announcing Crabbett Close, where they lived. To the left were Nicholson's bookshop and Appleblossoms Bakers and beyond that Nitpicks Trinkets and Treasures.

Mr. Nicholson would be inside as he always worked well into the evening and welcomed visits from anyone passing.

Ellen swung her umbrella back and forth to avoid bumping into anything. Had she not walked in these conditions before, it would have been unnerving.

Peering up through the fog, she saw the sign announcing the bookshop, and the lamp George always kept lit in the window when darkness fell.

"I have reached my destination!" she called out loud enough for Mungo to hear.

"Well, get inside then!" came his reply.

The roll of carriage wheels told Ellen that he was finally moving.

The bookshop was a favorite of the Nightingale family. They were often found there perusing the shelves and discussing titles with George Nicholson.

Placing her foot on the first step, Ellen stopped as tension gripped her. The vision that followed was of a man lying on the floor with blood staining his white shirt.

George?

Taking the four steps up, she pushed the door open and entered.

Behind the counter was a boy who she did not recognize. On the other side, with his back to her, was another. Both appeared to be searching for something.

"Where is Mr. Nicholson?" Ellen demanded.

Both turned to look at her as she spoke.

"Not here," the lad closest said. He was clutching money to his chest. She could see the corner of the banknote sticking out between his palm and finger.

"Well, where is he? And why are you behind his counter?"

The boys ignored her questions and continued doing what they were, dismissing her at their peril. Ellen took the two steps forward to reach them. Raising her umbrella, she then rapped it with some force on the shoulder of the one closest.

It was reinforced with a metal rod after she'd snapped the last one on a man's head.

"Ouch!" He leapt back and glared at her. "What'd you do that for?"

"I demand an answer. Where is Mr. Nicholson?"

"Not here," the boy she'd struck muttered, rubbing the injured spot. "You need to leave."

"Why are you going through his things if he is not here?" Ellen ignored his words. "Are you stealing from him?"

"He's not been in here all day," the other boy said, his tone as belligerent as the other one's had been. "If he left the door open, that's his problem, and we're taking advantage of that. Now, a pretty lady like you should go before we decide to check what you have in that little bag around your wrist."

He raised his fists. Rather than be frightened, Ellen

stood her ground and stared calmly back. "I don't think so. You need to leave here at once. That is Mr. Nicholson's money, and I won't let you take it with you."

The boy came round the counter and stopped beside his friend before her. Ellen guessed they would be about her sister Fred's age, around thirteen, but it was hard to tell.

"Who's going to make us, then?" one of them said.

"Me." Ellen raised her umbrella, and the boys laughed. "It's wrong to steal from others. You should earn your own money."

"It ain't easy to earn money, and if it's there to be stolen, why not take it?"

"Because that's stealing and unlawful."

They charged her, and she jabbed the first in the stomach, then spun and struck the next on the cheek with the metal handle.

Curses filled the shop.

Stay on the balls of your feet. It's easier to face an attacker that way. Keep moving.

Uncle Bram's words had Ellen shifting her weight from foot to foot. The boys lunged again. This time she ducked and caught the first lad in the shins, sending him onto his knees. Straightening, she then jabbed the second in the stomach. The boy yelped as he doubled over.

"Let's go, Snippy!"

The one on the floor tried to crawl away. Ellen beat him to the door.

"Leave what you have in your hands here."

She heard money hitting the floor seconds later.

"Pockets," Ellen said.

Keeping an eye on her, they emptied them too. More clattered onto the boards. Ellen stepped aside, and they fled out and into the night.

She locked the door behind them. Walking around the shop, she saw no sign of Mr. Nicholson. The place was filled with shelves of books, each grouped by author and alphabetized. She noted some were thrown to the floor.

"Where are you, George?"

Taking the lamp in one hand and her umbrella still clenched in the other, she headed through the door that led to the rear. Tense and uncertain what she'd find, Ellen wished one of her family or Mungo was here. But if George was in trouble, she could not wait for them.

"You can do this."

Exhaling, she walked into the room. Her knees went weak with relief when she found only books and other supplies in the small space.

"Okay, that's good. No George," Ellen said. She headed for the stairs.

Perhaps it was not George Nicholson she had seen in the vision?

Walking up, the fourth step creaked, making her jump. Instead of fleeing, which everything inside her was urging Ellen to do, she entered another room. The first thing she encountered was a pair of feet in black leather polished shoes.

"George," she whispered. "Dear Lord, no."

Approaching, she knew instantly he was dead because it was just like her vision. Dropping to her knees, she reached with her gloved fingers and gently closed his eyes.

"I am so terribly sorry this has happened to you, dearest friend."

Ellen remembered the hours she'd spent in here discussing books. She bit back a sob as grief surged through her. Grief for the gentle man who had not deserved this fate.

Another vision of a hand holding a knife, the blade red with blood, flashed through her head. She sat there waiting to see if more came, but when it didn't, she looked around and found something trapped beneath George's body.

Easing him over, she pulled it out by the tips of her gloved fingers. Horror washed through her as Ellen realized what she was holding. Surely this wasn't her uncle's knife? Rising, she studied the intricately engraved silver handle. It was exactly like the one Uncle Bram owned, but why was it here and covered in blood that was likely George's?

Removing her handkerchief Ellen wrapped the blade. She then tucked the knife into her sleeve with trembling fingers. Picking up the lamp, she hurried back down the stairs. Opening the door, she walked out, locking it behind her. She then made her way through the thick fog once more. The chill seemed to have invaded her limbs, and pulling her coat tighter achieved little as it seeped deeper into her bones.

George, her friend, was dead.

Ellen had seen the hand of his killer but not the face. She had to get help and then hurry home to tell her family what she had found. Tell them that their beloved uncle's knife was under the dead body of George Nicholson.

Chapter 2

When she was clear of the shop and heading toward Crabbett Close, Ellen cupped her mouth and yelled, "Help!" She yelled a further three times as she walked home clutching her umbrella.

Mungo would hear and come running. She collided with something large and solid seconds later.

"Unhand me!" she screamed when the person grabbed her. Ellen tried to kick him, but he held her close. She couldn't get her umbrella free, as it was pressed between them.

"Let me go!"

"Stop. I mean you no harm," a deep voice said.

Hands wrapped around her shoulders and gave her a gentle shake. She was then released.

"Back away, or I will hurt you," Ellen said, now gripping her umbrella in both hands.

"You called for help, and I came. What has happened?"

"Who are you?" Ellen raised the umbrella as she took

two large steps away from him. "If you touch me again, I will strike at you."

"As you should, but as I have stated that I mean you no harm, you can stay your fears, madam. Now, why did you yell for assistance?"

Even in the dark foggy night air, she could see his size. A hat obscured his eyes, but that face seemed severe. Cheekbones hard ridges, mouth in a line. Dressed in a long black overcoat, he towered over her. A noise had her turning away from him.

Something bumped into Ellen, sending her stumbling backward into the man. He didn't move, simply steadied her, and she had the oddest sensation run through her. Almost like a shiver of awareness.

"My dear Miss Nightingale, forgive me."

"Quite all right," Ellen said, backing away once more from the dark stranger.

"Was that you who screamed for help?" Constable Plummy asked. "I was some distance away but ran to your aid immediately."

"Thank you."

His moustache was twitching, immaculate as always in his uniform of a blue tailcoat with his armlets, white gloves, and top hat. In his hand he held a truncheon. He looked exactly as he had this morning when she'd seen him walking the same route he took every day.

"Plummy, do you know this woman?" the man at his side asked.

"Oh, Detective Fletcher," Plummy said, as if just noticing the man. "What has you here?"

"Work, Plummy."

"Right. Of course. This is Detective Grayson Fletcher, Miss Nightingale. He is a highly regarded man of consequence, you understand." The reverence in Plummy's tone told her he was in awe of the detective.

"That will do, constable." The man's voice was deep and gruff like she sometimes sounded after a dreadful night's sleep. "What appears to be the problem, Miss Nightingale?" he enquired. "Are you perhaps lost?"

"No, I'm not lost."

"The fog is thick. It is easy to become disorientated," he said. "There is no shame in admitting you cannot find your way."

"I live not far from here," Ellen said, sounding impatient.

"It's reckless, madam, to be out in these conditions alone. People have been known to stumble into the Thames. Especially—"

"If you say a lady, Detective Fletcher, I will not be impressed. I am more than able to care for myself without a man at my side, and I'm fairly sure the Thames is some distance from my present location."

His lips twitched. It was fast and over in seconds, but she saw it. She amused him, which annoyed her further.

Ellen had spent a lot of her life being amusement to men. Someone to leer at and tolerate. However, that was no longer the case, and she would ensure it never would be again.

"Miss Nightingale, what appears to be the problem?" Constable Plummy said, the breath wheezing in and out of his mouth, which suggested he had indeed been some distance away.

"It is Mr. Nicholson, Constable Plummy. I fear he is dead," she said, ignoring the large, disturbing male who was watching her intently.

"Dead you say?" The constable straightened. "On my

watch? Are you sure, Miss Nightingale? The light is poor, and—"

"I know when a person is deceased, Constable Plummy. They stop breathing."

The Nightingales knew the constable well because he was completely enamored with their housekeeper. He was often found on their doorstep under some guise or other. Yesterday it was checking nothing was missing as there had been several burglaries in the area, which none of the Nightingales had heard about, and they heard most things going on in Crabbett Close.

"And how is it you are aware Mr. Nicholson is deceased, Miss Nightingale?" Detective Fletcher asked.

"Obviously, I saw him, Detective Fletcher," she snapped. Her nerves were stretched tight. The visions were enough to upset even the most rationally minded person, but there was also the knife tucked in her sleeve to worry about too.

"Your delicate womanly sensibilities will be distraught after such an encounter, Miss Nightingale. You must allow me to escort you home. Please take my arm."

She ignored the arm Plummy raised. "I am not delicate and neither are my sensibilities. I am more concerned over the fact that my dear friend appears to have been murdered. You both must go at once and care for his body. Then ensure the killer is caught."

"Murdered you say!"

It was dark, so she couldn't see the constable's face clearly, but there was little doubting his cheeks would now be pale.

"Yes, I did. Now surely you wish to find out what has happened?" She pulled the key from her pocket and waved it before him. "I took the liberty of locking the bookshop."

He blustered.

"There was a large amount of blood on his chest——"

"Blood you say!" Constable Plummy gasped.

"Plummy." Detective Fletcher took the key from her hand. "There is a dead body that needs our attention." Their gloved hands brushed briefly, and she had a vision of a boy standing over a grave wearing black, crying, a gold bird, and then it was gone.

Had it been him as a child?

"Two boys were in the bookshop rifling through Mr. Nicholson's belongings when I arrived. One wonders why you did not notice the disturbance on your walk, as surely it carries you past the bookshop, Constable Plummy?"

"Ah yes... well, as to that, I was otherwise occupied in my line of duty, you understand, Miss Nightingale?"

In Mrs. Pettigrew's Pie Shop no doubt.

"You will find Mr. Nicholson through the door at the rear of his shop," Ellen said.

"I will have more questions for you, Miss Nightingale," Detective Fletcher said. "But now Plummy will walk you home, and I will go to the bookshop and check on this body."

"Do you believe I am lying, sir?" Ellen felt the weight of the knife in her sleeve. They must not see it.

"I believe you are upset and likely saw something," he said in a tone that had her wanting to slap him.

"I know what I saw. Just as I know those two young boys were about to steal from Mr. Nicholson's st-store!" She heard the quiver in her voice and cursed it. This was not the time to mourn her friend. This was the time for action.

"There now." Constable Plummy patted her arm. "No need to be upset. We are here."

"I don't need you to be here for me," she gritted out. "I need you to do your job. Mr. Nicholson had blood all over his chest," Ellen snapped. "Go and see to him at once. Good evening, Constable Plummy." She then turned to walk away, but a hand stopped her.

"You are not going anywhere alone, especially if there is a murderer on the loose."

She shook off the detective's hand.

"I have been walking these streets for two years."

"Miss Ellen?"

"Here, Mungo," she said, relieved to hear his voice and thud of his feet to her right.

"I told you to stay until I reached the bookshop!" He appeared. "Who the hell are you?" He glared at the detective. They were the same height. Both large and intimidating.

"I-I couldn't."

"What's wrong, Miss Nightingale?"

Ellen clutched his arm, and his large fingers settled over her hand.

"Are you well?"

"I fear something terrible has happened, Mungo."

"What?"

"May I have your name, sir?" the detective asked.

"She's told you, Mungo," he snapped.

"It's Mr. Nicholson. I found him dead… murdered," Ellen said.

His curse was muttered under his breath. "I knew I shouldn't have let you go in there without me at such an hour."

"Take her home, and I will call soon," the detective said. "This is no place for a lady to be out walking alone." His tone suggested it was Mungo's fault. Ellen bristled.

Mungo tugged her with him as he walked away without saying another word.

"You found the body?" Mungo asked her.

"Yes."

"And you saw other things?"

"I did, yes." He knew what the Nightingales were. He'd lived with them long enough now to understand.

He must have known she was shaking, as he started singing in his lovely brogue, and she listened all the way home.

"Is that you, Mr. Mungo?" A voice said to their left.

"Aye, it is Mr. Greedy," Mungo called back. "Are you well?"

"Just sitting outside enjoying the fog."

"I'll leave you to that, then."

Mr. Greedy resided in Crabbett Close like the Nightingales did.

"Here we are." He led her up the six steps to the front door of her uncle's house. Large, three stories. It had several windows facing the street, and two were blazing with light. The Nightingales did not like to live in the dark.

"Come along, in you go." Mungo placed a hand on her spine and propelled her forward. He opened the front door, and Ellen stepped into the light.

Home, she thought. Not in the best street in London as her last house had been, but it was a great deal more comfortable and filled with love.

"I'm all right now, Mungo. 'Tis just the shock."

How had Uncle Bram's knife found its way to being under George's body? Who had used it to kill him?

Chapter 3

"Ellen, finally you are home." One of her sisters, Frederica, came tumbling down the stairs as Mungo and Ellen stopped in the front entrance to remove their outer clothing. With her was Chester, their large dog, who let out a loud woof when he saw her.

"You have been gone for hours."

At age thirteen, Frederica was full of youthful enthusiasm and not tainted by what had occurred to change their lives completely. She'd declared at a young age that her name was far too long, and she wanted to be called Fred. Her siblings had obliged, her parents had not.

"Surely not hours. I simply went to drop off some food to Miss Marron as she has been unwell and now have returned. Is it not story time?"

"Of course it is," Fred said. "But I thought to wait here for you as it was so foggy out there, and I was worried."

Taller than Ellen, who was the most vertically challenged, Fred had an abundance of brown hair that curled in several directions at once and sparkling brown eyes.

"Thank you for waiting, and I am well."

"No, you're not." Fred looked at the hand she had clutched around Mungo's arm. "What has happened? Why are you holding onto Mungo?"

"I am so sorry to tell you this, Fred, but Mr. Nicholson passed away, and the news has upset me. As you know, he was our friend."

"Oh no." Her eyes clouded with tears. "He was such a lovely man."

"He was," Ellen agreed.

"We had word from Uncle Bram that he, Aunty Ivy, and Lottie are due to return any day now. They will be sad too," Fred said.

Uncle Bram could not have killed George, even if he'd wanted to, which he absolutely would not. He was taking a trip through the Lake District with Aunt Ivy, his wife, and their daughter. It was Aunt Ivy's birthday, and the nieces and nephews he'd stepped in to care for upon his brother's death insisted they go away, just the three of them.

"We all long to see them. But now, off you go, Fred. You don't want to miss out on the next chapter of Lord Hazel's adventures. Tomorrow is soon enough to discuss this further. For now, I too wish to wash and rest."

Her sister didn't move her eyes from Ellen.

"She's well, don't fash, Miss Fred. Go on now and do as your sister asked, and tomorrow we can go to Mr. Nicholson's shop and place flowers outside."

Mungo's words had the desired effect, and her sister left after hugging Ellen. Chester stayed.

"Go with Fred, you great big beastie," Mungo said to the dog. He didn't move.

Mungo and Chester weren't exactly friends, and the dog knew that and seemed to go out of his way to annoy the Scotsman.

"He stole one of my boots this morning."

"Funny how he steals nothing from us," Ellen said. She kissed Mungo's cheek. "Thank you for sending Fred back upstairs. I had no wish to upset her with details of George's death. I shall clean up now. Please tell Leo and Alex to meet me in the parlor."

Big and brash, Mungo Fraser had no more than six years on Ellen but was a great deal more world-weary. He'd been with Uncle Bram since they'd returned from their travels many years ago. The hair on his head was as thick and wild as his beard and the color of sunset. His face was tanned, and he seemed to have boundless energy.

"Will you tell me what it is you are hiding, Miss Ellen?"

Not much slipped by him.

"How is it you know I am hiding anything from you, Mungo?"

"Because I know you." He moved to stand beside Chester. The dog shuffled slightly until he could lean on the Scotsman's leg. Then they both stared at her.

Mungo might say he didn't love Chester, but the Nightingales knew better.

"I was going to do it when I saw Leo and Alex."

"But you'll tell me now," he said.

"I fear it is the weapon that killed Mr. Nicholson." She removed the bloodstained knife from her sleeve. Unwrapping it, Ellen held it out for him.

He took it and examined it. "Where did you find this?"

"Under the body. The handle was sticking out. I removed it from the scene. It was wrong, Mungo," she rushed to add. "But I panicked because I'm sure it's Uncle Bram's."

"I would have done the same." Mungo patted her shoulder. "And aye, it looks like your uncle's. For now, this will be a secret that does not leave the house. Go on up and clean yourself. I'll take this and call for the tea."

"George had so much blood, Mungo. His white shirt was colored red with it."

"And you'll remember that for some time and no doubt have visions. You tell us now if you do."

She nodded.

"We both know your uncle couldn't have murdered George Nicholson, Miss Ellen. It seems someone may have wanted people to think otherwise."

Ellen nodded. "My thoughts as well."

"Go on with you up those stairs and change. I'll collect your brothers and have Bud bring tea."

Ellen did as he asked.

"You go with her, wee beastie," she heard Mungo say to Chester.

She looked over her shoulder and watched the dog follow the big Scotsman toward the kitchens.

The house was the first real home the Nightingale siblings had lived in. The previous one had been large, prestigious, and they'd never really felt comfortable in it. Her parents had ensured their children were always subdued and quiet. Appearances had been everything to the late Lord Seddon.

This home was very different. Scuff marks, toys and books, and often a coat or pair of shoes were found in the hall. The walls and cabinets held her uncle's collections from years of traveling around the world. 11 Crabbett Close was full of all the things they loved, including the people.

The walls were painted in rich colors and trimmed with gold. An enormous mirror was the last item hung on the walls before descending the stairs. Aunt Ivy said this was to ensure they could check their shoes matched.

Treading the green-and-gold carpet, she took the next

set of stairs up to the third floor. Her room was at the end of the hall.

Opening the door, she walked into her sanctuary. Painted in soft mint green, there was a long shelf attached to the wall holding all her favorite books. In the corner, a piano Uncle Bram had insisted on buying her. A window overlooked the street below, and when they'd first come here, Ellen had spent hours just sitting and looking at life going on outside.

She washed the blood from her hands and tried not to look at the color the water had gone. After a quick look in the mirror, Ellen was tidy, and she then left to face her family.

Leo and Alex were up here with her, and the next level held the younger members of their family and Uncle Bram and his wife. Taking the stairs down to the second floor, Ellen opened one door quietly and poked her head inside. She found her three younger siblings. They were reading with Bonnie, their nanny.

"Good night, everyone," Ellen said. They all replied, and then she left, closing the door again.

On the ground floor, she made for the parlor the family used to gather in and heard the voices as she approached.

All conversation stopped as she entered another room painted in a deep rich sapphire. Ellen saw her two older brothers and Mungo debating something. Chester was stretched out before the fire on the rug.

She welcomed the warmth from the fire that blazed in the hearth and headed for it.

"What has happened, Ellen?" Leopold asked. "Mungo said something has, but said he'd leave it to you to explain."

Ellen moved to the fire and held out her hands. Finally,

she felt some of the ice in her veins thaw as the heat warmed her.

"I'm well, Leo, as you see. It has been a trying evening, however."

He was the biggest. Broad-shouldered, hair darker than Ellen's blond locks. He wore a scowl most often and usually said exactly what he was thinking and damn the consequences. Once, he'd been a very different man.

"Well, tell us what happened then," he demanded.

"Leo, for pity's sake. If you will back up a step, she may," Alexander, next in line from Leo, said. He came closer and took her arm. As tall as his brother, he had brown hair and eyes, like Fred.

Tugging Ellen around Leo, he led her to a chair and then nudged her down into it.

Even-tempered, gentle for the most part, and the peacemaker in the Nightingale family, Alex braced his hands on the seat he'd lowered her into.

"Are you well, Ellen?"

"I am unharmed, Alex." She patted his cheek.

"Here now, she needs a cup of tea. You lot leave her alone until she's got that," Miss Bud said, entering the room with a huge tray, which Mungo took off her and placed on a small table before Ellen.

Mungo and Miss Bud, or Bud as she insisted they call her, were the only two staff in the household who knew all there was to know about the Nightingales. Where Mungo was tall, Bud was short, close to Ellen's height. Slender with a head of long black curls she pulled back in a severe bun. They'd never been able to guess her age. Her nature was no-nonsense, and no one disobeyed her.

Constable Plummy adored her, but she had no interest in him. However, he was not to be deterred.

Tea was served, and plates filled with food, and then Miss Bud left.

"Now, speak," Leo growled.

"I went to drop off a book to Mr. Nicholson that I had loaned and found two boys in the bookshop." Ellen went through everything she'd seen.

"And you are sure he was murdered?" Alex asked.

"Yes. I saw him lying dead, also a hand holding a bloodstained knife. But seeing him with blood all over his chest would have alerted me," Ellen said.

"Yet more visions for you to live with, sister dear," Alex said.

"I'm all right, and it is no different for any of us."

"Some see more than others," Leo said. "Now tell us what you are hiding and what you have seen inside that pretty head of yours."

Ellen shot Mungo a look. He nodded.

"I found Uncle Bram's knife under George's body."

"We think it's his," Mungo amended. Pulling it from his waistband, he lowered it to the table before them, now clean of blood, next to the tea tray. It seemed more sinister in the room's light.

"It certainly looks like the one Uncle Bram brought back with him from his travels," Alex added.

"It was covered in blood under the body," Ellen said.

The Nightingales had suffered a lot in their lives since the death of their father and the disgrace that followed. The society they'd coveted had turned their collective backs on the children of the late perfidious Lord Seddon. They had been left grieving and alone.

It had been their father's younger brother, Bramstone, and his wife, Ivy, who had stepped in to support them. After removing them from London, he and Aunt Ivy had taken them to the country to heal. Only when he believed they were strong enough, did he return them to London, and this house.

"Ellen, it will be all right, as will Uncle Bram." Leo put an arm around her, sensing her worry. "No one but us knows about the knife, and we will keep it that way. With our talents, we will ensure he is not found guilty."

Ellen sniffed and pressed her face into her brother's chest. They would do what must be done, no matter the consequences. They were not called the Notorious Nightingales for nothing.

Chapter 4

Gray walked along Crabbett Close four mornings after meeting Ellen Nightingale. That night had been foggy, but his first impression of her had been clear. Beautiful and feisty. After some preliminary investigating of the case, he was now ready to speak with her again.

The anticipation he felt surprised him. Gray rarely got excited about anything, but he wanted to see her in the light of day. See if he'd imagined her beauty or if it had been a figment of a fog-shrouded night. But it was more than just her face that intrigued him. It was rare that a woman challenged him as she had.

Crabbett Close had a mix of homes. Some connected behind an iron fence that ran their length. Then there were the larger ones, like he was sure the Nightingale family lived in. The street looped at the end and circled a large park. Trees lined it on the side he walked, and through them he could see a handful of children playing.

"Good day to you, Detective Fletcher. What has you in Crabbett Close again?"

"Good day to you, Miss Alvin." Gray tipped his hat to

the elderly lady who was sitting on her doorstep in a rocking chair. She was wrapped in layers of shawls, and on her head was a tattered nightcap, or so he thought it was, as his mother had worn something similar. His guess was it was once white, but now it was gray and the lace torn around the edges.

"You'll not be after our Nightingales, is my hope? We don't like people who harangue them. They're good folk."

Behind her, the front door was open, and he saw the hall was lined with things, but Gray could not make out what.

"I make it a daily goal never to harangue anyone unless absolutely necessary, Miss Alvin," he said with as much gravity as he could muster.

When he'd knocked on Miss Alvin's door two days ago to make enquiries, she told him he needed to mind his business and that the Nightingales were wonderful people. She'd then shut the door in his face, so he'd not even been able to question her about George Nicholson.

"I know about you," she said, glaring at him out of rheumy eyes.

"Do not revile the king even in your thoughts or curse the rich in your bedroom because a bird in the sky may carry your words, and a bird on the wing may report what you say" came a voice from inside the house.

"Aye, Mr. Alvin, you've the right of it," Miss Alvin called to her brother, who was presumably nearby.

"I have no idea what that means," Gray said.

"It means a bird told me, and you should know that being one of them detectives," she hissed. "You need to read the bible and Ecclesiastes 10:20 specifically. Now off with you and leave our Nightingales alone."

"I mean them no harm."

She harrumphed, and he thought that was possibly his cue to depart, so he did.

"This is a very odd place," Gray muttered.

It was to number 11 Crabbett Close that he was heading. Reaching it, he climbed the three steps, then back down one and up again. He then knocked on the door twice.

Someone opened it minutes later.

"Detective Grayson Fletcher from Scotland Yard," Gray said, handing over his card to the huge Scotsman standing in the doorway. They'd met briefly four nights ago, and the man Ellen Nightingale called Mungo hadn't been impressed with him then either. In fact, no one in this street appeared to be.

"And what is it you'll be wanting?" The man's brows were like hedgerows and drawn together over bright blue eyes.

"To question Miss Nightingale," Gray said calmly. You didn't get to where he had in his career and life without being able to handle difficult people. His strength had always been the ability to remain calm in all situations. The residents he'd spoken to in Crabbett Close had admittedly challenged that.

"About?" the Scot thundered.

"The body she found. What she first saw upon entering Mr. Nicholson's establishment, and a few other questions that I would rather direct to her than you."

The man glared. Dressed in black trousers and a navy jacket, he wore a white shirt and necktie. He had the appearance of a gentleman, but that thick neck and those beefy hands suggested he could behave otherwise, if required. Which didn't bother Gray. He wasn't a gentleman either, no matter that he'd been born one.

"If you don't let me in, you are obstructing a murder investigation, sir."

"Mungo," the man snapped.

"God bless you," Gray said.

"It's my name," the Scot snarled.

He'd known that, of course, but it wasn't his nature to go easy on people if they didn't go easy on him.

"Well, Mungo, may I please speak to Miss Nightingale?"

The woman who had shown no fear over the fact she'd just found a dead body or that she was alone on a foggy night. He'd gotten close enough to her to see her face clearly. Gray had thought her beauty would be intimidating to some but not him. The woman had come to his nose, but her courage had been a great deal bigger.

Gray was sure Ellen Nightingale wouldn't be anything like the intriguing woman he'd believed her to be that night, but still. He wanted to see her.

"You'll wait here, and I'll see if Miss Ellen can speak with you."

"It would be in her best interest to do just that," Gray said pleasantly. Yet another door was slammed in his face, and he was left to cool his heels on the doorstep.

He'd heard stories about the Nightingale siblings since he'd started his enquiries. Ellen Nightingale had, after all, been the one to find the body, so he couldn't discount the possibility that she was the murderer.

He'd spoken to one man who manned the flower cart not far from the bookshop where Mr. Nicholson had been found dead. He had called them the Notorious Nightingales. Gray asked why. The answer had been "You'd need to speak to those who live in Crabbett Close to understand." Intrigued, Gray had done just that.

Each door he knocked on was opened with a smile,

and then when he'd mentioned he was looking for information about the Nightingales and Mr. Nicholson, the smiles fell. Doors were then politely yet firmly shut in his face. One Mr. Peeky who lived at 2 Crabbett Close had told him to mind his business. He'd added that the Nightingales were good folk and he should go in search of real criminals, and not waste his time on folk who weren't.

It had been extremely odd. Few were willing to shut a door in the face of a detective from Scotland Yard, but they had. One man simply said, "The Nightingales are the very best of people," before slamming his door.

He'd only knocked on five, as the response was always the same. No information was forthcoming.

Looking up at the walls of the Nightingales' red brick home, he thought it appeared a pleasant enough abode. If he leaned to the right, he could see in a large bay window. He didn't, of course. Gray didn't behave in a manner that might draw attention.

The gardens were weeded and yet planted haphazard with very little structure. He'd entered through a black iron gate and a brick fence that matched the house and bordered the property.

Leaning back slightly, he studied the top windows. Which room was hers? Miss Ellen Nightingale? The door handle rattled, and he straightened.

"Very well. Come this way, but I'll not stand for you upsetting her," Mungo said.

"The woman I met four nights ago did not appear someone who could be overly upset."

Mungo grunted and walked away, which Gray guessed was his cue to follow. He looked about him, which he always did, taking in his surroundings. Searching for clues as to the personalities of those that lived within the walls of number 11 Crabbett Close. A murderer could reside here, after all.

Deep, rich colors lined the walls. His booted feet sank into thick rugs. He saw a large mirror and a few paintings, plus a cabinet.

"A very nice interior," he said.

Mungo ignored him. He then opened a door and waved Gray inside.

"Miss Ellen will join you shortly."

"Excellent, it's my hope she does," he said with a smile that did not reach his eyes and his colleagues would interpret to mean he would not tolerate anyone obstructing his investigation.

Mungo left without further comment, and Gray wandered around the room. Wide windows drew him to look down upon a small garden. He found two older children he guessed were Matilda and Theodore. Gray had done his research, of course. He'd be a fool not to know exactly who he was about to meet.

What surprised him were the facts he'd uncovered.

Miss Ellen Nightingale. Eldest daughter of the late Viscount Seddon, who took a gun and shot himself when his debts had reached a point where he was to lose everything. He left behind a wife who now lived in the country at the only estate entailed. The family were left without funds as every penny had gone to paying the late Viscount's gambling debts.

Ellen had also been engaged to Lord Lester, a man old enough to be her grandfather, but he'd gotten cold feet once the state of the Nightingale finances was exposed. As far as Gray was concerned, this revealed the man to be a weak-kneed fool. To have walked away from a woman like Ellen Nightingale if everything he'd heard about her was accurate was cowardly.

Then there was the aunt and uncle. Bramstone and Ivy Nightingale. He'd learned from a source they had taken in their nieces and nephews and were still living together as a family.

Moving around the room, he came to a small side table. Farm animal figurines were scattered about on it in a random fashion.

Gray didn't like things scattered random or otherwise. Picking them up, he lined the horses facing the cows and the ducks facing the pigs. There was an odd number of cows, so he brought a horse over to join its bovine friends. Satisfied when everything was symmetrical in even rows, he walked on to a painting, which was hanging crooked. He straightened it.

"Detective Fletcher."

Gray looked to the doorway. Framed in it was Ellen Nightingale and a large white dog with black circles around his eyes at her side.

Something inside him tightened as he looked at her and then eased. Indigestion perhaps? He had eaten two slices of apple cake before coming here.

"Miss Nightingale." He bowed as she walked into the room.

She wore a deep blue and black checked dress. The bodice formed to a vee with the fitted top accentuating her small waist. The skirts were full to the floor. He could see why she was once considered a darling of the ton. Golden blond hair was pulled into a bun at the back of her head like most women wore and the front was pinned to the side. Deep blue, almost indigo, eyes were framed with long curling lashes and delicate arched brows. Her mouth was a cupid's bow.

His first impression of four nights ago had been accurate. She was exceptionally beautiful.

"Detective Fletcher, please take a seat. This is our dog, Chester."

He looked around them. "Is anyone joining you, Miss Nightingale?"

"The door is open, and my dog will attack if I command him to do so. If you are waiting for a chaperone, you'll have a long wait. Sit, Detective."

Gray looked at the dog. His mouth was open and tongue hanging out. He clicked his fingers, and it trotted over to him and sat on his foot.

"Appearances are not always what they seem," Ellen Nightingale said. "He is, of course, a dog that loves people, but he is always protective." This time she flicked her fingers, and the dog got off his foot, and blood started to circulate once more.

He waited for her to take the seat across from him and then sat too. She did not fuss with her skirts, simply placed her ungloved hands together in her lap. The dog collapsed, his legs seeming to give way at her feet.

There was little doubting to anyone looking at her she was the daughter of a nobleman, even one who had fallen on hard times. It was there in the elevated chin and erect posture. Her back did not touch the chair, and her ankles were neatly placed beside each other.

"I had expected a visit from Scotland Yard earlier than this, Detective Fletcher." Her tone held censure.

Grayson had a feeling Scotland Yard did not rank high in this woman's favor.

"I was investigating the case before I came to see you, Miss Nightingale, as you can imagine. It is a complex matter."

"Really? I am not sure how it could be too complex. After all, George was murdered. Yes, we don't know who did it but surely someone bent on nefarious intentions. As I found him, I concluded that I should be one of the people interviewed?"

Few could get the upper hand with Gray. He'd been raised by a tyrant and had a lot of his traits. His standard response was always to say a case was complex, and until today, no one had called him on that.

"Please walk me through what happened that night once more, Miss Nightingale," he said instead of "I know exactly what I'm doing, you little baggage."

She nodded regally and began. Gray could smell her scent, or something flowery and subtle, which was surely her, as no window was open.

"Halt!"

They both looked to the doorway. A tall man stood there, and the resemblance to the woman seated across from him suggested it was a brother. He was stalking into the room with a face that said murder would not be out of the question. Gray's murder.

He stomped closer. The dog rose at the same time, and they collided. Lord Seddon tried to leap over the rising animal and managed it just. He then staggered slightly and came to a halt inches from the fireplace.

"Nice save," his sister said.

Chapter 5

"You," the angry brother stated, pointing a finger at her, "should not be alone in a room with him." He jabbed the finger Gray's way.

Chester, deciding to give the angry man a wide berth, wandered to Gray again and collapsed, placing his chin on one of his boots.

"Oh, for pity's sake, Leo. The door is open, and I am merely recounting what happened the other night and nothing more. Don't be dramatic," Miss Nightingale said, rolling her eyes.

"I don't want you sitting in a room with a man and no one else, Ellen. Also, I have no wish for you to be interrogated without me, Alex, or Mungo present."

Leopold Nightingale, Viscount Seddon, stalked to his sister's side. Long-legged and Gray thought some would say handsome. He wore the dress of the gentleman he was.

"Chester was here."

"Chester couldn't terrorize a mouse, as you very well know."

Gray raised a brow at Miss Nightingale. She ignored him, so he regained his feet and bowed. "Lord Seddon."

Miss Nightingale laughed, and the sound was like a set of bloody bells it was so sweet.

"There is no need to be amused, sister dear. The title may be worthless, but I still hold it." Leopold gave her a small smile.

"Detective Grayson Fletcher, I believe," the man said.

Gray nodded. They had no idea who he was. He relaxed.

"Leo, there is no need for you to be here. Detective Fletcher is simply asking me a few questions, not a threat to my virtue, and clearly, he has done extensive digging because he knows who we are."

At the mention of her virtue, Gray had a sudden and unwelcome image of this woman naked in his bed, her golden hair over his pillow as she looked up at him adoringly. His body stiffened, and he willed the surge of lust away by thinking of his late Aunt Melinda's jowls.

"And yet I have no wish for you to be alone in a room with a man I do not know. Any man."

At least one of the Nightingale siblings worried about her reckless nature.

"Continue," Lord Seddon said, which made his sister's lips tighten.

Gray had a feeling he'd said it in that exact tone so he'd get that response. Siblings, he'd often noted, liked to annoy each other. Gray didn't speak to his brothers, so that was not something he understood anymore, but once they'd been close enough to annoy each other.

"Please carry on with your story, Miss Nightingale," Gray said.

Her brother sat on the arm of her chair, which highlighted how similar they were when close. He also read the subtle warning that Leopold would suffer no one upsetting or intimidating his sister because he was right there at her side.

"The two boys you encountered, Miss Nightingale," Gray said when she'd finished. "Do you see them as being responsible for the murder of Mr. Nicholson?"

"No. They just saw an opportunity to steal what was not theirs and took it," she said.

"And you can be sure of this how?"

She hesitated, and her brother patted her shoulder. Gray felt like he'd missed something but had no idea what.

"I can't be sure. It is just my observation. They were intent on taking the money from the box under the counter where Mr. Nicholson kept it. I doubt they would have appeared so calm when I entered if they had seen that body, as I had. It was not something I am likely to forget."

She was remarkably composed considering what she'd seen, as she had been the night he'd heard her scream help.

Nicholson had been murdered, his face contorted in horror, and while Gray had seen such scenes before, you never got used to it. Especially not a gently bred lady.

"And you closed Mr. Nicholson's eyes?"

"I did. He was my friend," she said simply. She then snapped her fingers. "Snippy. One boy was called that."

"You're sure."

"Yes, I am." Her tone suggested she was insulted Gray doubted her.

"You did not seem overly upset at seeing the dead body of your friend, if you don't mind me saying so, Miss Nightingale." Gray was good at interrogating people. He was usually called in if they had a particularly difficult person who would not tell them what they needed.

"What are you suggesting, Detective Fletcher?" her brother demanded.

"Just because I was raised in society does not mean I fall about the place at the first sign of blood or murder," Ellen Nightingale said. "I gave up simpering and having fits of vapors many years ago."

"Most men would not cope with seeing what you did," Gray said.

"That's because most men are weak."

Her brother rolled his eyes at that.

"Have you seen a body before, Miss Nightingale?"

He'd thought she'd shake her head, but instead to his surprise, she nodded.

"My father shot himself, as you know, Detective Fletcher. It was me who found him."

Christ. He'd seen people who'd been shot in the head. That she'd found her father after he'd done that to himself must have left a stain on her memory.

"I'm sorry for your loss. It was not my intention to insult or upset you," Gray said, wishing he'd been aware of that piece of information. Clearly it was not common knowledge, as no one he'd spoken to about this family had mentioned her being the one to find the late Lord Seddon.

"Thank you," she said in an icy tone, which he guessed was something she'd learned to do to disguise the hurt. Gray understood building walls. He'd erected a few himself over the years.

"If that is all, Detective Fletcher, I'll ask you to leave before you upset my sister further," Lord Seddon said.

Had he not still been watching, he wouldn't have noticed the moment Ellen Nightingale's eyes dulled and her gaze became fixed. Her brother, however, was instantly aware that something was off with his sister. He put a hand on her shoulder again and squeezed. It was several seconds before Miss Nightingale blinked, and when her eyes returned to his, they were focused and alert once more.

"Are you all right, Miss Nightingale?"

She nodded. "Why would I not be?"

"You appeared to go into a trance of some sort," Gray said.

She forced out a laugh. "I certainly did not."

"You did." Gray studied her.

"I have no idea what you are accusing my sister of again, Detective Fletcher, but I assure you I will not tolerate it," Leopold Nightingale said, sounding every inch the viscount he was. "Firstly, you wanted to know why Ellen was not more upset than she appeared over seeing George Nicholson's body. Now you are accusing her of lying about a trance of all the absurd things."

Gray was sure the man was trying to divert his attention, but he kept his eyes on Ellen Nightingale. She did not look away or flinch. Her expression remained cool, but she was paler now. Almost white. He remembered seeing someone else look exactly as she just had throughout his childhood.

"I had an aunt who used to slip into a trancelike state as you just did, Miss Nightingale. She called them her moments," Gray said. "It wasn't until later in life I understood them."

"Moments?" She smiled, but it didn't reach her eyes.

"My aunt was eccentric," Gray said. "She—"

"Ah, of course," she interrupted him. "A lady is always thought eccentric when they exhibit signs that are in any way different from what society dictates or sees as normal."

She had a point. Gray had never understood his aunt, and it was only when he was older that he'd talked to her about her moments and begun to understand perhaps she saw things others didn't.

Aunt Tilda's family kept her away from society due to her "moments," and to his shame, he'd not stood up for her even when he was old enough to do so.

"Your face changed, Miss Nightingale," he persisted.

"I assure you, I was just thinking about the bodies of Mr. Nicholson and my father. The memories are fresh, but I'm sure they will fade."

He looked at her brother, whose brows were drawn together and large fists clenched on his thighs. Gray backed off for now.

"Give yourself time, Miss Nightingale. The images will ease but never completely."

"You sound knowledgeable on the matter, Detective Fletcher," she said.

"It is the nature of my job that I have seen murder victims before, Miss Nightingale."

"Of course."

"Is your uncle home?"

Both siblings subjected him to a hard stare, and the temperature in the room dropped several degrees. Had he been anyone else, like that bumbling fool Plummy, he might be intimidated. Gray was not. He simply stared back.

"He is traveling with our aunt, his wife, and their daughter," Leopold said.

"And when do you expect their return?"

"Soon," Ellen Nightingale said. "Why do you need to speak with him?"

"How well did you know the deceased George Nicholson, Miss Nightingale?" Gray asked instead of answering their question.

"Very well. He and I talked regularly about literature or the latest book of Captain Broadbent and Lady Nauticus."

Gray didn't pinch the bridge of his nose, but the need was there. He'd never understood the craze that swept London about those books. Plenty of his colleagues read and loved them.

"Did you meet his family?"

"Only his sister once. She was in the bookshop when I called one day," Miss Nightingale said.

"Did you know much about Mr. Nicholson?"

"I'm not sure why we would," Lord Seddon said.

"This is a murder investigation, my lord. I am attempting to investigate by asking questions," he said.

Gray had excellent instincts, and something was off here. He just couldn't put his finger on what.

"Well, I think you are finished with your inquisition here, Detective Fletcher?" Lord Seddon regained his feet, every inch the aristocrat he should be. He then held out a hand for his sister to join him. It was clear they were close and protective of each other. Gray experienced a tug of something that horrified him when he realized it was longing.

He had no one that made him feel this strength of emotion. His work was his life, and he'd always believed that was enough.

"Chester, let the detective rise," Lord Seddon said.

"It is not an inquisition," Gray said with a calm he was far from feeling. Being in this house near Ellen and Leopold Nightingale should have been a straightforward interview. It was turning out to be anything but.

"Yes, well, whatever it is, are you done?" Ellen said. Her face was a closed off mask.

"For now," he said.

The large dog got to his feet with a grunt and went to Ellen and Lord Seddon. Gray rose too, then bowed. "If you can think of anything more from that night or your dealings with Mr. Nicholson, I would be grateful if you contacted me." He handed her his card.

He held it in the middle, so her fingers brushed his when she took it. Both gloveless. The contact shot up his arms, and because his eyes were on her, he saw the moment she flinched.

It should not have made him happy that he wasn't the only one who felt something when they touched, but it did.

"Good day to you both."

The siblings nodded but did not follow him from the room. When Gray reached the street, he took his first deep breath. There was something deeply disturbing about Ellen Nightingale but even more so was his reaction to her.

Was she like his aunt? The rational part of Gray's mind said that was not possible and yet his aunt had convinced him otherwise. That look on Ellen's face had reminded him of Aunt Tilda.

Was he imagining things?

Chapter 6

"Bud, do you know I think your apple cobbler is superior to any I've eaten before?" Teddy said from his position seated on the floor with his back against Ellen's chair.

"And yet, you're not getting anymore," Leo said.

The Nightingale family was in their favorite parlor after their evening meal. Once, they would have been preparing to go out, but now they played games or lounged around furniture reading.

Ellen's brothers sometimes left the house to find entertainment. She'd told them once she'd wanted to go. Leo had laughed, explaining that their circumstances might have changed, but she'd not enter a drinking or gambling establishment while he still had breath in his body.

"Why can't I have more cobbler, Leo?" Teddy asked.

"Because I want the last piece," Leo said. "But we will share."

Theodore was sixteen, and still growing into his body. He tripped over most things, and especially his feet. His hair was darker, and he had Ellen's eyes. He was also the mischievous Nightingale, and constantly tormented his younger sisters.

Once he had confided in Ellen that he liked this life better than the last one, as it was a great deal more fun. Mainly because his elder siblings were around a lot more and spent time with him, where once they hadn't.

Teddy, Matilda and Fred knew they'd left their mother behind in the country and their father was dead, but had been given no other details of what occurred, and they were determined to keep it that way until they were adults.

"I think Detective Grayson Fletcher could be a problem."

"What?" Ellen put her finger on the page she'd been reading so she knew where she was. "He is surely just doing his job?"

Leo was seated before the fire watching Alex and Fred, who were playing checkers at his feet. Matilda sat on the sofa reading beside Ellen, sideways, with her legs wrapped over the arm. Chester had his head in her lap, having his ears ruffled.

"He's dangerous. There's something about him that sets my teeth on edge," Leo said.

There was something about him, and she'd felt it that night she'd found Mr. Nicholson. Detective Fletcher was far too handsome and disturbing.

Ellen did not like the flutter she'd experienced in her belly when their fingers had touched. It was a good thing that she would not see the man again.

"How can a detective who Plummy said is one of the most respected in Scotland Yard cause us trouble?" Alex asked. "Surely he will find who murdered George Nicholson, and it will absolve Uncle Bram?"

"Plummy is a fool who knows little about anything," she scoffed. "And as yet, I'm unsure what the detective is."

"But our local constable is an excellent font of information. After all, Plummy is an even bigger gossip than many we encountered in society. I saw him today and questioned him about Fletcher," Alex said.

"What did he say?" Ellen asked. Not because the detective had intrigued her but because it was always good to know who you were dealing with.

"Plummy said the man was difficult to pry anything out of."

"Now that doesn't surprise me," Leo said. "He had a way about him that suggested he kept his secrets close. Arrogant too."

"He sounds exactly like you, Leo," Ellen said.

"Very amusing."

"Who did that?" Fred had risen from the floor, and was pointing to the side table where she always left her farm figurines.

They all looked and saw the neat rows.

"Not me," Ellen said. The others shook their heads. Her thoughts went to Detective Fletcher. Could he have done it?

A tap on the door had Bud appearing.

"I think it's bedtime. Harriet is waiting for you three upstairs."

"We are hardly children anymore," Matilda said. "If we were in society, I would be presented at court soon."

"How lucky for society we are not then," Leo mocked her. "Now off you go. Yes, even you, Teddy. You can read the girls a story."

There were groans and debates, but eventually the younger Nightingales left, leaving peace to settle on the parlor. That was until Mungo appeared.

"Mr. Douglas has called and is in need of our help, my lord."

"Why must you 'my lord' me, Mungo? Leo, Leopold, or Master Leo if you must, but my lord isn't necessary."

"You're a bloody lord, so I'll put a 'my' in front of it," the Scotsman said, glaring at Leo. "Now, if you're done telling me what to do, Mr. Douglas is waiting for you at the back door." He then stormed from the room.

"Such a winning personality has our Mungo," Alex said. "He's like a little ray of sunshine."

"Sunshine!" Leo and Ellen yelled, getting to their feet. "What did Teddy say we had to do this week when someone said sunshine?" Leo asked.

"Hop for four," Alex sighed. "But as he is not in the room, perhaps we could forgo?"

"He'll know," Ellen said.

The Nightingale children had only ever had one tradition that they still followed from when Fred, Matilda, and Teddy were young.

Matilda had been a sickly child. Fred had told her once she must choose a word each week for the Nightingale siblings to use in a sentence. Leo had added that whoever selected the word also chose what actions they must carry out when it was spoken. Many years later, they were still doing this game.

"Get moving, Alex," Leo said.

He hopped toward the door with Leo and Ellen on his heels. They then left the room looking like the children of the viscount they'd been raised to be.

Walking under the stairs, they made for the back door. Even though they'd told locals to come through the front one, none of them did. Passing the kitchens that always smelled delicious, she found Bud at the open door talking to Mr. Douglas from number 24 Crabbett Close.

"Good evening to you, Mr. Douglas," Ellen said. "What has you here at such an hour?"

The man had tugged off his cap. Gray tufts of hair stood off his head, and the worry was clear in his lined face. He and his family had lived here for many years. Now that all but one of their six children had left, the home was usually filled with grandchildren and baking smells. The three youngest Nightingales spent a lot of time there.

"My Sally's girl, Penny, has gone missing, Miss Nightingale."

"How long has she been missing?" Leo asked.

"She didn't come home from work the day before yesterday."

"Penny is the seamstress, or is that Lolly?" Ellen asked. Since moving into Crabbett Close, the Nightingales had learned what it was like to have neighbors that wanted you to be part of their lives.

"That's our Penny. She's not one to worry her mother, so this is out of character for her. She'd never do this to her family. It's that scoundrel who's behind it. I'm sure."

"Scoundrel?" Alex asked.

"Barney Forge, he's a young lout from Smiley Street. Lad has been bothering Penny. Said he likes her, but she didn't feel the same. Five nights ago, he stood outside my Sally's house and yelled at Penny. Said she'd be sorry if she didn't pay him attention," Mr. Douglas said.

"Is there a chance she could be with friends or went somewhere else, Mr. Douglas?" Ellen asked.

He shook his head, his hands worrying the brim of his cap. "Penny always comes home from work each day at the same time to take tea with her ma. She'd have told her if she wasn't. I went to her work, and they were worried Penny hadn't come in because it's not like her, and she's their best seamstress."

The Nightingale siblings had found out quickly when

they'd moved into their aunt and uncle's house that the people in Crabbett Close didn't keep to themselves. Residents had started knocking on their back door the day after they'd arrived. They'd been dropping off baking, meals, and other items ever since.

The week they'd arrived had also been the week the Samuel twins from 7 Crabbett Close had been abducted by their father, who had recently left prison. Desperate, the residents had taken turns going out to look for the boys, but no one had found them.

A vision had alerted Ellen where to start searching.

"Where else have you looked, Mr. Douglas?" Alex asked.

"I've been to his house, that Barney Forge. He wasn't there, but his father was and told me to leave when I started accusing his son of harming my Penny. The man has two other boys. They were there too. Right intimidating the three of them, and I left before they made me."

Mr. Douglas wasn't young and could easily have been hurt by three younger men. The thought of anyone harming this lovely, kind man did not sit well with Ellen.

"We're all worried. Her father has been out looking too but so far nothing."

"Then we will come and help you find her, Mr. Douglas," Alex said. "Is it possible to visit Penny's house first? So we can start where she lives in our investigations?"

"Of course." Mr. Douglas wasn't surprised by Alex's request. "We can collect something of hers from there for you, Miss Ellen."

While that statement might seem odd to anyone not from Crabbett Close, it wasn't for its residents. Mr. Greedy had called them the Notorious Nightingales once, and the name had not gone away. Their reputation had been embellished over time because they had helped many people in need.

Their neighbors knew they were different and had no issue with that. In fact, they embraced it and showered the Nightingales with support and love, plus taffy cake, a particular favorite of the entire family.

"'Tis a thirty-minute walk if you wish to call a carriage," Mr. Douglas said.

"No indeed," Alex said. "We love a good evening walk."

"Since our little Sydney passed, it's been hard on Sally. If Penny—"

"Sydney is your grandson who died?" Alex asked.

Mr. Douglas nodded.

"We will be with you shortly," Leo said. "We just need to collect our coats."

The siblings ran back up the stairs and to their rooms. Ellen grabbed her umbrella and pulled on her thick black wool coat. Tying her bonnet in place, she then picked up her gloves and left the room at a run.

Nightingales competed over everything these days, and beating her brothers back down the stairs was no exception. Jumping the last three stairs, Ellen ran to the door. Her brothers were already waiting for her.

"Ready?" Leo asked, smirking.

"What took you so long, sister dear?"

She elbowed Alex in the stomach as she passed him and out the door.

"That will do," Mungo said, already dressed and waiting outside.

"Lead the way, Mr. Douglas," she said.

"Stay alert," Leo said falling in behind him. He swung his cane back and forth with every step.

Alex was at Ellen's side, with Mungo behind them. She'd walked these roads many times in the daylight hours, but at night, they took on a more sinister air. Especially with the fog beginning to swirl around their ankles.

Gossip had a way of reaching all corners of London. It had not taken long for the residents of Crabbett Close to learn the Nightingales were children of a viscount. It had humbled them when no one treated them differently.

"Step left," Leo said.

Ellen raised her skirts and stepped around the large pile of manure.

It wasn't late, and the streets were still full of people. Some returning home. Vendors still selling their wares.

"I say—"

"No," Ellen said. "We are not stopping for more food. The matter is clearly urgent, Leo."

"I didn't even finish my sentence."

"I know you two. You're both always hungry."

Her brothers muttered something, and they continued on.

The road they turned into thirty minutes later was narrower than Crabbett Close. The houses were smaller and stepped out their front doors directly onto the street.

Once, she'd never have contemplated walking about at any time of the day in a street like this one. Ellen and her brothers would be preparing for their evening's entertainment at this hour. She would have spent a night chatting with her friends, dancing, and flirting.

A memory of her laughing with Dorrie, Somer, and Samantha slipped into her head. Her friends would have been worried when she disappeared, and she'd made no effort to send word she was all right. The tug of guilt had her wondering if it was time to write that letter. Time to tell them she was well. They were perhaps the only three women who had been her true friends.

No. No good could come of thinking about them and the life she'd once lived. Parts of this life were so much better, and parts... far worse.

Chapter 7

"My daughter lives here." Mr. Douglas's words snapped Ellen out of her contemplation. They had stopped by a door. No steps up or gate to unlatch.

The Nightingales stood back, Mungo behind them, while Mr. Douglas knocked. It was flung open seconds later, and a pale-faced, small woman stood there. Light from behind her showed she was tearful.

"Have you found her, Pa?"

"I've not, Sally. But I've brought help so we do."

"Good evening." Ellen moved closer. "I am Ellen, and these are my brothers, Leo and Alex. With us is our friend, Mungo. We wish to assist you in locating Penny."

"Are you them?"

"Them?" Ellen asked.

"The Notorious Nightingales. I've heard what you've done for others. What you do for those that live in Crabbett Close." She could hear the hope in her words. "Pa talks about you often."

Ellen nodded.

"Please find my Penny." The woman grabbed Ellen's hands.

"Now, Sally. They'll do what they can," Mr. Douglas said.

"It will help if you would bring us something of your daughter's, Mrs. Tompkins," Alex said in his lovely, soothing voice. He could charm anyone to do anything. Everyone loved Alex. Unlike Leo and Ellen, who were cold and prickly.

"Clothing?" She didn't hesitate.

"Or a book," Alex said.

"She doesn't read." Mrs. Tompkins stepped inside.

"I always forget that we were privileged to have learned to read," Alex muttered after she'd hurried away with her father. "It's wrong, you know, that people can't," he said, stuffing his hands in the pockets of his overcoat.

"Very wrong," Ellen said.

"How is it we didn't realize how indolent, spoiled, and atrociously behaved we once were?"

"Because everyone around us was the same," Leo said.

"True," Alex agreed.

"I'm quite sure I was never atrociously behaved." Ellen tugged off her gloves. She then stepped to the open doorway.

"It's my feeling you're making up for lost time, Miss Ellen," Mungo said.

"Never a truer word," Alex agreed.

"Haha," Ellen said, moving closer to the house.

"What are you doing? Stay here, Ellen," Leo cautioned.

"I'm just looking inside and am where you can see me, Leo. I'm hardly likely to get into trouble two feet from you, now am I?"

"Would you rather I did not care about you?" the eldest Nightingale said, sounding testy.

"You are a trifle overbearing, Leo," Alex said. "Ellen is not about to run into danger right before our eyes."

"I am not overbearing. I am cautious. Someone needs to be in this family."

Ellen ignored her brothers as they bickered, which they often did. Mungo would interfere if required. She then looked into the house. There was a small lamp that sat on a table. Four chairs and a fireplace but little else. The room was small but tidy. No clothes lying about or other clutter as there would be in their parlor.

The vision hit her fast and hard. She was not prepared and stumbled. Hands settled on her shoulders, steadying her, and then she was once again back in the present.

"What did you see?" Alex said from behind her. "Easy now."

"Take a deep breath of lovely smoggy London air, Ellen," Leo said, squeezing her shoulder. "That's it."

"Now tell us what you saw, darling," Alex said. He took a lemon drop out of his pocket and tapped her chin. Opening her mouth, he dropped it in.

The sharp bite of lemon shocked her senses.

"Are you well, Miss Ellen?" Mungo asked.

"I'm fine. I saw a man. Not overly tall but big. He stood outside a wooden building. There was a window. Four," she said, waving a hand in front of her.

"Four?" Alex asked.

Ellen made a two-fingers-down-and-across movement with her hands.

"I have no idea what you're trying to get at," Leo said.

"Four panes in the window?" Mungo asked.

"Yes." Ellen nodded. "And a lamp sitting there."

"In the window?" Alex asked.

"Yes."

"I'm sure that Penny Tompkins has not passed over," Alex said. "But then sometimes a new spirit takes time to get through."

"I hope no one ever overhears us. We'll be locked away for life," Leo muttered.

"Here is my girl's scarf," Mrs. Tompkins said, reappearing in her front door. She handed it to Leo while Ellen tried to recall everything she'd seen in her vision.

"Thank you, and we will start looking now. You say this Barney Forge lives on Smiley Street?"

She nodded. "I went to see them Forges again. My Bob is searching with his friends, but I thought to see if Barney was there, but he wasn't."

"Sally, no!" Mr. Douglas said. "Them's bad, those three boys and their father."

"I don't care, Pa. We have to find Penny! Bob has been out there for two days looking. He's not eaten or slept."

"Did anyone answer when you called to see Barney Forge, Mrs. Tompkins?" Leo asked her.

"No." She sniffed back tears. "We can't lose Penny too, not after Sydney, passed."

"We will do our best to find your daughter, Mrs. Tompkins," Leo said.

"Pa and me will keep searching too." Mrs. Tompkins grabbed Leo's hand and squeezed. "Please bring her home."

"We will find her," Leo promised, and Ellen hoped he was right.

"Mrs. Tompkins, does your daughter wear any jewelry?" Leo said.

If she was surprised by the question, it didn't show on her tear-blotched face.

"My ma's pin. It's in her coat and has a small bird on

the top of it. No jewels but shaped into a bird by my da when they were courting. I have one too."

"Could I see it?"

No one spoke as she ran back into the house. When she returned, she handed him the small pin. Leo studied it before handing it back.

"We shall find your daughter, I promise."

Leo then took Ellen's arm, and they started along the street. They reached the corner and stopped under a lamp.

"Sydney," Alex said. "Perhaps I need to meet Mrs. Tompkins's son."

The siblings all stood close, shoulders touching, and Mungo slightly back, watching them and their surroundings. A big silent presence who had simply accepted the lost and broken Nightingale children into his life and that they now needed him as much as their aunt and uncle.

"Focus," Leo said.

When Uncle Bram had first asked them if they had visions three months after he'd taken them to his home in the country, they'd been shocked.

Ellen had been the first to speak on the matter. Alex had later admitted that he felt like people were trying to communicate with him who were dead.

Leo, however, was still in complete denial about what he could do. He had learned to fight with Uncle Bram and the rest of them and was lethal with his cane. But he had never acknowledged his uncanny ability to locate missing things.

"Sydney Tompkins," Alex said. "I'd like to speak with you if you're about."

Ellen snickered. It always amused her when he spoke this way, as if Sydney Tompkins would be lurking on a street corner.

Beside her, Leo was running the scarf through his fingers.

"Lungs," Alex said, rubbing his chest. "He died of something to do with his lungs. Young. He was a boy when he passed. I'm seeing a pin of some kind. It has something on the end. A flower," he added.

"Like a pin you'd wear in your hair, do you mean?" Ellen asked him.

Alex opened his eyes. "I have no idea. I just saw a sharp pointy end and a flower."

"In the vision I had outside the Tompkins house I remember thinking, the man, he was wobbly," Ellen said.

"As in on-a-boat wobbly or drunk wobbly like Alex gets?" Leo asked.

"I protest. I definitely do not get wobbly!"

"Drunk wobbly, I think. I don't know," Ellen said.

"Why is it your visions don't simply say go here now and find what you're looking for?" Alex asked Ellen.

"Well, your dead people are not very forthcoming either," Ellen snapped. "And Leo is simply ignoring what he can do."

"I am not ignoring it. There is nothing I can do," Leo said in his best haughty tone.

"Is that why you studied the brooch Mrs. Tompkins gave you so intently?" Mungo said. Leo didn't reply.

"There is none so blind as those who have no wish to see, brother," Alex said.

"Could he have been outside some kind of drinking establishment?" Mungo asked.

"And he was wobbly from being inside?" Leo said. "That could make sense."

"A tall wooden-sided public house with a four-paned window and lamp," Alex mused. "Should be easy to find."

"Is that sarcasm?" Ellen glared at him, and as they were inches from each other, he saw it clearly.

"Well, sister dear, it could be any public house."

"Could it?" Ellen frowned. "I have not been in many."

"And that is not about to change," Leo said.

"I just feel the window is right there for all to see. The lamp too," Ellen persisted. "Plus, wherever this place is, and if Penny is near, it must be close."

"Hope and Anchor," Mungo said suddenly.

Alex snapped his fingers. "By God you're right, Mungo. It has a window that people sit in and watch the ships, but I'm not sure about the lamp."

"Let's go," Leo said.

Chapter 8

They hurried along the streets, ducking down alleys and weaving around people who stood in their way.

"I'm not sure this Barney Forge will have her here," Ellen said. "Surely he couldn't smuggle her inside. The place will be full of people drinking and the other things they do in such establishments like the Hope and Anchor."

Leo made a choking noise, and Alex snorted.

"What?" Ellen demanded.

"Nothing. Sailors and drinking," Leo said. "There will be a lot of noise."

"Wonderful, just the right combination to create stupid men," Ellen muttered.

"Not all who imbibe are stupid," Alex protested.

"Oh please. I've heard you and Leo arrive home inebriated and singing or stumbling about the place. You turn into fools. One wonders why women don't behave in such a way... oh wait, clearly, we are the inferior and therefore less intelligent sex, so we have no wish to make fools of ourselves."

Mungo snorted.

"You have an extremely cutting tongue, Ellen. I wonder when that happened. I'm sure you were once quite sweet-natured," Leo said.

"I was an excellent actress. Now I don't have to be."

Both brothers sighed.

It took them half an hour, but they arrived at the docks. Rigging clanged, and hulls creaked as they stood looking around them. It was busy, sailors and people lugging cargo on and off ships. Hackneys rolled along, and the air had a tang of salt and refuse.

"Gah." She pressed a sleeve to her nose. "That stench is horrid."

"Perhaps your stomach is not as strong as you think it is." Alex looked smug. "Leo, Mungo, and I aren't worried about a few smells."

Nightingales never missed an opportunity to poke at each other.

"Where is your umbrella, Ellen?" Leo demanded.

"Bud made me a loop to hang it on. She said, and I quote, 'not sure why you need to lug that bleedin' thing about even on fine days, but a woman needs her hands free, so I put loops on your skirts.'"

Ellen opened her coat.

Her brothers moved to Ellen's right to inspect the loop and umbrella hanging from it.

"That's handy," Alex said.

"Very," Ellen agreed.

"Unhook it then," Leo said. He carried his cane, and she knew Alex would have his sticks.

"Please," Ellen said.

"Cease," Mungo demanded. "You three are always at each other. I'll bang your bloody heads together if you don't stop."

"It really is not the done thing to bang a lord's head

with the empty caverns of his siblings' heads." Leo smirked. "Come along."

"I see the window and the lamp from the vision," Ellen whispered as they drew closer to the Hope and Anchor.

"Excellent," Alex said.

"You stay out here with Mungo, Ellen. We'll find him," Leo said.

"I'm coming inside too."

Her brothers looked at her. Mungo sighed.

"You will stand out."

"I'm wearing a black wool coat. How will I stand out?"

"The Hope and Anchor is a drinking establishment for sailors who want a good time. The women inside will want to give them that," Mungo said in a cold, hard voice.

"What he said," Leo agreed.

Ellen untied her bonnet.

"What are you doing?" Alex asked.

"Unpinning my hair. That should help me blend."

"Unpinned hair will not achieve that." Leo grabbed her hands. "You are a gently bred lady to your toes no matter that you act like a hoyden. Now stay here. We'll be back."

"I have spent my entire life being a lady and behaving as others have dictated I should. I no longer have to or, for that matter, want to."

"I hate that tone," Alex muttered. "She's being reasonable and speaking to us like we're five-year-olds."

"We'll watch her in there," Mungo said. "Let's go, or we'll stand out here arguing for another hour. People will think she's some kind of Good Samaritan come to save ruined souls and keep their distance."

"What?" Ellen glared at him.

"Be quiet, and do not open your mouth again until we

are back outside," Leo said. A large hand then clamped around her wrist and dragged her forward.

"But you can?" Ellen huffed out a breath.

"We did not make up the rules that men are superior. It is simply common knowledge," Alex said. He then took two large steps out of her reach and hurried inside the Hope and Anchor.

"Like that will keep him safe," Mungo said. "Does the lad not realize yet that revenge is a dish best served cold?"

"He's an idiot. What can I say?" Leo added.

Ellen walked in behind Leo and was instantly hit with smells and sounds. Singing, laughing, and talking. There was music coming from a fiddle somewhere. The scents were a mix of alcohol and sweat.

"Stay close," Mungo whispered in her ear. He then nudged her into Leo's back.

They moved through the room slowly, looking for anything that may alert them to Barney Forge and Penny Tompkins's location.

"We don't need your sort in here. There are no souls that want saving."

The woman who said those words moved close to Ellen. Her breasts were spilling out of her dress and her hair was loose. But it was the pink cheeks and lips that caught Ellen's attention.

"What are you staring at?" the woman demanded.

"I was just thinking how lovely you look," Ellen said.

The woman's fierce expression softened. "You could be too if you weren't dressed in that outfit, looking prim and proper," the woman said.

"We're actually searching for a man. His name is Barney Forge. Would you be able to help us with locating him at all?"

"Him and his brothers just left. You stay clear of the likes of them, love. They're a bad lot."

"Ellen," she said. "And thank you so much for your help."

The woman smiled. "You come and see me if you need any work, Ellen. My name's Dottie."

"Oh, I will, and thank you again."

"Are you finished with your chat?" Leo hissed from in front of her.

"The Forges just left," Ellen said. "And there is no need of sarcasm, seeing as I have found them, and you did not."

Leo muttered something and then told Alex they were heading back out the doors. When they stepped into the foggy night air, they found a group of men several feet away.

"Mungo did tell you your appearance made you look like a Good Samaritan trying to save souls," Alex said. "The lovely Dottie simply confirmed that."

"Stay back, Ellen," Leo said. "And be quiet, Alex. Now is not the time."

"We've been over this, Leo. I can fight as well as you," Ellen said.

"No, you can't. You're tiny, Ellen, and it would take one punch to knock you out."

"Then I'll make sure no one punches me."

"Excuse me," Alex said, moving away from his arguing siblings and toward the group of men. "Are you the Forges?"

"The lapel," Ellen whispered when she, Leo, and Mungo joined Alex. A flower pin in the lapel of one man's coat told her they were talking to Barney Forge.

"Who's asking?" He stepped closer.

"Who's asking what?" Mungo said, moving to Ellen's right. Alex and Leo were now to her left.

"Who's asking if we're the Forges?"

There was no doubting the three well-built men were brothers.

"We are," Leo said. "We're also asking you to tell us where Penny Tompkins is."

"I don't know what you're talking about," the man wearing the flower pin said.

"That pin on your jacket would suggest otherwise, Barney Forge. Now where is she?" Alex asked.

"You're talking nonsense, and if you don't want the lady hurt, you'd better leave."

"What lady?" Leo asked.

A meaty finger was jabbed her way. "That one."

"That's our sister. She's no lady."

Leo swept his cane and dropped Barney Forge on his ass, and all hell suddenly broke loose.

Chapter 9

One of Gray's informants had told him the two boys who had broken into George Nicholson's bookshop to steal money often lurked around the Hope and Anchor. They preyed on drunken patrons, picking their pockets. He was now on his way there to see if he could locate them.

Walking down the street toward the tavern, he thought again about the Nightingale siblings and, more specifically, Ellen. Why did she disturb him?

Gray had met many women in his lifetime. Some had intrigued him, one in particular, but that came to nothing when she realized he was married to his job. Which was the truth. He loved his work, and it took all his focus, and while he was sometimes lonely, the feeling soon passed.

Ellen Nightingale had been a society darling and fallen hard from grace. The woman he met was cool, collected, and nothing like he thought she'd once been. Her beauty would have had men falling at her feet and likely still did. It had definitely caught Gray's attention. Yet, he had a feeling there was a great deal behind that pretty facade she'd once kept hidden in the ballrooms of fancy houses.

At least he'd walked away from society by choice. She'd not been given that.

Something hard hit him, and he stumbled but stayed upright. Gray reached out and grabbed the arm of whoever had ran into him.

"Sorry, mister," a boy said.

"No harm done. Do you know someone called Snippy?"

A second boy appeared. "Why do you want him?"

"Are you Snippy?"

"Him." The boy nodded to the lad Gray was still holding.

"I'd like a word with you if you please. I am Detective Grayson Fletcher from Scotland Yard, and I'm investigating a murder, which I believe you may be involved with."

"What? No, I'm not!"

"A bookshop was being robbed. A lady stopped you, and she heard one of you call the other Snippy," Gray said. "She then found a dead body. Now, if you don't wish to be brought in on murder charges, you will talk to me."

"We didn't kill anyone," Snippy said. "We were just taking the money, but the woman stopped us. There was no dead body!"

"How old are you?" Gray asked both boys.

"Eleven," Snippy said. "Both of us."

Gray released the boy. "If you run, I'll follow, and I will find you. Do you understand?"

They both nodded.

"When you entered the bookshop, did you see anyone?"

They shook their heads.

"We just went behind the counter to look for money," Snippy said.

"And then the woman arrived?" More nodding.

"She was a right big one, like a man in size. Came at us with her fists," the other boy said. "No woman I know can fight like that. It ain't right."

"I spoke to that lady who was no taller than either of you and defeated you with her umbrella. So don't think to lie to me again. And how is it not right for a woman to be able to defend herself?" Gray asked.

The boys looked at each other, clearly unsure how to answer that question.

"Do you have mothers and sisters?" They nodded. "Wouldn't you like to know they could take care of themselves?"

They shrugged.

"So, the woman fought you both with her umbrella?"

"She was quick. Got me on the floor with it and Snippy in the belly. She then told us to empty our pockets and go, so we did."

"And you did not see the proprietor lying on the floor or anyone leaving?"

They shook their heads.

The sound of a fist hitting flesh reached Gray through the fog, and then raised voices. The boys took the moment he'd turned away to flee.

Moving closer to the lamplight that he knew was just inside the Hope and Anchor's front window, he found a group outside fighting. Elbowing his way in through the crowd forming, Gray caught sight of a tall, dark blond head.

Surely not? Stepping to the right of the large man in front of him, he found the Nightingale brothers. He guessed it was the other brother Alexander, as from what he could see of him, he had the look of his siblings. Mungo was also there, fighting alongside them, as was Ellen

Nightingale. Gray actually blinked, sure he was imagining what he was seeing.

"Wouldn't mind a night with that one. Methinks she'd be a right handful in bed," the giant to his left said. Gray elbowed him hard in the ribs before he joined the fray.

"What the hell are you doing?" He reached Ellen first.

"Get out of my way, Detective Fletcher." She feinted right and then dodged left and around him. Before he could stop her, she'd hooked the handle of her umbrella around a man's ankles and dropped him on his ass.

"Get out or in, Detective Fletcher!" Lord Seddon yelled. He then swung his cane and another fell.

Gray's count had them outnumbered. The three Nightingales and Mungo against at least six men.

"Your sister should not be here!" Gray said, raising his fists.

"Good luck telling her that," Alexander Nightingale said. He carried what appeared to be two sticks connected by rope. He did a nifty maneuver with them, and the man he was fighting stumbled back a step.

Gray punched and jabbed, then hit the man with a right hook and dropped him.

"Where is she?"

When he looked for her, Gray found Ellen with her umbrella pressed down on a man's throat. The rest of the men had melted away except for two. They were being subdued by the Nightingale brothers.

"Where is Penny?" Ellen put more weight on the umbrella, and the man made a gagging sound.

"Miss Ellen, he can't speak if you do that," Mungo said.

"Oh, right." She eased up a bit. "Tell us what you have done with Penny, and I may let you live or at the very least be able to speak, which would mean I won't crush your windpipe."

"Go to hell. She's mine!" The man lying at her feet wheezed. "Get off me, you bitch!"

Mungo sighed. He then stood on the man's hand, making him howl with pain.

"Ask him again, Miss Ellen."

"What the hell is going on?" Gray demanded.

"Sssh." Ellen waved her hand at him. "Now, Barney Forge." She bent at the waist and peered into the man's eyes. "Where is Penny? You're wearing her pin on your lapel."

"Who is Penny?" Gray asked instead of are you mad. "What the hell are you doing in such a place, fighting of all things? Get home at once to safety."

The brothers were still fighting but had the upper hand, and soon both had knocked their opponents to the ground.

"What did he say?" Lord Seddon demanded, joining his sister.

"I insist someone tells me what is going on," Gray said, his voice louder this time.

"Detective Fletcher, I believe?"

Gray looked at the hand Alexander Nightingale held out to him. Manners were the true sign of a gentleman, his mother once told him, so he shook it.

"Answer her if you please, Forge, or I'll let her put more force on her umbrella. Believe me, the end is very pointy," Lord Seddon said to the man on the ground. Ellen now stood on his chest. "I've had it jabbed in my side many times, and it leaves an impression."

"Are you all mad?" Gray asked anyone who would listen.

"That man has abducted the granddaughter of one of

the Crabbett Close residents," Mungo said. "We're getting her back."

"You should have spoken to one of the bobbies."

Alexander Nightingale scoffed. "I don't mean to sound disparaging, Detective Fletcher." He smiled, and Gray knew right off this brother was less serious than the other one. "But there are not bobbies on every corner, you understand. Nor is Plummy that easy to get on task."

This he knew as he'd tried. The man was a good enough sort, if a little simpleminded.

"We could wait no longer to retrieve the woman this scum abducted. We have the skills to see it done, so we are doing it," Alexander continued.

"That's completely reckless with a disregard for your sister's welfare, who you have plunged into danger."

"Yes, because it's quite clear she can't look after herself," Alexander said.

The woman was now straddling the man's body with her feet. Her umbrella was under his chin, which she was forcing upward.

"That as it may be—"

"Perhaps the lecture could wait?" Lord Seddon cut off Gray's words.

Looking at those watching and the men lying on the floor, Gray realized he was right.

"And I was not in danger," Ellen snapped. "Get him up, Leo. He needs an incentive to tell us where Penny is."

Lord Seddon dragged the man to his feet and held his hands behind his back. "Right then, let's get this done, as the crowd is growing restless, sister."

"I want the address of where you have taken Penny Tompkins, Barney Forge. If you don't give it, I'm letting my brothers loose on you," Ellen said, her face now inches from the man's.

"As if we could hurt him more," Alexander muttered.

When Forge didn't answer, Ellen jabbed him in the belly with her umbrella.

Alexander Nightingale and Mungo watched on as if it was a normal occurrence for Ellen to behave in this way. *Was it?*

Gray took a step closer, no longer able to be a bystander. The man could head butt her or kick out with a large, booted foot at any time.

"What is going on?" he asked to anyone who would give him an answer.

"This man has abducted a woman," Lord Seddon said.

"Yes. Penny Tompkins. She told this rodent many times she has no interest in succumbing to his revolting advances," Ellen snapped. "And yet he persisted, and when she demanded he stop, he kidnapped her." She finished that statement with another jab of her umbrella into the man's stomach. She then reached for his lapel and wrenched the small pin from it.

"She's my woman!" he wheezed.

"Now, that's not the truth, is it?" Alexander said.

"What's your name?" Gray asked the man. When he didn't answer, Ellen jabbed him again. "Yes, thank you, Miss Nightingale, I have it now." He grabbed her arm and tugged her back a few feet.

"Hey!"

"Release him, my lord," Gray said. The nobleman raised his hands in the air and moved to where his siblings and Mungo stood.

"Run, and I'll let them have you," he said to the man before him. "Name?" Gray barked.

"Barney Forge."

"Do you know the location of the woman called Penny Tompkins?"

The man hesitated.

"I will have you incarcerated in Newgate if I find you've lied to me, and I will be in no hurry to get you released. Now I will ask you again. Do you know where Penny Tompkins is?"

"You should lock him away where he can't hurt Penny or anyone else again," Ellen Nightingale snapped.

"That will do." He shot her a look he hoped held authority. Her brothers snorted.

"Good luck getting her to shut her large mouth," the eldest said.

"Leo," Ellen growled.

He'd thought her cool and contained. Emotionless. It seemed he'd been wrong.

"Answer the question, Mr. Forge. Where is Penny Tompkins?" Gray said while he attempted to tamp down the anger that smoldered inside him.

What the hell were these people thinking coming here and finding this man? Anything could have happened to them. Right now, this crowd of onlookers could have turned on them.

"She's not hurt," the man said. His shoulders dropped, and Gray saw defeat when faced with it.

"You will take me to her now."

He nodded.

"I just needed time to make her see," Barney Forge said.

"A small lesson in how to woo a woman, Mr. Forge," Alexander said. "Never force yourself upon them. They tend to react badly."

Chapter 10

"Go home, Miss Nightingale. In fact, all of you go home, and I will retrieve this woman with Mr. Forge."

"No," Ellen said, refusing to be impressed by the detective. He had a way about him that was steady and yet authoritative. He'd not raised his voice, but Barney Forge had capitulated. "We will come, and I will help Penny. You could be overpowered by this scumbag."

"Exactly," Leo said from beside Ellen. "We will all go with you, Detective Fletcher."

The muscle in Grayson Fletcher's jaw ticked. Clearly, he was not accustomed to having his orders disregarded.

"I do not need your help and have been dealing with this kind of scumbag, as you so eloquently put it, for years."

"As you are alone, and he has his brothers here, we will stay with you," Leo said. "Granted, they are just now waking up, but they could be offended at you taking their brother away."

"These are his brothers?" the detective asked, nodding to the two men who were struggling to their feet.

Alex nodded.

"Then, if you will not leave, I suggest we move before they realize what is happening," he said in a hard voice. "Lead the way, Mr. Forge."

Ellen walked with her brothers and Mungo behind Barney Forge and the detective.

"He's going to lecture us when this is over," Leo said.

"I have that feeling too," Alex added. "He's bigger than you said and very authoritative."

"I never mentioned his size," Leo snapped.

"I'm sure you did, or perhaps that was Ellen."

They walked on discussing the angry man in front of them, which she was sure he could hear.

Grayson Fletcher thought she should be home safe. Ellen would never simply sit and wait for life to come calling again, just as she would not wait for a man to offer her protection.

Her uncle and aunt had ensured she could always look after herself. They had shown Ellen how to be strong when for so long she'd simply known how to behave like a lady should and little else. It had been a revelation to know she could, in fact, take steps to keep herself safe if she needed to.

The place Barney Forge led them to was a small narrow building about a ten-minute walk from the Hope and Anchor. He then did something very foolish and tried to make a run for it.

Detective Fletcher stuck out his foot, and the man hit the ground hard. He then hauled him to his feet. Pulling a rope from his pocket, he tied his hands.

"Clearly trusting you was a mistake, Mr. Forge. I will not make the same one again."

Ellen shivered at the cold tone.

"I bet he's a right mean bastard when he wants to be," Alex whispered.

"Open the door," the detective said. Mungo did it without comment, which surprised the Nightingale siblings. He usually had an opinion on most things.

The hinges made a loud squeaking noise, which simply added more authenticity to the dark eerie night.

It was as cold inside as it had been out, and the thought of Penny Tompkins in here somewhere alone was terrifying. Ellen hoped they found her.

"Leo—"

"She's here and so is the brooch."

His tone did not brook questioning. He found things but never wanted to talk about why he had that skill.

"Where is she?" Detective Fletcher asked Barney Forge.

When he didn't speak, the detective put his hand on the man's shoulder and squeezed. Forge yelped.

"I'll ask you one more time. Where is Penny Tompkins?"

"At the end of the room! Walk straight ahead," Forge said, clearly in pain.

"You lot wait here and watch him," Detective Fletcher said.

"Not bloody likely," Ellen said.

"Agreed," Leo added.

She heard the angry hiss of breath from the detective.

"Hand him here. I'll ensure he doesn't run again, and you get the woman," Mungo said. He then grabbed Forge by the arm and forced him to his knees. The man dropped with a whimper.

"Penny?" Ellen called the woman's name as they started moving again. A muffled sound came from somewhere ahead of them.

Running around the detective, she hurried forward with Alex and Leo.

"Halt!" Detective Fletcher called. "It could be a trap."

"You'll find it easier to try stopping a waterfall," she heard Mungo call. "They're impulsive."

Ellen tapped the floor with her umbrella as Leo did the same with his cane. She touched something and dropped to her knees. A woman lay there on her side. Hands and feet bound, mouth gagged.

"'Tis all right now, Penny. You are safe," Ellen said. "Come, let's get you unbound and home."

Leo pulled out his knife and freed the woman's hands and Alex her feet. Ellen removed the gag from her mouth.

"You're safe, Penny." The woman collapsed into her arms sobbing, and Ellen simply held her as tight as she could, telling her that everything would be all right now.

"She's chilled, Ellen. We need to get her home," Leo said.

Leo helped Penny rise, and Ellen was lifted to her feet by Alex, or she thought it had been, until she turned to face Detective Fletcher. This close, she could see his anger.

"Everyone outside now," he said in a carefully controlled voice.

Leo shrugged out of his coat and draped it around Penny's shoulders. They then did as the detective said. Once they were free of the building, she took Penny's hands and rubbed them. They were ice cold.

Mungo had Barney Forge by the shoulder.

"You're safe now, Penny," Ellen said.

"I-I was so scared." She was pale and her face smudged with dirt and tears.

"You're my woman, Penny," Barney Forge growled. He was clearly too much of an idiot to see he had lost.

Penny tugged her hands free from Ellen's and moved to

where he stood. She then drew back her hand and swung it in a fist. It connected nicely with the jaw of her kidnapper, snapping his head to the left.

"You don't own me, Barney Forge, and never will! If I see your face anywhere near me or mine, then I'm telling these people. They'll make sure you'll pay."

"Have no fear he will harm you again, Miss Tompkins," Detective Fletcher said. "I'll see to it."

"Th-thank you."

"I will deal with Barney Forge if you'll take Miss Tompkins home?" The detective looked from Leo to Alex and Mungo and lastly to her.

"We can do that. Thank you, Detective Fletcher," Leo said. "Are you quite sure you don't need one of us to go with you?"

"I do not," he snapped. "I will come to speak with you tomorrow."

"Have you found who killed George?" Ellen asked him.

"I have not. I want to address this... this reckless behavior that you all exhibited tonight."

"I wouldn't bother," Mungo said. "I've been trying for years."

"I'll succeed," the detective snapped. "Good evening."

"Good evening, Detective Fletcher," Alex said. "I hope your night improves."

The man growled. He then walked away, urging Barney Forge before him.

Chapter 11

Penny was weak and stumbled a few times. Ellen stood on her left and Mungo on her right. Between them, they kept her upright.

"Did he feed you?" Ellen asked.

"No. He said he was starving me until I said I was his woman. I-I told him I'd rather die hungry."

"I'll get you something," Alex said. He then vanished into the fog.

If anyone could track down food, it was Alex or Fred. Both were ruled by their stomachs.

Leo took the lead, his cane swinging from left to right.

"Are you them?" Penny asked.

"Them?"

"Them Notorious Nightingales. I heard you were gentry and that you help people, and live in Crabbett Close."

"We are," Ellen said.

"Thank you." Penny sniffed. "It was me pa who came to you, wasn't it? He lives there."

"He's a good man, your grandfather," Leo said over his shoulder.

"The best," Penny agreed.

Alex reappeared with a slice of spiced fruit cake that had Ellen's mouth watering. Penny fell on it like a starving child.

They reached the Tompkins house soon thereafter. Leo banged on the door, and it opened seconds later. A red-eyed Mrs. Tompkins shrieked and then caught her girl as she fell into her arms.

"We can't thank you enough," Mr. Douglas said from behind his daughter and granddaughter. "But I'll be finding a way."

"There is no need, but perhaps one of Mrs. Douglas's taffy cakes if she's a mind to make one," Leo said.

The brothers bowed, Mungo nodded, as did Ellen, and then they were walking away.

"You ate some of that cake, didn't you?" Ellen glared at Alex.

"As if I would do that?" he said, but the innocent look fooled no one.

"I want cake," Leo grumbled.

"He's coming back tomorrow, you know," Mungo said as they headed to Crabbett Close.

"We did nothing wrong, Mungo," Ellen said. "Detective Fletcher can be angry that he sees us as pathetic noblemen amusing ourselves, but the fact is we had as much right to be there as anyone."

"I don't think he believes we're pathetic," Leo said. "We certainly showed him we can take care of ourselves. However, I believe he sees our actions as vigilante."

"Which they are," Mungo added.

"You know as well as I that there are not enough peelers about when you need them. We've also established that Constable Plummy is harmless and entirely useless," Leo added.

"Agreed," Alex said. "But back to the detective. To me, he seemed most upset about Ellen being there, and he certainly had an appreciative look in his eye when he was staring at her."

"Oh please," Ellen scoffed, refusing to acknowledge the sudden thudding of her heart at her brother's words. "There was no way you would have seen his eyes as you were fighting, and when you weren't, you couldn't see a foot in front of your face."

The disturbing detective did not see her differently from any other woman. *Did he?*

"He's a handsome man, and you have tolerable looks, I suppose. Surely you can't believe that no man will have you," Alex teased her.

Leo, who was still walking ahead of them, stopped, and Alex ran into his back.

"Ouch!" Alex grabbed his nose.

"Thank you, my favorite brother."

"Welcome," Leo said to Ellen. "And that cold, calculating detective is not getting near Ellen."

She absolutely did not feel another flutter in her belly at the thought of getting close to the dark, handsome Grayson Fletcher.

"I wonder if he has any leads on George's murder?" Ellen said.

"I've been thinking about that," Alex said.

"Which will not bode well for any of us," Mungo added. "You thinking always spells trouble."

"The point is, someone used Uncle Bram's knife and that means it involves us. Did they deliberately take it to implicate him? Or did they steal it from him, and he hasn't realized it yet? You know how forgetful he is," Leo added.

"We can't really do much until he returns and we speak to him about it," Alex said.

Ellen shivered at the thought of anything happening to the wonderful man who had saved them. He and Aunt Ivy had stepped in to gather up the distraught Nightingale siblings and given them a home. She would not allow him to be incarcerated for something he would never do.

There had to be another reason his knife was there in that bookshop.

"We've all made enemies at some stage in our lives, and it's not always our fault," Mungo said in his gruff Scottish burr. "But your uncle is the best man I know. He'd never intentionally hurt anyone."

"I need to talk to George," Alex said. "But so far, he's not wanting to chat with me. Clearly, he is not quite settled in the spirit world. Your great uncle Hamish, however, Mungo. Now he is a constant visitor."

"Well, ask him what his recipe for bannock is. He put something secret in them, and they always tasted the best."

"I'll try."

"I'd like to get into that bookshop," Leo said. "Have a look around."

"I'm sure I can pick that lock," Mungo said.

"Excellent. Then we shall do so tomorrow," Leo added.

When they reached 11 Crabbett Close, the lights still shone from a few rooms. Clearly Bud had stayed up to await them. Letting themselves into the entranceway, Ellen heard a deep bark of laughter and started running, followed by her brothers.

Bursting into the parlor, they found their uncle and aunt seated before the fire. Bud was there too.

"Uncle Bram!" Ellen ran at him as he rose. His big arms settled around her.

Beside her, Leo and Alex hugged Aunt Ivy.

"Is Lottie asleep?" Ellen asked when he released her.

"She is and was exhausted. She will be pleased to see you all tomorrow, as she has mentioned your names constantly."

"We missed you all," Ellen said. "Did you have a wonderful time?"

"Yes, it was lovely, but we were ready to come home to you lot." He had a deep voice, a voice that had told her the world would once again be set to rights soon, the night she'd lay in his arms weeping for the loss of her father.

"Hello, Aunt Ivy." Ellen was wrapped in a sweet-smelling hug. Small like Ellen, Ivy embraced like a much larger person. She held on until she was ready to let you go.

"Hello, my darling Ellen. How are you?" She gripped her shoulder and stared intently at her.

"I am well, thank you."

Ivy was the exact opposite of her husband in appearances. Small and pale, but that was where the differences stopped. They both loved each other openly and included Ellen and her siblings in that love, along with Lottie, their two-year-old daughter, who was doted on by her older cousins. Not once had they doubted that having the Nightingale siblings thrust upon them had been anything but a wonderful thing.

Of course, Leo and Alex were old enough to set off on their own, but they too had been reeling from their father's death. Uncle Bram had insisted they stay together, and together they'd stayed. Although lately they'd both been murmuring about moving out.

Thinking about not having her brothers close saddened Ellen, but she also knew they needed to find their independence. It had taken all the siblings time to heal, but now they were, they were ready to begin living.

"I'm not sure you are well, dear, but I know you will all tell us what is bothering you, given time and cake."

Bud rushed off to get more food and tea, even though the hour was well past midnight now.

"Mungo. Thank you for keeping an eye on this rabble." Bram greeted his old friend.

"As you can imagine, it was not without its trials."

"Harsh but true," Alex said.

"We decided to push on and not stop on the road as we missed you all," Uncle Bram said. "Now tell us what happened to make you all tense and anxious. Bud said something had upset you, Ellen."

Uncle Bram sat beside Ivy. He then took her hand and trapped it beneath his on his lap. They were always touching, and Ellen now knew this was what she wanted one day. She'd have never had that with her ex-fiancé, who had broken their engagement swiftly after her father had killed himself.

The Nightingales and Mungo settled in the other seats.

"Ellen will tell the story," Leo said. "She lived it."

She recounted everything, from the night she'd entered Nicholson's bookshop, right up to encountering Detective Inspector Fletcher and Constable Plummy.

"How sad. George was a wonderful man," Aunt Ivy said.

"He was," her husband agreed. "Which knife was it, Ellen?" Uncle Bram asked.

"The intricate handled one you got in Mongolia," Mungo said.

"Good lord, really? That was stolen about a year ago."

"What?" Leo and Ellen said.

"I did not want to worry you. But I had it on me one night. You know how I always like to carry a weapon that I've brought home with me from my travels—"

"How is it I am not aware of this?" Aunt Ivy demanded.

"I had no wish to worry any of you. A man confronted me demanding money. I disarmed him, but it was as I was walking home, I checked and found my knife gone."

"So, whoever stole it murdered George?" Alex said.

"Or he sold it and another did," Uncle Bram said. "I understand why you did what you did, Ellen, and I'm grateful to you, but we have tampered with evidence," he said. "And now we must come clean to this detective."

"No. He may not believe you, and I won't have you taken away from us." She could not imagine their lives without this wonderful man in it.

"Never," he said, holding out a hand to her. She gripped his fingers briefly.

"Now about this Detective Fletcher. His first name is not Grayson, is it?"

Leo nodded to their uncle.

"Cold, emotionless type of fellow and extremely unhappy that we were doing what we did tonight," Alex said.

"By jove," Uncle Bram said. "Grayson Fletcher. I wondered what happened to him."

"What do you mean, Uncle?" Ellen asked.

"He's the Earl of Draven's son, or so I believe. The eldest, Christopher, was at Eton with me. An obnoxious sort, but we tolerated each other on the few occasions I was unlucky enough to see him," Uncle Bram said. "Last time we met, he was with his mother. I asked after his brothers, and when he didn't mention his youngest, Lady Draven told me her son had joined Scotland Yard. Christopher was not pleased she'd mentioned him."

"Snobbish nobleman." Ivy sighed.

"Exactly, my love."

"Grayson is not a common name, and becoming a detective would be the height of embarrassment for Christopher and his father," Uncle Bram said.

Could it be true? Ellen wondered again about the vision she'd seen of a boy standing at a graveside. Was it Grayson Fletcher or someone else? And who was he mourning?

"And now let us tell you about tonight," Alex said. "And the reason Fletcher thinks we're indolent noblemen with little to occupy our time but be vigilantes."

"Not quite true," Ellen said. "He has no idea what we get up to other than tonight."

"But he saw us fight," Leo added. "And wasn't happy you were in the thick of it."

She sipped the cup of tea Bud handed her.

"Tomorrow we are paying a call on this detective, Ellen. He needs to know what you do and that I was away from London when George was murdered."

"Oh, but—"

"We do not break the law, niece."

She lapsed into silence as Alex started retelling the story of Penny's rescue. Ellen didn't know why the detective unsettled her, but there was no doubting something about him did. After tomorrow, she would make sure never to see him again.

She'd vowed after leaving society, no man, other than family, would ever be important to her, and she had a feeling the detective spelled trouble for her and the Nightingale family.

Chapter 12

Gray woke in his room, as he had every day since he'd inherited his aunt and uncle's town house. Six bedrooms, several parlors, and too many floors for a single man. He'd loved it since he'd stepped foot in it. Their furnishings had filled the place and made it home. Gray had changed nothing.

The day he'd been told this was his, he viewed it and then had ridden home to his father's town house and told his family he was moving out. At twenty-four, they could not stop him. He'd left and never gone back. What he'd told them he was about to do had confirmed that he was from that moment on his own.

His mother's brother had been a second son of a duke but not happy to live off his family. He'd chosen to study law. He'd then amassed a considerable amount of money with his wife's help, investing. That money had all come to Gray, as they'd had no children of their own, much to his family's horror.

"Your bath is drawn, sir."

"Thank you, Albert."

This room had soft beige walls, cream trimmings, and drapes. A huge fire and two big comfortable armchairs set before it. It had been the one Gray chose out of the rooms to make his.

He'd been lucky to have relatives he'd loved. His grandfather, Aunt Tilda, Uncle Henry, and Aunt Louisa. They had made sure to spend time and love the third son of an earl when no one else would. He'd been surplus to requirements and therefore left with a nanny more often than not.

When his aunt and uncle visited, they'd always spent time with him. Telling him he could be whoever he wanted to be. Not to live in the shadow of his family. He hadn't, and his family had never forgiven him.

After a bath, he ate his breakfast while reading the morning papers. His staff were quiet and kept out of his way, which he liked.

After ensuring Barney Forge would no longer be a danger to Penny Tompkins, he'd wanted to storm around to 11 Crabbett Close and demand to know what they were about. He hadn't, and instead he'd gone home to calm down.

What the hell had her brothers been thinking to allow Ellen Nightingale out at such an hour and near a place like the Hope and Anchor? Yes, clearly she knew how to look after herself, but still, she was a lady and should not have been there.

What was their story, these Notorious Nightingales? Their neighbors were fiercely loyal to them, but why? Were they actually some kind of vigilante group? His blood boiled at the thought of a bunch of spoiled noblemen taking to the streets to seek justice.

"Yes, what is it, Albert?" he said when his butler appeared in the doorway.

"A Mrs. Nicholson has called to speak with you, sir."

His butler was tall, rail thin, and bald. Unlike many who liked their butlers to look elegant and stately, Albert was anything but and the best of men. He'd served Gray's aunt and uncle.

"Where did you put her?" Gray got out of his chair.

"The parlor nearest the front door, sir."

"Thank you." What the hell was she doing calling at his house? George had no wife, so it was his mother downstairs in his parlor. Taking the stairs, he nodded to his aunt and uncle's portraits. Entering the room, he found the short, round figure of Mrs. Nicholson looking out the front window.

"Mrs. Nicholson."

She turned, and her face was pale, eyes red-rimmed. She wore the dark colors of mourning.

"What has you at my private address?" Gray was not a man to mince words.

"Forgive me for the intrusion, Detective Fletcher. But I-I need to know what is happening with the investigation into my George's murder."

"How did you get my address?"

She studied him through tired, sad blue eyes that made his anger dissipate. This was a grieving mother. He needed to remember grief made people do what they normally wouldn't.

"I spoke with Constable Plummy, who was stationed outside my son's bookshop. He was kind enough to give me your address."

He was going to kill that fool.

"You should have called at Scotland Yard, Mrs. Nicholson, not my personal address." He kept his words gentle.

"I was standing at the window when you came to tell

my husband of George's death, Detective Fletcher. I remember watching his face pale as you talked to him."

Gray also remembered the moment he'd told the man about his son. Devastation had him staggering, as if his knees could no longer hold him. He'd told him that his son was a great man and those who knew him spoke highly of him. The words had straightened the man's shoulders.

"I remember thinking that was a good man standing on my doorstep," Mrs. Nicholson continued. "Even as I knew the news you'd delivered to my husband was going to devastate me too."

"Mrs. Nicholson—"

"I couldn't go to Scotland Yard," she said quickly. "I'm not very brave for all I work in our sweet shop."

Nicholson's Sweets, Gray remembered.

"My husband is the strong one."

Gray doubted that. She'd birthed and raised two children as well as kept a home for her family. She also worked. It sounded to him like she was the strong one.

"So I came here to ask if you have any idea who killed my boy. Our house is in mourning, you see, and we can't find anything to change that and won't for many years. But to know that wh-whoever murdered my boy is caught would help."

"I'm sorry for your loss, but I have no news of your son's killer yet, Mrs. Nicholson. I will come to you when I do."

Her shoulders hunched forward in defeat.

"I'm sorry I do not have more for you," he added, feeling totally out of his depth. Gray was not used to comforting victims. He left that to his colleagues who actually had empathy.

"Have you ever lost someone, Detective Fletcher? Not just lost them but had their life brutally ended in such a way?" She pressed a handkerchief to her mouth. "Someone you cared for deeply?"

"I have buried relatives, but their deaths were not brutal." He'd lost his grandfather. Two aunts and an uncle. All he'd cared for in his own way. But he couldn't imagine that even came close to being the same as losing a child to murder.

"You should never have to bury your child," he said, remembering someone saying that to him once, when they'd been called in to investigate the murder of a young boy.

"It is the worst kind of hell," she said in a shaky voice.

"Would you like tea?" Gray was never good at feminine distress. Tea was the best he could come up with before sending her away.

"I met your mother once."

"I beg your pardon?" Gray hid his shock behind the harsh demand.

"You look identical to her. She came into our sweet store. She has a weakness for the toffee we make. It's the best in London, you see. Her smile was small and sad. We used to talk, her and I. Two women from completely different lives who, for a brief moment in time, chatted as if there were no barriers between us."

He couldn't speak. There weren't many things Gray was irrational about. His family was one of them. But to know this woman and his mother had spoken about him was almost unbelievable.

"We talked one day about sons. She was sad as she said she no longer sees her youngest boy. That Grayson Fletcher, her son, was a detective at Scotland Yard. She'd said the words with pride."

He wanted to scoff at that. No one in his family was proud of him... were they?

"She said her husband and other sons could not condone that, so they didn't see him, you," she added gently.

He saw his mother once a year, if that. He'd receive a note stating a date, time, and place, and they would meet and take tea. It was stilted, uncomfortable, and he was pleased when it was done. Not once had she talked about what he did.

"It was June 19th, the day she came in to pick up her standing order of toffee."

His mother had a standing order that she collected herself? Gray was sure no one but her knew about this.

"I remember saying to her I hoped she had a lovely day. She looked sad and told me it was her youngest son's birthday, so she didn't think she would, as she wouldn't be seeing you."

He didn't move, not a facial muscle or finger twitch. But inside was another matter. *His mother had talked about him.*

Why had she done that with a complete stranger? She didn't care... did she? Gray knew his father had complete control of her life. She made no move without asking his permission. It would take a strong woman to break away from that. His mother had never been strong.

"I had the feeling she loved you."

If she loved me, she would have fought harder to show it.

"I have nothing to tell you, Mrs. Nicholson. Please return home, and I will call when I have information."

"Very well, and from a mother who has lost a child she loved, you need to visit your mother more and forgive her for the grudge you hold against her."

He didn't answer that. She kissed his cheek and then left.

Gray fell into a chair. His mother had spoken to a complete stranger about him. What did that mean?

Thirty minutes later he was still sitting in the same position when his butler appeared.

"Mr. Bramstone Nightingale and Miss Nightingale have called, sir," Albert said from the doorway with an excited gleam in his eyes. "I tried to usher them inside, but they said they would rather wait for you to invite them."

"What? Why?" Gray demanded.

"As I have just stated, they wish to speak with you before entering your house, sir."

Ellen was here. Gray never had visitors, so this would be his butler's idea of heaven. Why had his heartbeat suddenly increased at the thought of seeing Ellen Nightingale again?

Because I'm still furious with her and her brother's antics last night, that's why.

"Fine. I will come and see what they want," Gray said, getting out of the chair.

"It is the correct procedure to invite them in. This parlor is suitable for such company," Albert said.

"Do you even know who these people are?" Gray asked.

"I have a copy of Debrett's Peerage & Baronetage. Your aunt gave it to me."

"And what? You dashed to your rooms to check for their names?" Gray asked.

"I have read the book many times," Albert said in a haughty tone.

"Well, good for you," Gray said.

"I will prepare tea."

"Don't bother. I'm sure they are not staying."

He walked away with his butler muttering something

unflattering, wondering if he should slip out the back door and run away.

Life had taken a strange and odd slant since the night he'd found Ellen Nightingale in the fog. His mother had spoken about him to a stranger. Not just any stranger, the mother of the man whose murder he was investigating, and now he was receiving visitors.

He couldn't lay it all at Ellen's door, but he wanted to.

Chapter 13

"Good day," Gray said, standing in his doorway. Two steps below him was the man he knew was her uncle. Ellen stood three steps lower, still on the path. Her hands were clasped around her umbrella, the weapon she'd wielded with lethal force just last night, as she swung it from side to side. She wore lavender today. Not a simple color but splashed through with mint and orange, which should be hideous but was lovely. Her lavender pelisse was a darker shade. Her bonnet had two fat ribbons tied beneath her chin and framed her pretty face. She looked sweet, disturbing, and nothing like the harridan who had threatened the man's voice box with the tip of her umbrella.

"Hello, Detective Fletcher. I hope you don't mind us calling. I'm Bramstone Nightingale, and of course you know my niece, Ellen."

He was a tall man, well-dressed. His hair was darker than his nephews', and eyes that were sharp and saw a great deal were focused on Gray. He'd learned to read people many years ago and had a feeling this was a man who knew exactly what he was about.

"How did you get my address?" Gray said for the second time that day. He stood on his doorstep, blocking entry to his town house. He didn't know why, but he had a feeling he didn't want Ellen Nightingale or her uncle inside his domain, as it would never be the same again.

"Constable Plummy," Ellen said from the step below her uncle.

Gray bit back a curse. Plummy knew where he lived because he was nosey and would have asked someone, and that someone would have let it slip. He'd now told three people, and they had all presented themselves on his doorstep.

He would have harsh words with the constable when next he saw him.

"He called to see us today," Mr. Nightingale said. "He's in love with our housekeeper, you see." The smile he threw his niece was genuine and full of affection. She returned it, but it didn't reach her eyes.

Gray realized then that she was about as comfortable as he was with this situation. She might appear calm swinging her umbrella, but she was far from it. Her eyes kept darting from left to right. She was nervous.

"Can we come in?" Bramstone Nightingale asked. "I think after last night it would be better if we chatted here in the comfort of your home, don't you? Plus, Ellen has something of a sensitive nature she wishes to discuss with you."

"I fail to see why here is any better than at your house. You could have sent word, and I would have called. Further to that, it is not a sound notion for your family to storm about London like... like vigilantes doing work better suited for—"

"If he says men like Plummy, I won't be responsible for my actions," Ellen Nightingale interrupted him.

"I'm sure he wasn't about to say any such thing," Bramstone soothed his niece. "Were you, Detective Fletcher?"

Gray hesitated. He never hesitated. What was wrong with him? He was known as the cool head in any situation.

"He also has no wish for us to step foot inside his home, Uncle Bram, and likely sees us as quite mad after last night," Ellen said. "Which is perfect, as I have no wish to either."

"That is not the case at all," Gray lied. "But it is highly irregular for me to speak on work matters here."

"Of course it is, but the matter we wish to discuss is of a sensitive nature. We do not want anyone to overhear," Bramstone said. "One never knows in Crabbett Close who would be listening."

Gray pinched his nose.

"Headache?" Ellen's uncle asked him.

"It has been a trying day. Mrs. Nicholson just called."

"Ah, I can only imagine her pain," he said.

"Poor woman," Ellen said from the bottom of his steps.

Something made him look to the gate, and he saw a carriage had stopped there, and the occupants were staring at him and the Nightingales.

"It seems we are drawing attention."

Ellen and her uncle looked. She then quickly returned her gaze to him. Her uncle watched a while longer until the carriage moved on.

"Like you, Detective Fletcher, we no longer walk in society, and as you are aware, our fall from grace was a spectacular plummet, which was in no way the fault of my nieces, wife, or myself but has tarnished us with my foolish brother's shame. However, we may no longer walk among them, but we are still fodder for gossips."

They knew who he was, just as he knew who they were. If he was honest, his identity was not something he hid, but it was rare anyone recognized him. But today, not only Mrs. Nicholson knew but the Nightingales too.

"I was at Eton with your brother, Christopher," Bramstone Nightingale said.

"How unlucky for you, sir," Gray said.

He let out a great bark of laughter. The lines deepened around his eyes, and Gray thought that he quite liked the idea that Bramstone Nightingale had been there to support his nieces and nephews when their parents had not. And why he cared, he had no idea.

"He is not someone I spent a great deal, if any, time with, I must admit."

"That makes two of us," Gray added and then wished he could shut his mouth.

His colleagues would be shocked. He never spoke unless he had something to say, and yet here he was, running off at the mouth in front of Ellen Nightingale and her uncle.

"Well then, my sweet niece, if the detective has no wish for us to enter his house, then you must tell him here what you did. However, keep your voice down."

"What did she do?" After last night, not much had the power to shock him, but he had a feeling that the next words coming out of her mouth would.

"Good God!"

The Nightingales and Gray looked to his gate at that shriek. Two women were standing there with two tall, dark-haired men at their backs. The women were identical, and the men had the look of them too. Something tugged at Gray's memory.

"Ellen?" one lady said, and then they were surging forward.

His eyes went to Ellen. She appeared frozen. A statue

of stillness. Gray wasn't sure she even breathed. Then a strangled sound came from her throat.

"Dear Lord, it is you!" The two women ran the last few steps and fell on Ellen Nightingale, hugging her.

Her uncle moved closer and placed a hand on her back, letting Ellen know he was there, Gray guessed.

"They mean her no harm, Nightingale." One man approached. "They were once friends, you see. My sisters have been searching for your niece for some time."

Bramstone nodded, stepping away from the gaggle of weeping women. "I shall leave them to their reunion, then."

He didn't move too far away from Ellen, however, remaining close enough should she need him. Gray wondered what it was like to have that kind of support.

"Sinclairs," Bramstone said, holding out a hand to the man who'd spoken to him. "'Tis good to see you again."

They exchanged greetings, and then the three men turned to look at Gray, who was still in his doorway.

"Lord Sinclair, Mr. Sinclair, this is Detective Fletcher of Scotland Yard. It is his path that we are standing upon."

The eldest had penetrating green eyes, and his dark hair was liberally streaked with silver. The other, younger, was not as big but tall. He had the same coloring.

"Good day to you," the younger man said. "It's my hope you have a full pantry, as we will all probably need to come inside so these three can continue their reunion away from prying eyes, and I'm exceedingly hungry."

Gray glanced to the street and saw that they were indeed attracting attention. He invited no one into his house. It seemed that was about to change.

"Come along, you three," Bramstone said. "You can have a catch up away from prying eyes."

Between them the two Sinclairs and Bramstone Nightingale herded their women inside his home.

"Bring refreshments please, Albert," Gray said, unsure as to how he'd lost control of everything and he now had guests.

"At once, sir." Beaming with excitement at the prospect of presenting a tea tray worthy of not just one simple detective but several people of noble birth, Albert all but skipped away.

"This is nice," Mr. Sinclair said, turning on his heel to take in Gray's entrance way.

"Thank you."

"Was this your aunt and uncle's home?" Lord Sinclair said. He was behind the women, who were still talking. Or the two dark-haired ones were and Ellen was pale and silent.

"It was, did you know them, my lord?"

"Indeed, I did, and they spoke of you often. Your uncle had great hopes you would follow through with your dreams. They were friends of my aunt and uncle, and wonderful people. I was very sorry to hear they had passed."

"They were." *Yet more family who had talked about him.*

"These are my twin sisters, Mrs. Dorset Charlton and Mrs. Somerset Charlton," Lord Sinclair said. "They weirdly married brothers, but there you have it. Weird encapsulates my family. They are a touch overwrought at the moment, but I'm sure will find their manners shortly."

Gray nodded again.

"I am Dev, Devon, or Devonshire, if you must, and this is my younger, and far inferior brother, Cam or Cambridge."

"Now we all know that for the lie it is," Cam or Cambridge said.

Gray had woken up alone and happy with that circumstance. His house was usually silent and ordered, yet right in this moment he felt like he'd lost complete control. As if everything had suddenly tilted slightly, and he had a terrible feeling he couldn't right it again.

He looked at Ellen Nightingale. Saw the panic she was struggling not to show. All the signs were there. Her hands were clenched in fists, eyes wide and she was pale. A lump formed in his chest. Which couldn't be good, but perhaps he could put it down to the overindulgence of crumpets he'd eaten this morning.

Yes, of course, that was it.

But Gray knew when someone was panicking because once he'd had episodes like that. Remembered the feeling gripping him when he was about to fall apart. It had happened often when he'd first left his family to live alone.

Looking at Ellen Nightingale he knew he had to do something to help her, because no one had helped him when he needed them to.

Chapter 14

Dorset and Somerset were here. Ellen couldn't seem to find a rational thought in her head. The minute she'd seen her friends, heard their voices, everything inside her had frozen.

For so long, she'd avoided contact with anyone from her previous life. Avoided the hurt and humiliation of what had happened.

"You vanished, Ellen. You and your family. We spent six months searching for you, but there was no word," Somerset said.

Her dear friends were pretty, vivacious, and the only people to ever really see the woman she was behind the facade Ellen had always upheld. The dutiful daughter with the expectations of her family on her shoulders.

You are so beautiful, daughter. Royalty or a duke for you, my girl. Oh no, Ellen, you must not associate with someone like her. She is beneath you. That dress, dear. It shows your body to perfection. You will trap your husband in that.

Her parents had constantly spoken this way to her.

Groomed her to be the shallow, self-centered woman society saw.

"Where did you go?" Dorset asked her.

"Sit," Cambridge Sinclair, the twins' brother, said. "And do not harangue your friend. I am sure she had her reasons for what she did."

"We do not harangue!" Somer said.

"We are simply pleased to find her well." Dorset took Ellen's hand. "It is wonderful to see you again, dear friend."

Ellen had told herself that tears were something for the weak. She'd wept until she had no more after her father's death and then vowed no one would make her cry again. But she could feel them building inside her. Soon she'd burst into loud, noisy sobs right there in Detective Fletcher's parlor in front of him and the Sinclairs.

Dear Lord, what must he be thinking?

`Her fingers started to tingle. She needed to get out of this room and compose herself. Rising before she lost control completely she said, "M-may I have the use of—"

"Of course, follow me," the detective said interrupting her. He moved to the door waving her ahead of him.

"Ellen—"

"I'm all right, Uncle Bram. I will return shortly." She could feel the panic welling up inside her. It had been many months since her last episode like this, but Ellen knew the signs of what was happening. She just needed a moment to collect herself.

She walked from the room, passing the detective who held open the door. Behind her, her two dear friends would be upset, wondering why she was walking away from them again. Uncle Bram would want to come after her.

"I will return your niece shortly," she heard the detective say to her uncle and then a hand settled on her spine. Warm and solid. "Come, this way."

Ellen walked as if in a trance. Willing herself to stay controlled and let no one see what she was feeling.

"Through here, Miss Nightingale." He reached around her and opened a door.

"Thank you. I will only be a few minutes."

He didn't leave, just nudged her through and shut it behind him.

"Please go," Ellen got out without a stammer. "I need a moment."

"Ellen, you need to breathe slowly. You will pass out if you continue at that rate."

The hands that turned her were gentle.

"Slow breaths in, Ellen."

"I-I can't."

"Sit." He placed a hand on her shoulder and forced her down into a chair. He then dragged another forward to face her.

"What are you doing? I just need a m-minute." Ellen tugged off a glove and clenched her hand, making her nails dig into her palm. The small sting of pain had often helped her to focus.

"Ellen, look at me."

Her eyes shot to his. He was seated so close now. Dark eyes intent as they willed her to look at him.

"Inhale and exhale with me."

"I-I can't." There was no point denying it. Her chest was being squeezed in a fist. It felt like she was breathing through a tiny opening.

"Listen to my voice, Ellen. Inhale for three."

He counted as she struggled to haul in a breath.

"Out for four. That's it, good girl."

It felt like his voice was the only thing keeping her from

collapsing at his feet. Her friends were here. The people she'd walked away from. The people she'd told her uncle she never again wanted to see.

"Again, Ellen. Breathe in, one, two, three."

She looked at him. Focused on his eyes and the feel of the warmth of the hand now holding hers. He talked in a steady, deep voice, and panic began to ease. Minutes later, she could take her first deep breath.

"Thank you."

"You're welcome." His smile was small but all the more powerful, as she'd never seen it before.

"How did you know?"

"That you were panicking?" She nodded. "I used to have episodes like that. I saw it in you," he said.

A vision of him in a garden filled her head.

"You walked here, outside," she said before she could halt the words.

His eyes were steady on hers. "How did you know that?"

She shrugged. "I'm sure a house like this has a lovely garden." She said the words quickly, and when she stopped, a silence settled between them. It should have been uncomfortable, but strangely, it wasn't. He still held her hand, and she didn't want him to release her.

"What did you see, Ellen?"

"What? I mean, pardon?" He couldn't know. If anyone knew what she saw, they'd turn from her, like society had.

"You had a vision. What did you see?"

Her laugh was high-pitched.

"Wh-what made you panic? Why did you have those episodes, Detective Fletcher?"

She held her breath as she waited to hear what he'd say. Luckily, he did not pursue the answer to the question he'd asked.

"Because I left everything I knew."

"When did they stop, the panic attacks?"

"It took many months, but eventually they did. And yes, being outside in the garden helped." He was still looking at her, his eyes seeking answers she would never give.

"I will remember what you taught me about the breathing."

"I learned that from my butler." He smiled again.

"Thank you, I will not forget."

"Do you want to leave, Ellen, and not speak with those women in there? I can make that happen and tell your uncle."

"No. They deserve more from me than that. I will talk to them. But what of you? This is your house, and now it is full of people you have no wish to have here."

"That's true. So far, I've avoided all contact with the life I once had... until today."

"I'm sorry." And she was. Ellen knew how important it had been to her she left that life behind. She had gone into hiding after the humiliation and devastation she and her family had suffered after her father's death. She'd vowed never to return to society. Her uncle and aunt had respected those wishes, as had her brothers.

"I loved those two women in that room. The Sinclair twins were my friends, and I walked away from them without a word of explanation," Ellen said.

"I'm sure they understood why."

"Perhaps, and while I will never return to that life, I should have told them I was at least well. I ran and hid." She never talked about this. Gave no one insight into the woman she was. She'd chosen to be strong and closed off. Even her family rarely understood what was really going on inside Ellen's head.

"I understand."

"I'm sorry. You don't need to hear this, and I'm not sure why I'm telling you." But in that moment, she felt close to this man. That would change. After all, they were strangers. But he'd helped her, and that deserved some kind of explanation.

"Sometimes the time is right," he said. "Turning your back on society takes courage, Ellen."

That forced a dry laugh from her. "It was a necessity. My mother refused to even leave the house, therefore, my uncle removed us all from London. We lived at his country home until he decided we were ready to return."

She realized she wanted to stay in this room with this big, strong man. He was a calming presence. Ellen was aware of him, and even more so now that he'd helped her. He'd shown her some of what lay beneath that cool exterior.

"Are you ready to return then?" he asked.

"Yes."

He rose and held out a hand to her. Ellen took it and regained her feet. She hesitated for a second and then leaned into the detective, pressing a kiss to his cheek.

"Thank you for helping me and knowing I was about to fall apart."

"You're welcome." His dark eyes held hers again.

A tap on the door had her pulling away. Her uncle appeared.

"Are you well, Ellen?"

She nodded. "I am, thank you, Uncle. Detective Fletcher has been very kind."

"Well, now that's good and completely understandable that you would feel panic when faced with someone from your past. Even if they are friends."

Ellen walked to her uncle. His arms closed around her,

and she laid her cheek on his chest. A place she'd spent a lot of time since her father's death.

"Thank you, Fletcher," she heard him say.

"It was nothing."

"Oh, it was certainly something. Come now, Ellen, we will face your friends, or do you feel the need to slip out a side door?"

"You've wanted me to do this for a long time. I guess my hand is now forced." She looked up at the face of the man she owed so much to. "I will, of course, meet with them."

"I am pleased, my love."

Ellen knew Detective Grayson Fletcher was watching them. She'd told him more than she'd told anyone about herself in many years, if ever.

He'd asked about her visions. What did he know of such things? He'd told her his aunt had moments. Was she like Ellen? Had he believed her or thought it nonsense? Whose grave had he stood over weeping?

Chapter 15

Gray followed the Nightingales back to his parlor, deep in thought. His cheek burned from her kiss. How could a simple touch of her lips have branded him like that? He'd been with women, but none had made him feel as Ellen had. A simple, chaste kiss and he'd had to fight with himself not to pull her closer. Not to hold her as her uncle had.

The emotion that woman stirred inside him was dangerous. Seeing her fierce fighting outside the Hope and Anchor or vulnerable as she'd just been. The many faces of Ellen Nightingale intrigued him far more than they should. And what of her knowledge that when he panicked he'd often walked in his garden? No one could have known that.

His Aunt Tilda once told him she'd seen him outside. He'd been on the highest branch of the biggest tree in his father's gardens. A place he'd spent a great deal of time in his youth. She'd said he'd had a book titled *Harry Hamlet's Adventures*, in his hands and was reading, nestled between branches.

He'd only taken that book up there once to read. Her words had made the hair on the back of his neck rise. Gray had told himself to dismiss them as her ramblings, like the rest of his family did. Mad Aunt Tilda. But he'd never forgotten.

Did Ellen Nightingale have visions like his aunt had?

Reaching the parlor, he entered with the faint hope that his guests had left. Unfortunately, it had not happened.

"Wonderful. The tea tray has arrived and now you. All is right with the world," Cambridge Sinclair said. "And may I just add Fletcher, that it is a superb tea tray. Expect regular visits from me henceforth."

Gray found the man seated in front of the tray staring at it. He looked like a salivating dog.

Ellen was back with her two friends.

"I'm not here often," Gray said, hoping to dissuade the man.

"Never mind. Just tell your staff to expect me."

Lord Sinclair laughed. "He's not serious, Detective Fletcher, even though food is more important to my brother than many things."

"I am still growing. I need sustenance."

Gray was raised taking tea with people he neither liked nor respected. He knew social chitchat better than most and loathed it. But it had been some time since he'd done this.

"Come. Sit, Fletcher," Bramstone said, waving to the seat to his right. He was next to Cambridge now. Albert handed him a cup of tea out of cups Gray didn't think he'd ever seen before. Delicate white and trimmed with gold around the rim.

"Let them talk. They have much to catch up on," Lord Sinclair said, waving to his sisters and Ellen. They were now seated on his sofa. She was in the middle and still pale but at least breathing more freely.

She had panic attacks as he had when he'd left his family. The first one had shocked him because he'd never experienced anything like it before. Albert had been there to help him through it.

"What crime are you working on at the moment, Detective Fletcher?" Mr. Sinclair asked.

Albert handed him a plate of cake. His plum cake.

"I cannot discuss any cases with you, Mr. Sinclair."

"Come now. Detective Sadler is quite chatty. I often get information for my newspapers from him."

"Newspapers?" Gray asked.

"He owns the *Trumpeter* and the *Bugler*," his brother said. "They have a law-and-order section in each, I believe?"

It surprised him that Cambridge Sinclair owned newspapers and even more that the staid and proper Detective Timothy Sadler talked to this man about Scotland Yard.

"I see it has shocked you that I would dabble in such things."

"Not shocked, no. As I am not living the life I was born into," Gray said.

Cambridge shrugged. "It is not for everyone. Someone needs to keep us safe, Detective. I don't suppose you have a copy of Captain Broadbent and Lady Nauticus tucked away somewhere?"

Gray couldn't stifle the shudder.

"Right then. Clearly, you are a sturdy, unimaginative soul to shudder at such a literary genius. Have you read it?"

"I have not." He really should be offended by that, but he wanted to laugh at the excitement in the man's eyes.

"I'll have a copy sent around," Bramstone said. "Try

before you mock, Detective Fletcher. Broadening the mind comes in many guises."

"All true," Cambridge said, waving his cup for Albert to refill it.

His butler was simply in heaven. After refilling the cup, he scooped up the now empty tray and said he'd have it replenished at once.

"When you have read it and understand the author's brilliance, we will conduct a literary salon here. I will have to run it by the Duchess of Yardly—"

"Good Lord, is she still alive?" Gray said.

"Most definitely and as crotchety and awkward as ever," Cambridge said.

"This is your parlor, Fletcher. For pity's sake, sit," Lord Sinclair said.

Gray was confident in the work he did but not in social situations. Mainly because he avoided them now. But even when he had been attending them, he'd stayed in the background. The Sinclairs, he could tell, were extremely confident.

He'd heard their name, of course, and in connection with the powerful Duke of Raven. Other bits of information also filtered into his head. A sister had wed Mr. Huntington, one of the wealthiest men in England.

Gray picked up the last available chair in the room, a spindly, uncomfortable thing, from under the desk his aunt had written her letters at. Unsure where to place it, he put it beside Bramstone Nightingale.

"Now, tell us about your latest case, Fletcher," Lord Sinclair said.

"I don't discuss my—"

"Have you ever been to Nicholson's bookshop?" Ellen Nightingale said, drawing all the eyes in the room.

"I have not. Should I?" Lord Sinclair asked.

"It's an excellent shop and not far from where we live, but it's very sad that the owner, Mr. Nicholson, was murdered there recently. Detective Fletcher is investigating that."

Gray shot Ellen a look. He didn't want her discussing the case, but he guessed it would be no secret George Nicholson was murdered if anyone asked after the man. He was sure a paper somewhere in London had printed the story.

"I remember hearing about that," Cambridge said. "Must have been terrifying to know it happened so close, Ellen." He then sniffed loudly. "Is that fruit cake I smell?"

"It is fruit buns, sir," Albert said, returning with a fresh pot of tea.

"I love fruit buns." Cambridge Sinclair's expression was like that of a small child presented with a treat.

Albert lowered the pot and left the room once more. Presumably he would reappear with fruit buns.

"I can't believe you were here in London this entire time," one of the Sinclair women said to Ellen.

She looked down at her hands, uncomfortable. "I wasn't here all the time. We spent some time in the country after father's death. I'm sorry I didn't send word. I just wasn't sure what to say."

"Hello, I am well. You do not need to worry," the other woman said. "Which we still would have done, but at least we would not have imagined you somewhere you shouldn't be?"

"They had you working in a brothel or enslaved in a workhouse," Cambridge said.

"Yes, thank you, Cam," one of the dark-haired twins snapped.

"I'm sorry I worried you," Ellen said. "But there was so much change."

"Completely understandable," Lord Sinclair said. "And on behalf of our family allow me to tell you we are very sorry for what you and your family endured." He looked from Ellen to Bramstone Nightingale. "Now that is enough from you two," he then said to his sisters. "You have found her so no more interrogating is required."

Gray could tell the twins didn't think that was anywhere near enough but didn't say anything further on the matter.

"More visitors have called, sir."

"What? Who?" Gray said exasperated. He couldn't imagine who else would be here. His family never visited.

"Mr. Ramsey Hellion."

"Hello, Gray." The tall man standing in the doorway looked nothing like his old childhood friend.

"Ramsey?" The name came out louder than he'd intended and then Gray was hugging his cousin.

"It's a busy day in the Fletcher household, it seems, what with reunions and making acquaintances. This bachelor establishment hasn't seen this much action for some time is my guess," Cambridge said.

"What the hell are you doing here, Ram?" Gray said, emotion thick in his throat.

Ramsay Hellion was his cousin and once best friend. His parents had moved to India when he was young. They'd not seen each other since. But they had written regularly. In fact, Ram was the only relative he'd kept in contact with, which was ironic when his siblings and parents were under an hour away.

"Well, I think it may be time for us to depart, Ellen," Bramstone Nightingale said. "We shall call on you tomorrow to discuss what information we have, Detective Fletcher. But now we'll leave you to your reunion," he added.

"Don't depart on my account," Ramsey said, smiling at the ladies.

Gray had the sudden urge to punch him when he looked at Ellen, which told him it was important not to spend too much time in that woman's company going forward.

Brief introductions were made, and then they were all leaving.

"I'll call again soon, Detective. You can give me an interview for one of my newspapers," Cambridge Sinclair said. Gray noted he had a fruit bun in his hand.

He looked at Ellen, and she gave him a small smile before turning and walking out of his parlor.

When it was only him and Ramsey left in the room, Gray fell into the nearest chair and wondered what the hell was happening to his life.

"I'm so sorry about Uncle Henry, Ram."

His cousin nodded and took the seat across from him. "It was a quick death, Gray, but we miss him dreadfully. Mother came back with me but is now closeted away with her sister in Cornwall after visiting with your family. Her brother, as you can imagine, was a cold, emotionless bastard when we arrived."

"Yes, my father is the most soulless, unemotional man I know."

"Amen," Ram said.

Tall, with hair the color of a burnished chestnut, Ramsey had bright blue eyes and a large personality. He'd always been the exact opposite of Gray, and that was perhaps why they'd been the best of friends.

"I will bring more tea," Albert said, still smiling. He then bustled about collecting up plates and cups and left.

"We were invited to your brother's wedding, which as you can imagine will be a crushing bore, but needs must when it comes to family. Or so mother told me," Ramsay said.

"Which one of them is getting married?" Gray asked, not surprised in the least that he hadn't received an invitation. However the ache in his chest told him it still hurt.

"Don't tell me you are not going?" The horror on his cousin's face made Gray feel marginally better.

"We don't talk often, and clearly, I'm an embarrassment. How would they explain to the haute ton that one of them was a detective at Scotland Yard?" He told himself he wasn't hurt.

"That pompous bloody twit," Ramsey seethed. He'd always been the louder of the two of them. "I've a mind to refuse. In fact, I will if they do not invite you."

"No, go, I have no issue with not being there," Gray lied. "Which brother has found a woman to have him?"

"Christopher. He's marrying Lady Mary Smythe. A perfect match from what I gather. She was there when we arrived at the Seddon town house. She's as cool and emotionless as Christopher."

"You're right, that is a perfect match."

Pushing aside the gnawing ache deep inside that his family was so ashamed they hadn't even invited him to his eldest brother's wedding, Gray reminded himself they'd been ignoring him for years. This was just another occasion.

He drank more tea and caught up with his cousin for the next two hours, and by the time Ramsey left, he knew he had his best friend back. Gray thought that was a bloody amazing thing. A relative who didn't care what he was and only that he was a friend.

Chapter 16

Ellen and Uncle Bram had decided to visit Detective Fletcher at Scotland Yard instead of his house as he'd clearly he'd been uncomfortable having visitors in his home.

Leo and Alex had wanted to come, but they had recently ventured into business, and today were viewing a large building with the hopes of purchasing it. They would then convert it into a variety of shops all under the same roof. It was a concept others had achieved, and they wanted to try.

Her brothers were no longer the bored indolent nobleman they'd once been, and she knew Uncle Bram was behind this and their current venture.

"Don't be nervous, niece. Detective Fletcher is a good man."

"I know. He was kind to me in his house that day."

They were at present sitting in hard chairs inside Scotland Yard, waiting to see if the detective had time to speak with them.

"He will not judge us harshly."

"I hope you are right, Uncle Bram."

He patted her hand.

"I like him."

"You do?"

"He's firm but fair, he will treat us the same."

Ellen looked around the stark brown walls and hoped he was right. The information they had could cause a great deal of trouble for her and her uncle.

"Hello." Looking to the doorway, she found Detective Fletcher standing there. Ellen felt that jab of excitement in her belly seeing him again. Tall and somber in charcoal trousers and a black jacket. "If you would like to come this way."

She held Uncle Bram's hand as they walked along a hallway with more brown walls and little else adorning them. He then waved them into a room. Following, the detective shut the door.

"Please, sit."

He took the chair behind the desk, and she and Uncle Bram the ones opposite.

"I gather this is what you wanted to discuss when you called at my house?" His voice was unemotional, his dark eyes passing over them coolly.

"We thought it better to come here so we would not be interrupted," Uncle Bram said.

"Yes, it got a trifle busy in my house." The corner of Detective Fletcher's lip twitched. "Please, tell me what brings you here."

"Have you nothing you could put on the wall to liven it up a bit in here?" Ellen said, looking around them. It was stark and empty. Not a terribly welcoming environment to work in daily.

"I come here to work, Miss Nightingale, not liven things up," he said.

He'd been gentle with her when she panicked. That man was now gone.

"Right, at least we've established that then," Uncle Bram said, shooting her a look that suggested she stay focused. "When you're ready, Ellen. Tell the detective what you did."

Now the moment had come. She felt nervous. What would he say or think about her hiding evidence?

"I found a knife under the body the night I came upon Mr. Nicholson dead in his bookshop. It looked the same as my uncle's. I panicked and took it from the scene."

The silence that followed her words filled the room. Detective Fletcher's expression had not changed, but there was now tension in his shoulders. Ellen fought to keep any visions at bay. This man seemed to have them filling her head when he was close.

"And is it yours?" he asked Uncle Bram.

"It is. It was stolen from me months ago one night when I was returning home. I wrestled with my assailant, and he ran away. I hadn't realized he'd taken the knife from my pocket with him."

"You walk about London carrying a knife, Mr. Nightingale?" the detective said calmly.

"Don't you?" Ellen demanded. Uncle Bram placed a hand over hers and squeezed.

"I always have a weapon on me, Detective Fletcher. On my travels I collected many and usually have one with me if I am to walk about London at night," Uncle Bram said.

"Why do you walk about London at night if you don't mind me asking, when there is surely a carriage available to you?"

"I enjoy it and am more than capable of protecting myself."

"As you have taught your niece and nephews to do?"

"He did yes. My uncle, unlike many men, believes a woman should be able to protect herself," Ellen said. "I learned at the same time as my brothers to defend myself."

"It was not an insult, Miss Nightingale, but a query. If I had a daughter, I, too, would wish for her to defend herself. Had Miss Tompkins been able to, then Barney Forge would not have achieved what he did."

She huffed out a breath.

"Do you have the knife on you?" Detective Fletcher asked.

Uncle Bram rose and took it out of his pocket. He then laid it on the desk between them.

"Tell me what you did that night in the shop when you saw this, Miss Nightingale."

She went through everything she could remember.

"You realize, of course, that what you did was wrong and could have jeopardized the case."

"My niece was protecting me, Detective Fletcher. I will not have her censured for her loyalty." Uncle Bram rarely used that voice, but when he did, people listened.

"I understand, and her loyalty to you was admirable, but in taking this evidence, she stopped us from investigating another avenue. That of who had this knife in their possession the night George Nicholson was murdered."

"We understand what she did is wrong, but the reasons were pure as I have explained," Uncle Bram said. "Surely if I was guilty, we would not have come forward but kept the knife hidden and my name out of anything to do with George's death."

"Your wife can vouch for where you were on the night Mr. Nicholson died, I presume?"

"Now, just a minute!" Ellen got to her feet, panic flaring to life inside her. "You know he was out of town, because we told you."

"Ellen, sit down. The detective is simply doing his job."

"I don't care. He will not insult you with the notion that you could have done this. You are not capable, nor would you. George was your friend, as he was ours."

"I have to ask the question, Miss Nightingale. It is my job."

Ellen braced her hands on his desk, ignoring the sigh from her uncle. "My uncle is the best man I know, and he would never do such a nefarious deed. Had I my way, I would never have given you this information, but he insisted."

She and the detective stared at each other. His eyes cool, hers shooting fire.

"Sit, Ellen." A hand on her shoulder had her pushing off the desk. "Heartwarming though your words were, this will get us nowhere, love."

"I won't have him insulting you," she muttered, retaking her seat.

"I don't believe I insulted anyone. I am doing my job, Miss Nightingale." The words had a snap to them now.

"I have several people you can approach to vouch for my whereabouts on the night George Nicholson was murdered, Detective Fletcher. I can give you their names. We were with the Fairweathers. We stayed there two nights on our return to London."

Detective Fletcher took out a piece of paper and wrote in silence for several minutes while Ellen fumed. She'd learned control early in life. It deserted her when someone she loved was threatened. Especially this someone. Bramstone and Ivy Nightingale had believed in the Nightingale children. Believed and loved them and helped them to become the people they were today.

"It's all right, love." Uncle Bram leaned across and kissed her cheek. "Thank you for your ferocious defense."

She managed a nod.

"If you would give me those names, please, Mr. Nightingale," Detective Fletcher said in his cold voice.

She sat in silence and fumed some more that he had not taken her uncle's word at where he and Aunt Ivy had been.

He's doing his job.

She was fiercely protective of her family since her father's death and perhaps a bit irrational when someone challenged them too, if she was being honest.

"Can I ask you something, Miss Nightingale?" Detective Fletcher said suddenly. He'd lowered his pen and was studying her.

Ellen nodded.

"I questioned you that day in my house, when you were panicking, if you saw visions. You did not answer me. Will you do so now?"

"No." Her uncle said the word in a hard voice. "Come, Ellen. Let's go. I believe you have everything you need from us. If you are not arresting me, then we are leaving."

"I mean your niece no harm, Mr. Nightingale. I had an aunt who had visions. None of her family, including me, took her seriously. It is only later, after she passed and with age, that I've begun to wonder about her and what she saw. More so since I met Miss Nightingale."

"I will not have my niece ridiculed or—"

"No. I would never do that. I merely wish for her help."

"What? How could I help you?" Ellen asked him.

"In truth, I don't know, but perhaps you could help find a lead. Anything to point us in the right direction of the man who killed Mr. Nicholson."

"You believe I do see things?" For so long, Ellen had hidden who she was, and now her family and some of the

Crabbett Close residents knew. But did she want Detective Fletcher to have that information too?

"The rational part of my mind tells me I shouldn't, but I can't discount it without more research."

"You think I can assist?" That shocked her. The man was someone who did things by the book. A rule follower. Not that she knew him, but she knew his type. Was sure he was a man who ate the same breakfast at the same time each day and liked routine. He had that look about him, even if it was a handsome look.

Not handsome! She had to stop thinking of him that way. The problem was, a spark of attraction had broken through the numbness and cold inside her that she feared would never let her feel anything for another person, other than those that carried her blood, again.

"In truth, I'm not sure, but I wish for you to walk through the bookshop with me. See if anything comes to you. I can find no clue as to why Nicholson was murdered. If, as I know will happen, your uncle was away from London and his alibi turns out to be solid, then I have no suspects."

"No," her uncle said.

"You said you saw me in my garden," the detective continued, ignoring Uncle Bram. "I used to walk about there when I was gripped by panic. The day when I came to speak with you after the murder, you had another vision, didn't you?"

Ellen nodded.

"What was it?"

"I-ah, I've had a few, actually."

"Ellen—"

"It's all right, Uncle Bram. If he tells anyone, we will put it about that he's mad. I'm sure, even tarnished, we have a few friends in high places who could destroy him.

Plus, let us not forget the residents of Crabbett Close, who can make his life hell."

"You could try," Detective Fletcher said slowly.

"Before she tells you what she saw, let me make something very clear to you, Fletcher. I would be your worst nightmare as an enemy. Never forget that. I will do whatever it takes to keep my family safe. Anything," Uncle Bram said in a hard tone.

The man simply nodded, not appearing overly worried about the threat to his safety, even here in his offices, but he didn't speak. His eyes stayed on Ellen.

"I saw a hand holding a knife after I found George lying on the floor dead that night when he was murdered in his bookshop."

Detective Fletcher wrote more notes.

"I had a vision of you as a young boy standing over a grave in a black jacket. You looked alone and were crying."

His head shot up at her words. "I wore a black jacket to my grandfather's funeral but then so did many."

"I saw a gold bird."

Color drained from his face.

"I'm sorry if my memory hurt you," Ellen whispered.

He shook his head slowly, as if to clear it. "My grandfather was buried with a set of golden wings that were his father's."

"Wings," Ellen whispered. "Not a bird."

He nodded this time.

"So now you know what I can do," Ellen added.

"I do."

"You're not sure that you believe me, but you're willing to take a chance that I can help you with this case?"

He nodded. "Will you assist me with my enquiries, Miss Nightingale? Help clear your uncle's name?"

If it meant Uncle Bram was no longer a suspect and the killer caught, then yes, she would.

"I can do this," she said to her uncle. "I trust him to not tell anyone what I can do. Besides, who would believe him?"

"Very well. But remember what I said, Fletcher," Uncle Bram said.

"I don't take well to threats, Nightingale, but if it eases your mind, your niece is in no danger of exposure from me. I simply want to find a killer. If she helps with that, I would be grateful."

Uncle Bram took her hand after those words and led her from the room, and Ellen had a strange feeling that something monumental had just happened. Her life was about to change completely, but she just wasn't sure how.

Chapter 17

Gray had thought long and hard for four days about calling at 11 Crabbett Close. He'd spent that time following leads and getting nowhere. But the memory of what he'd talked to Ellen Nightingale and her uncle about in his office had stayed in his head.

Was it really possible she could see things as his aunt had claimed to?

It had shocked him when she told him of her vision of Gray standing over his grandfather's grave, weeping. Gray had loved his grandfather. No one could have told her that.

Ellen Nightingale was intriguing. The fiery woman who'd protected her uncle and then said she'd help him.

When the carriage stopped in front of the Nightingale family home Gray climbed out. After instructing his driver to carry on around the circle until he was ready, he walked up the path and knocked on the front door.

"Good day to you, Detective Fletcher!" A voice said from over his shoulder.

"Hello, Mr. Greedy." He raised a hand to the man who

had told him he wasn't right in the head if he believed the Nightingales anything but good folk.

"Good day to you, Detective Fletcher," the housekeeper then said after opening the door. She raised a hand to Mr. Greedy too. "What can I do for you?"

"Could I speak to Miss Nightingale please, Miss Bud?"

"I'm right here, Bud. Step aside, and I'll see what he wants," a voice said.

The housekeeper moved, and there she was, Ellen Nightingale, looking lovely. So lovely he felt like someone was standing on his chest, and it was suddenly hard to breathe.

He battled down the need to smile and instead scowled.

"If you want to get information from people, if I may suggest a smile, Detective. That will work a great deal better than that expression," Ellen said.

"I have no time to smile." *Why had he said that?* She made him addled. "I am here to ask you to accompany me, Miss Nightingale."

"Am I being arrested then?"

She wore multiple shades today. Pinks, grays, and greens all blended into patterns. It should be odd and yet on her it was perfect.

"No, of course not. I wish to have you with me when I go to the Nicholsons' house. See if you can get anything from the family. They have requested I visit with them and give them an update on the case."

Surprise had her mouth forming a perfect and kissable O. Not kissable. *Damn.*

"I thought you wanted me to come to the bookshop?"

"I do. But if you have the time, I would like you to accompany me to the Nicholson's as well."

"You have no leads and are desperate?"

She was on to him.

"What of the knife? Have you found anything there?"

He gritted his teeth. Then, exhaling through them, he shook his head. Gray was good at his job. The best, if he was honest. But he could get nothing on this case.

"And how will you explain my presence?"

"I'll say you're my assistant."

She folded her arms, just like he did when he wanted to convey his annoyance to someone without words.

"Yes, because we would not want anyone to think a woman actually had a brain and could do detective work also."

"Then what would you like me to say you are doing?" he said as politely as he could, when in fact he wanted to snap the words at her. She had a smart mouth, this woman. "I do not make up society's rules, Miss Nightingale," he added.

"Can I not be an adviser?"

"Of what?"

She thought about that. "I see the problem. We can't say I'm going to try to see visions."

"Exactly."

"Oh, very well. I will just collect my coat then."

"Is your family home? Do you need me to speak with them on the matter?"

"No." Her smile was sly. "You are safe from a lecture, as they have all gone to the museum. Not that I need you talking to them on my behalf. I am capable of making my own decisions."

"Fine," he muttered as she left. The door was open, and even though she did not invite him in, he stepped inside anyway. There was every chance the protective males in her household would want to throttle him for this.

The click of nails on the floor had Chester appearing

with a black shoe in his mouth. He wandered to Gray, dropped it on his foot, and barked once, loudly.

"What is it I'm meant to do after you bark at me, Chester? Say good boy for stealing that shoe?"

The large head tilted to one side, studying Gray.

He had no experience with pets or children. His family had none, and he had no friends he visited in their home with either.

The dog let out a big woof again. Gray leaned closer to pat his head, and the brute sat, so he continued to do so. He was sure the dog was making a purring sound when he saw Miss Bud reappear.

"You'll take care of her."

"She is simply going to consult for me."

"What does a consultant do exactly?" the housekeeper asked. Her green eyes were narrowed and focused on him.

What was it with people in this house not trusting him? He added the neighborhood to that.

"Advise." He wasn't used to having his actions questioned, and especially not by the housekeeper. "We are visiting some people, and I would like Miss Nightingale to tell me what she thinks of them." Why was he explaining these details to her? She was a housekeeper, for pity's sake.

And therefore, did not deserve his respect? Was he such a hard man he didn't respect those beneath him on the social ladder of life? He thought about his staff. They were paid well, but he did not get close to them. Albert, of course, pushed those boundaries, but he didn't really know much about him.

He blamed Ellen Nightingale for stirring all these thoughts up inside him. Before her he'd never even considered if his staff were happy in his employ.

"Well, you make sure to watch over Miss Nightingale or her family will not be best pleased."

He nodded.

"Right. I'll be back soon, Bud." Ellen appeared now in her coat and bonnet.

"Will you be wanting me to come with you?"

"I won't, no. But thank you." Ellen kissed the housekeeper's cheek. She then looked down at Chester.

"Is that Alex's other shoe? You are a good boy." She patted his head and then waved Gray out the door.

She'd kissed her housekeeper's cheek as if she was… what? *Important?* Worthy of her attention? Damn the woman. She was confusing him.

He waved down his carriage. Opening the door, he took Ellen's hand and helped her inside.

"Why is Chester a good boy for stealing your brother's shoe?"

"You have met Alex. Surely the reason is clear. He, like Leo, can be infuriating. It's quite funny, really. Chester only takes Mungo's and Alex's things."

She then leaned out the window, which he'd had open.

"Good day, Mrs. Varney! How is your foot?"

"A great deal better!" The woman wandering down Crabbett Close called back.

"Excellent!" Ellen replied. She then sat in the seat across from Gray once more.

The woman was unlike anyone he knew. Born into nobility, she could now not be further from it.

"Do you often shriek like a fishwife from the carriage window?" Gray asked.

"Asking after someone's welfare, out a carriage window in the street you live in, is not shrieking like a fishwife. It's being supportive."

"Right, silly me." It didn't sit well with him that she had no one with her, but it had made his job easier of getting her into the carriage.

"It's quite freeing not needing a chaperone," she said.

"There is no way you could have known what I was thinking."

"No, I didn't, but I knew that thought would be in there." She pointed to his head. "My brothers are not dissimilar to you, Detective Fletcher. They may no longer live in society, yet sometimes they are sticklers for propriety."

"I'm sure they would disagree with you."

"About being similar to you?"

He nodded.

"Possibly that is true," she said.

That had him snorting.

"How do the visions come to you?" Gray asked, intrigued. To his shame, he'd never shown his aunt any interest because his family had wanted it that way.

"'Don't encourage your aunt, she's addled in the head,'" his father would say. But his aunt hadn't been addled. She'd been, for the most, a sensible, if colorful person, or so she'd seemed to him. Not that his family had allowed him to spend much time with her.

"I see things that were or are going to be, but, I cannot tell when they will appear."

"Visions?"

She nodded. "Take the night with Mr. Nicholson. I saw the hand holding the knife clearly, almost like a picture. Just as I saw you as a boy. But sometimes they are not that clear and a great deal more cryptic, which can be vexing."

"Do all your family know?"

"This family does. But before, when I was in society, I did not allow myself to believe the visions were anything. But I knew." Her voice was small now.

"Knew what?"

"Many things about what was to happen or at least

some visions leading to my father's death."

"I'm sorry. That must have been hard." He could only imagine the hell she went through seeing what she had and trying to deny them, as she'd never acknowledged what she could do.

"I'm not sure why I told you that." Her eyes went to the window. "It's not something we like to talk about."

"We share that in common. I don't like to talk about the life I once lived, either, but I did not suffer as you did. Leaving was my choice."

Her eyes came back to his. "Why did you leave?"

Gray shrugged, suddenly uncomfortable. He didn't like to speak of that time either. But he found himself talking just the same. "My aunt and uncle passed, and they had no children and were fond of me, so they left me enough money to change my destiny."

Her smile was small, but this time it reached her lovely eyes. That heat settled in his chest again.

"I'm glad you had a choice to change your destiny, Detective Fletcher."

Gray managed a nod around the lump in his throat that her words had created.

"Were you the one to inform the Nicholson family of their son's death?" She changed the subject.

He nodded. "I spoke with Mr. Nicolson."

"That must have been terrible."

"It was." He hated informing people of a loved one's death. But as he'd seen George Nicholson's body, he'd decided he'd visit the family.

"Now tell me about these people we are to meet," she said.

Gray told her who they were going to speak with.

"The Nicholsons have made their money through their sweet shop but also have other business investments. Mr.

Nicholson is a savvy businessman from what I have learned, as was his son. The mother who called to see me is Mildred. They have a daughter, Olivia, three years younger than George. Mrs. Nicholson told me they were close."

"Poor girl, losing her big brother. It would devastate me if anything happened to one of mine. While I want to shake them constantly, they are the best of men."

Gray couldn't remember ever feeling like that about his brothers.

"George and I discussed books but never family. I feel bad about that now," Ellen said.

He lapsed into silence, unsure of what to say.

"I'm sorry, I'm being maudlin. Now the Nicholsons have asked you to call, but you want me to go with you to see if I have any visions. What do you hope to achieve, as surely you do not suspect his family?"

Gray shook his head. "You can never discount anyone, especially those closest to the murder victim. I also thought having you there would help Miss Nicholson feel more at ease." Gray struggled with weeping women, and it was possible that at least one of the ladies they were to see could be that. "I have met her mother but as yet not the daughter."

"She has just lost her brother, Detective Fletcher, it's entirely possible she is ravaged with grief."

"I understand that, but I want to ask some questions about her brother."

"And I will repeat, she is in mourning," Ellen said. "If you speak to her like a brisk, emotionless man, then I imagine she will be too intimidated to reply. Perhaps if you smiled and offered a please or thank you. Maybe even state that you are incredibly sorry for her loss?"

"I beg your pardon. I am not there to be her friend but

ask questions of them."

"But surely to achieve what you want, if they are comfortable around you, you would have more success. The family we are about to meet are grieving. Surely that allows them some of your small supply of sympathy, Detective Fletcher? Being polite and kind does not mean you are making lifelong friends."

His eyes narrowed as he looked at her. She had a smart mouth, this woman. He couldn't help but enjoy talking to her, even if she was attacking him.

"Let me ask you this, Detective Fletcher."

"If you must."

She flashed a white-toothed smile at him, and he knew she'd used it as a powerful weapon in the London ballrooms in her time. It certainly had an effect on him.

"Do you believe that to achieve the results you want, you must intimidate people with your dour face and cold words?"

He stared at her. No one spoke to him like this.

"You weren't exactly the friendliest when first I met you, Miss Nightingale, may I remind you." When Gray was cornered, he went on the attack.

"Because you were interviewing me about the murder of my friend, whose body I'd found. Plus, as you know, I'd taken my uncle's knife from the scene, unknowing that, in fact, it had been stolen from him a few months before."

"Which was breaking the law," Gray added.

He'd never doubted Bramstone Nightingale's story, even after he'd investigated his alibi. The man's knife had been stolen from him. Gray knew people. He'd not been lying. However, he hadn't known his niece had been when he'd interviewed her. But he admired her loyalty for all that she tampered with evidence and broke the law.

"Don't change the subject. You are trying to deflect,

Detective Fletcher."

"I'm very good at my job," Gray said. He felt alive sitting here, verbally sparring with Ellen Nightingale. Which said what about him? "I get results, Miss Nightingale."

"I bet all the women you interview are terrified or in love with you."

"I am not terrifying. I am professional. Please note the difference." He ignored the "in love" part of her statement.

When was the last time someone had spoken to him like this? Gray couldn't recall, if ever, anyone had. Then he remembered Ramsey. His cousin had always challenged Gray. He was happy his old friend was back in London.

"We are here," he said as the carriage rolled down a street filled with large town houses.

"You are my assistant and write up my notes," Gray said.

"Is that actually something you would do? Or anyone, for that matter?"

"Not me personally, but I doubt the Nicholsons would be aware of that."

"Well then, have no fear. I shall not blow our cover. After all, I was a superb actor for years."

With those cryptic words, she threw open the door and stepped from the carriage before he could assist her.

Gray had a sense of foreboding but swallowed it down and followed.

The first thing they saw was a wreath of laurel tied with black crape, hanging on the front door to alert passersby that a death had occurred.

He took Ellen's arm and walked up the steps to knock on the door, suddenly glad he didn't have to face the mourning Nicholson family alone.

Chapter 18

The pall of death hung over the Nicholsons' home as they stepped inside. Ellen knew George had been buried two days ago, but there was no doubt the house was in deep mourning. Dark and silence was everywhere.

They were ushered by a butler into a parlor lit by lamps. The Nicholson family were gathered in the room.

Ellen took the seat beside Detective Fletcher. Across from him were George's mother and father, with their daughter, Olivia, between them. The girl had red eyes and a pale face, and after a small weary smile for them, she had kept her head down. Clearly, she was distraught over her brother's death.

Also in the room was Mrs. Nicholson's sister, Miss Denton. Olivia and her mother had their hair in a severe bun but not the other woman.

Hers was styled perfectly, with ringlets framing her face. The dress was deep gray with black lace marching down the shoulders and black satin bows around the hem. She presented a picture of demure gentility, and her eyes had been on Detective Fletcher since he entered the room.

"George was a wonderful man," Miss Denton said, sending Detective Fletcher a flirtatious smile, which, to Ellen, signaled her interest in the man. He was oblivious, his face serious as he continued to ask questions. "We loved him very much." She leaned forward slightly and gave him a wide-eyed, innocent look. He simply nodded, which had annoyance flashing across her face.

Did the woman not understand that the Nicholson family was in mourning? Surely flirting with the detective who was investigating her nephew's murder was the height of unacceptable behavior.

Ellen swallowed her smile as the detective turned from Miss Denton to speak with Mr. Nicholson, and her lips clamped into a hard line. She bet that women had thrown themselves at him many times, and he'd failed to notice. The man was handsome, articulate, and had good breeding, and he did not make her heart flutter, she told herself.

The detective was not for the likes of her. Ellen had vowed no man would be. She would spend her life unwed. Never again to be a pawn for a man to discard.

"And you are Detective Fletcher's assistant, Miss Night?" Miss Denton asked her.

They'd decided not to use her actual name, so the detective had shortened it.

"I am yes," Ellen said.

"How wonderful. I can imagine how thrilling it must be to work for a man such as him," Miss Denton said.

"Oh yes. Every day is a thrill. And so exciting. I go home some nights and barely sleep due to the day I have just spent in his company."

Ellen tried to converse with Miss Nicholson, but she did not speak more than a few words, and often her aunt answered for her. In fact, none of the Nicholsons offered any conversation unless directly questioned. They sat together and were clearly a family grieving deeply for their much-loved son and brother.

Mr. Nicholson had the look of George, only taller, and he had a solid presence to him that reminded her of Uncle Bram. Mrs. Nicholson had red-rimmed eyes and dark smudges underneath. Ellen's heart wept for them. George had been her friend, and she missed him, but she had not known him all her life.

"Do you remember George arguing with anyone? An enemy from his youth? Anyone that may have held a grudge against him?" Detective Fletcher asked.

"Everyone loved my brother," Olivia said softly. "He was the very best of men." She burst into tears and pressed her face into a handkerchief.

The vision came fast. George talking to his sister in the bookshop. Olivia was crying. The vision changed suddenly, and she saw another man with dark hair. He was lying on his side and unclothed. One arm was raised in the air, and then that vision was gone too.

"He had no enemies," Mrs. Nicholson was saying when Ellen came back to herself.

Detective Fletcher shot her a look, and Ellen managed a smile. She was faintly nauseous and wanted to blush at the same time over the fact she'd just seen her first naked man.

When the dreams were strong, the emotions vivid, she sometimes felt them.

"Not quite true, Mildred," her husband said, drawing Ellen's eyes.

She concentrated on breathing slowly to push aside the nausea.

"There was that man who wanted to purchase the bookshop, but George got it before him. He was not happy and said he had been cheated in some way. Vowed he would own that shop if it was the last thing he'd do," Mr. Nicholson said.

"I'd forgotten about that," Mrs. Nicholson said. "He was not a nice man." Her nose wrinkled.

"Do you remember his name?" Detective Fletcher asked.

"Dunston, Michael Dunston," Mr. Nicholson said. "He threatened George, but that stopped when I got Bow Street involved."

"Do you know where he lives?"

"I'm sorry, I don't. But the Bow Street runner I talked to on the matter was a Mr. Brown."

"Thank you," Detective Fletcher said. "If you think of anything else, please let me know."

Had the vision been of this Michael Dunston? Was he the angry man?

"We will," Miss Denton said. She then sent the detective another flirtatious smile.

Ellen had never thought about a man's plight in life. She'd just believed they had the best of most things. They could go to school and university. Their reputations stayed intact even when they had affairs. But she'd never given much consideration to what it felt like to be pursued by women.

Only a small negative in a list of positives, it had to be noted, but still, it must be uncomfortable. Especially if you were handsome, like Detective Fletcher and her brothers. Not that she'd ever tell Leo or Alex that.

"Please find whoever killed my darling nephew, Detective. We cannot rest until you do." Miss Denton held out her hands to him, and Ellen stifled a snort at the look of panic that came over his face.

"Ah, of course." He held the tips of her fingers briefly

and then stepped back and bowed. "Come, Miss Night. We must leave." His words sounded urgent.

"I have my son's latest account ledger here, Detective Fletcher. You said you'd like to see it," Mr. Nicholson said. "If you'll come this way, I'll get it for you."

Mr. and Mrs. Nicholson went through a door with Olivia. Gray followed, and Ellen prepared to do the same.

A hand on her arm stopped her.

"Is Detective Fletcher married? Do you know, Miss Night?"

"Detective Fletcher is a very private man. He does not speak of his personal life, Miss Denton."

She smiled, her hand going to Ellen's wrist, where she squeezed gently. "Come, Miss Night, from one woman to another. You must tell me what you know of him. He is quite simply divine. So handsome, and those shoulders." She made a humming sound. "Does he have a woman in his life or not?"

"I'm sorry, I don't know," Ellen said.

"How disappointing. I shall have to make enquiries for myself."

Relieved the detective chose that moment to return, Ellen dropped into a curtsey and murmured her goodbyes demurely. She was rarely demure. Once it had been expected of her, but no more. Her uncle and aunt encouraged her to be outspoken and loud if it was her wish to do so.

Detective Fletcher helped her into the carriage, aware that eyes were on them. Ellen took his hand and stepped inside. She then settled on the seat. He joined her, and soon they were moving.

"What did you see?" he sounded irritated.

"Your tone would suggest I've done something to annoy you?"

"I'm—"

"Because you'll pardon me if I'm wrong, Detective Fletcher, but didn't I just sit there quietly, observing as you'd asked me to?"

"Miss Nightingale—"

"A please would have been nice, considering what I saw made me nauseous," Ellen added, knowing she sounded testy.

He raised a hand when she opened her mouth to speak again.

"If you will allow me to talk," he said in a rigidly polite tone. Ellen nodded. "Forgive me, I find that kind of thing difficult."

"Interviewing parents of a son who was murdered or the flirtatious aunt?"

His eyes narrowed. "Whichever way I go will be the wrong way with that question."

She laughed, and he replied with a smile.

"I'm sorry, and thank you for being there. Are you all right? Can I get you anything? Are you still nauseous?"

"That apology was very well done, and I'm sure didn't hurt you too much," Ellen said.

"Are you always this annoying?" He frowned.

"Yes."

This time it was him who laughed. A great bark of it that seemed to surprise him. Ellen wondered why the detective didn't laugh much because it suited him. But then again, perhaps considering how appealing it made him look, it was better he didn't. Women like Miss Denton would be falling all over him.

"Will you please tell me what you saw in the Nicholson household, Miss Nightingale?"

"The first vision was of Olivia and George. She was crying in his shop. I don't know why, but I was sure they were both angry. The next was of a man with dark hair." Ellen felt color fill her cheeks.

"What?" He leaned closer.

"He was, ah, naked and lying on his side."

"Naked?"

"I only saw his back view," she rushed to add. "I mean… well, you know what I mean."

He looked out the window of the carriage.

"Are you laughing at me?" Ellen demanded when she noted the side of his mouth twitch.

"Absolutely not. I was just thinking."

"You are laughing at me!"

His face might be serious, but his eyes were alive with humor.

"Yes, yes, very amusing. Now tell me what you got out of that interview," Ellen said.

"Do you think the naked man could have been this Dunstan fellow?"

"I wondered about that, but until I see him, I can't know."

"Was he big or small? An Adonis or…?"

"Are you teasing me now? Because if you are, I will never again go to an interview with you."

"Miss Nightingale, do I appear to be the type of man who teases people?" he said solemnly.

"There is a type?" she asked in an excruciatingly polite tone.

"I'm just attempting to work out who I am looking for or if I come across a naked man draped in scarlet velvet how to identify him," he said.

His face was serious, so she couldn't be absolutely sure but thought he was teasing her.

"Miss Denton asked me if you were married or had a

special woman in your life. She seemed very interested in you," Ellen said to annoy him.

"She what?" His dark brows drew together.

"I think she sees herself as the next Mrs. Fletcher. Of course, I told her you were actually a nobleman's son, and that interested her further, so expect some kind of communication going forward, as I also gave her your address."

He shuddered. "That was cruel, Miss Nightingale, and if I thought you were serious, I would be extremely angry right now."

"How do you know I'm not?"

He shrugged. "You have brothers and would hate for one of them to be subjected to women like Miss Denton."

"She is not bad, just spoiled is my guess."

"Yes, I would agree with that," he said. "Would you recognize this man if you saw him, Miss Nightingale? The one in your vision?"

"It was only a rear view, but his arm was raised… a mark," Ellen said, closing her eyes as she recalled the memory. "I remember it now. At the time, I was still recovering from George and Olivia Nicholson's anger."

"You feel things when you have these visions?"

She nodded, eyes still closed. Something warm settled on her hand, the one she hadn't realized she'd clenched in her lap.

"Don't distress yourself."

Her eyes opened, and he was close now, and staring at her intently. His hand was warm on hers, encasing it in heat. Their eyes caught and held. Ellen was suddenly breathless.

"What mark did you see, Ellen, Miss Nightingale?" He removed his hand and sat back in his seat, and she could breathe again.

"Something on his forearm. A black…" Ellen tried to remember.

"A mark he's had since birth?"

"No. It was drawn there. I've seen things like this in my uncle's books. A circle, I think."

"Would you be able to draw it?" he asked.

"I believe so."

The carriage rolled to a stop outside 11 Crabbett Close, and Ellen hadn't even realized they'd arrived.

"What is the time, please, Detective Fletcher?"

He pulled out his watch. "4:30 p.m."

Teatime, Ellen thought. She knew her family would all have returned and would be waiting for her. Some happy, others angry. It was the angry ones she was worried about.

"Good day to you," Ellen said. She needed to get out of this carriage and inside before Leo or Alex realized she'd returned.

"I'm coming in," the detective said, and the look on his face told her she would not be able to dissuade him. "I wish to see if you recognize this mark on the man's arm in one of your uncle's books."

"Not necessary, I assure you. I will come to you or send word if I remember anything else." Ellen reached for the door. A large hand stopped her.

Chapter 19

"Not this time." Gray lifted her arm. He then opened the door and stepped down. She glared at the hand he then held out to her but placed hers in it, and he helped her out of the carriage.

"I can step from a carriage."

"I'm sure you can, and as a gentleman, I can assist you."

"Detective Fletcher—"

"Miss Nightingale." Gray cut her off and then bowed. He wasn't a man who liked to tease or annoy people. If something needed saying, he said it. The rest he left to other people, and yet right then, he was enjoying teasing her.

"Why are you bowing?" Her brows drew together.

"It's called respect."

She muttered something, which he was sure would be unflattering, and stomped a few feet toward the steps that led to her home. Ellen then turned and came back to him.

Gray had been shocked after what she'd told him in the carriage about her visions. About the mark on the naked man and the argument between the Nicholson siblings. He couldn't imagine the burden of seeing what she did. The sadness, the fear, and the anger. Trying to find sense in some of the ramble of imaginings she no doubt saw.

It was a wonder she was sane.

He'd felt the need to comfort her when she'd closed her eyes in the carriage. After she'd told him about feeling nauseous. He'd wanted to touch her hand to make sure she was all right. The look that passed between them had said so much, even though a word had not been spoken.

Ellen Nightingale felt the spark of attraction as Gray did. In that moment he'd wanted to lean closer and kiss her soft lips.

He had urges like any man, but he controlled them. But if Ellen Nightingale had touched him in any way, he would have touched her back.

"Take the carriage home please, Bentley, I will call for a hackney later."

"Very well, sir."

"I think it best I go in alone, Detective Fletcher. You return to your carriage before it leaves."

"I'm coming in, Miss Nightingale." He nodded to Bentley, and his horses clopped away.

"There really is no need, and my brothers can be a trifle—"

"Protective? Overbearing?"

"Yes, all of that." She waved a hand about.

"But I thought you said they would not mind if you came with me?"

"Yes, well, perhaps I was stretching the truth slightly, but I can handle them. I'll look at my uncle's books and let you know if I see anything. Good day."

Nervous, Gray thought. She was suddenly extremely

nervous. His eyes went to the still closed door behind her, then back to Ellen.

"I am not frightened of your brothers, Miss Nightingale, and I would like to see if you can draw the mark you saw while it is fresh in your memory. I can then take it back with me and examine it to see if it connects to other cases. Lead the way." For some reason, he felt the need to accompany her inside. Was it a protective need? Possibly. Gray did not investigate the emotion too closely.

Before she could utter a word, the door opened behind her, and her eldest brother stood there looking like he was ready to rip Gray limb from limb.

"I think you should leave," she hissed.

"No."

"Ellen!" Leopold Nightingale barked.

"Inside please, Leo. There is no need for all our neighbors to hear you barking at your sister on the doorstep," someone said from behind the angry lord. This voice Gray didn't recognize.

"Good day to you, my lord."

They all turned as one to look over their shoulders, and there stood a lady swishing her skirts from side to side while she smiled at Leo.

"Who is that?" Gray moved closer to Ellen.

"Tabitha Varney. She's in love with Leo, well anyone really. But he's her favorite," Ellen said. "We've tried to explain to her she has poor taste," Ellen said but louder this time so her brother could hear.

"Good day to you, Miss Varney." Leo smiled, and it was genuine, which was some feat, considering he'd been scowling not two seconds ago.

"Right. Now inside all of you," the voice behind Leo said.

Leo stepped back at those words. Ellen climbed the stairs with Gray.

"For pity's sake, Leo, why were you roaring at me like that?" Ellen said as she entered the house.

Gray followed.

"Hello, you must be Detective Fletcher. I am Ivy Nightingale, Bram's wife."

She was small, with brown hair and eyes a color he'd never seen before. They were pewter and ringed with black.

"You were expressly forbidden after the last time you took it in your head to leave the house alone, notifying no one—"

"I told Bud!"

Ellen and her brother were now yelling at each other loudly in the front entrance, and it did not seem to bother Mrs. Nightingale.

"Leo, Alex, and Bram were worried about Ellen. Leo shows it by roaring," she added for Gray's benefit. "We don't like her to leave the house without one of us, but she continues to do so. Stating that she no longer has a reputation to worry about, therefore she can do as she chooses."

"Which is not a sound notion and could lead to her falling into trouble. Especially considering how lovely she is," Gray said and then wished he'd chosen his words better.

"I'm glad you think she's lovely." The woman was happy about that. "And she can look after herself. We made sure they all could do so after their father's death."

Gray stared at her.

"I know you are aware of what happened to my family, Detective Fletcher. I don't believe in talking around the truth."

"I told you, Ellen. It is not safe for you to leave the house without us!"

The siblings were now standing toe to toe to their right, still yelling. Gray lived in solitude. He couldn't imagine this kind of chaos going on around him constantly.

"I was not alone! I had a member of Scotland Yard with me," she shrieked at her brother.

"They love each other really," Mrs. Nightingale said, patting Gray's arm, which he thought might be to comfort him but couldn't be sure. She could just be one of those demonstrative types of people. He'd never been that way and rarely liked to be touched. Strange how he didn't mind Ellen's hands on him.

"You are entirely too reckless and innocent. Anything could have happened to you!" Leopold roared.

Gray could handle most things, and clearly this was how the siblings communicated by their aunt's reaction. But it was a direct hit to his honor to suggest he would not keep Ellen safe when she was in his company.

"I can protect myself, Leo, but there was no need," Ellen said.

"You are a woman. There was every need!"

"That will do, Lord Seddon," Gray said, his anger tweaked. "I asked your sister to assist me, and she consented. She was in no danger, nor would I allow that to happen. You insult your sister and me to suggest otherwise."

He caught the flash of surprise on Ellen's face before her brother stalked toward him, blocking her from his sight. Gray didn't back away. He'd confronted more dangerous men in his lifetime than this one.

"I don't know you," he growled, his face inches from Gray's.

"Not quite true. I believe I fought alongside you the other night."

Something flashed across Seddon's features, and then it was gone before Gray could read it.

"She is my sister and therefore mine to protect," Leo gritted out.

"I understand and admire that, my lord. But she was in no danger."

"Leo, cease."

"We've told her not to leave the house, Aunt Ivy." Leopold looked at his aunt.

"And you have been reassured she was safe. Enough now." The small woman wedged herself between Gray and her nephew. "She is, as you see, her usual beautiful, strong-willed self."

"Trouble?"

Gray looked left and watched Bramstone Nightingale enter the fray. He held a small girl in his arms, and with them was Alexander Nightingale.

"Ellen has returned," Ivy Nightingale said.

"Hello, niece."

"Hello, Uncle Bram."

"Are you well, Ellen? Has Detective Fletcher harmed you in any way?"

"Of course he hasn't," she said quickly.

"Then I see no need for Leo to continue roaring or scowling. Let the detective and my wife go if you please, nephew. Our afternoon tea is to be served. We will discuss whatever needs to be discussed while seated, in a civilized manner," Bramstone said.

"I shall leave you to your tea and call again tomorrow," Gray said.

"I'm sure we can find room for a member of Scotland

Yard," Bramstone added. "As long as you don't eat all the treacle cake Mrs. Douglas recently dropped off."

"Did she?" Ellen made a humming sound.

"He's not staying. How do we know he believes you about that knife and is not just infiltrating the house to get more information?" Leopold said.

The man had a lot of anger, Gray thought.

"Had I believed your uncle was guilty, my lord, I would have arrested him, or at the very least questioned him further. He has alibis, and was far from London, as has been verified already by a few people we have tracked down."

"Well, there you have it then. I am not to spend the night in Newgate," Bramstone said.

"Leo, don't be a goose," Ellen said. "I wonder sometimes if the men who decided titles should only pass to other men, realized just how foolish some of you could be. The world would surely be a better place if women ran it."

"Amen to that," a young girl with brown hair and eyes said, appearing from behind her uncle.

"Fred, this is Detective Fletcher." Bramstone placed the hand that was not holding the little girl on her shoulder.

"Hello, Detective Fletcher. Can you come and share tea with us so I can ask you questions about being a detective?"

"Well, I don't—"

"Do you have somewhere else to be?" Ivy Nightingale asked him.

Gray shook his head. He didn't lie unless absolutely necessary.

"Excellent. You will eat with us then," Bramstone said. He then took Fred's hand, and they walked away. "Come along, everyone," he called over his shoulder.

Gray found his arm taken by Ivy Nightingale and was soon following the other members of the family.

Bloody hell, he could usually get himself out of any situation that did not sit well with him. However, not this one. Looking at the swish of Ellen's skirts, he thought perhaps he knew exactly why he was still here.

Dragging his eyes from her hips, he stared at a painting on the wall of an austere man dressed in flowing robes.

"That is Chodrak. He is a monk my uncle met when he was at a monastery in Tibet," Frederica told him, leaving her uncle's side. "Uncle Bram learned a great deal from him. My uncle and aunt have traveled everywhere," she added.

"That must have been exciting for them," Gray said.

"I want to travel."

"And you will, Fred," her aunt said, blowing the girl a kiss.

There was love in this house. Even the grumpy Leopold cared deeply for his family with all that he had inside him. Gray thought about who loved him this passionately and came up with no one.

Why did that bother him today, when yesterday it hadn't?

Chapter 20

"We do not even know this man," Leopold hissed from behind Gray to Ellen, who had dropped back to walk with her brothers. "And yet you got into a carriage with him."

"He is a detective, Leo." Gray could hear the exasperation in her voice. "He has been to our home and helped us the night we rescued Penny Tompkins."

"Do you think because he is a member of Scotland Yard he is therefore above reproach, sister? Let me persuade you otherwise," Alexander added in support of his older brother.

"I protest," Gray said over his shoulder. But he knew the words were correct. Unfortunately, some of his colleagues were corrupt and easily bribed to sway from the path of right. He was trying not to be annoyed about Ellen's brothers' opinion of him. They were, after all, protecting her.

"Ignore them. They will blow themselves out. My theory on their behavior is that they were uptight and restrained for many years and did not much care for each other. They are now the opposite. The shackles were released, and they are free to speak their minds and do as they wish, which includes loving openly," Ivy said.

"I was once in the same situation as them. It was freeing to be removed from it." And why he'd said those words, Gray had no idea. Clearly these Nightingales were having an odd effect on him.

She patted his arm again. "I know. My husband told me."

"I will leave and return in the morning," he added, coming to his senses. He felt the need to put some space between himself and this family, especially Ellen. Gray didn't sit down to take tea with other peoples' families he didn't know. Any families, if he were being honest. He never did things impulsively either, so why was he still in this house?

"No, you will not. From what I understand, you are as yet unmarried and therefore have no one waiting for you at home, so you will take tea with us. We always have enough food," Ivy Nightingale added.

He could pull free and leave anyway, but instead, he allowed her to usher him into a room that was dominated by a table and chairs. Large windows looked out to the rear of the property, and the fading early evening light showed him plenty of trees and grass, plus a glass house.

"We eat at the table or there is a horrid mess," she said.

"He is aware of my visions," he heard Ellen say.

"I know that. Uncle Bram told us. But that does not mean he trusts us, as we are unsure if we trust him."

"I had an aunt who had them." Gray found himself speaking again about something he never discussed. After all, they were talking about him loud enough for him to hear. If they had wanted privacy, they should have sought it.

"Ah, it all makes sense now," Alexander Nightingale said. "Do you have elderly relatives who have passed?"

Gray nodded.

"And was there an aunt who loved the brightest shade of orange?" he added, making the hair on the back of Gray's neck stand.

"Yes."

"Well, that explains the reason I am seeing the color when you are near. Tell me, Detective Fletcher, do you love treacle?" Alex asked.

He nodded again because he couldn't speak. His throat was dry. He used to eat bread and treacle as a child when he snuck into the kitchens.

"I thought so."

"How did you—"

"Enough for now," Ivy Nightingale said.

"This is Matilda and Theodore, the youngest members of our family," Bramstone said. "You have already met Frederica."

Gray acknowledged the children, still thinking about what Alexander said. His Aunt Tilda had loved orange. The brighter the shade, the happier she was. Why had he said that? Why had he mentioned treacle?

"Greet the detective, please," Ivy said.

The children reluctantly got out of their chairs and bowed or curtseyed, and Gray returned the gestures.

The younger Nightingales were a mix of their elder siblings' features and would become more like them with age, he was sure.

"Sit." A hand nudged him into a seat between Frederica and Matilda. "You will be doing us a favor. If they are separated, they can't argue," Ivy Nightingale added before she walked around the table to sit next to her husband, and she leaned in to kiss his cheek and then her daughter's.

Across from him, Leo and Ellen were still arguing, but their voices had lowered. Alex was next to Ellen, adding a comment when he felt it was required.

"They're always like that, with Alex chirping in," Frederica said. "We place bets to see who will win the argument."

"Pardon?" Gray looked down at her.

"Leo and Ellen never used to be fiery natured, and few see it when they are, so clearly they are comfortable around you," Teddy said. "But we place bets when they start. It can be either of them. Sometimes Alex too."

"I protest," Alex drawled. "You brats are hardly the best tempered of all of us."

"True," Matilda said. "But the fieriest Nightingale has to be Leo."

The other two hummed their agreement to that.

"Do you have brothers or sisters, Detective?" Fred asked him the question.

"I do, yes. Two brothers, both older."

"Do you argue with them?" The innocent brown eyes looked up at him, and Leo and Ellen took that moment to stop arguing.

"I don't, no. We don't see each other." Gray had to force the words out of his tight throat.

Matilda nudged him with her elbow, so he turned her way.

"Why don't you see them?"

"We are busy."

"We're busy, but we see our siblings all the time now," Teddy added.

Gray knew everyone at the table was listening to the

conversation because there was now absolute silence, not even the clink of a glass.

"That's nice."

"When did you last see your brothers?" Fred persisted.

And this, Gray thought, was why you didn't take tea with company under the age of eighteen.

"A year ago."

"What's your name?" Matilda asked. "Your first name."

"Grayson."

"I like that. Can we call you Grayson? Because Detective Fletcher is too long."

"Matilda," Bramstone cautioned her. "Don't push, sweetheart. Not everyone is as comfortable using their first names as we are."

"It's all right," Gray managed to get out. "You could call me Gray if you like."

She smiled, and it was like her big sister's and lit her entire face.

"I'm Fred," she said.

"I'm Teddy," the young boy said, reaching around his sister to hold out his hand.

Gray shook it.

"Bram," her uncle said with a smile.

"Lottie!" the little girl shrieked.

"Ivy."

"Alex," he said.

"Ellen," she said softly.

All eyes then turned to Leopold.

"Leo," he snapped, which had them laughing, and the tension was broken.

"Right, now I want to know where you went today and what you learned, Ellen," Bram then said.

"Are you happy to speak about this, Gray?" Ellen used his name for the first time.

He liked how it sounded on her lips. Not many people called him Gray. In fact, no one.

He rarely talked about his cases, but this situation was different. These people were entwined now. The knife, Ellen finding the body, and her visions. She would tell them anyway if he didn't.

Gray looked at the children.

"We don't hide things from them, but not too much detail if you please, Gray," Ivy said.

"I was like a consultant," Ellen said.

Leo made a scoffing sound that had Ellen's lips tightening.

"I was, and very useful too." She poked out her tongue, and Gray had an urge to nibble it.

What was wrong with him?

Gray found himself talking about the Nicholson case, seated between Matilda and Fred, with the disturbing Ellen across from him. Plates of cakes, fruits, and sandwiches appeared, carried by the man called Mungo and Bud. Plus another young lady who kept sending Alex flirtatious looks.

He'd never seen so much food for afternoon tea.

"Like debating, eating is a sport in our household," Bram said, noting the bewildered expression on Gray's face.

The food was consumed with gusto, and he'd never eaten with so much noise before. It was a revelation. He thought about the solitary life he led and loved. But did he really? Suddenly, it seemed lonely and sterile when faced with so much happiness.

Was this what mealtimes were always like? Loud, with the children present? He ate slowly and read the paper or just sat and reflected on the day. No way would a person reflect on anything with this noise.

Why did his existence suddenly seem lonely?

"So you really have no leads on the case yet?" Alex asked him.

"It's early days, but no, only what your sister has told me and of course, the knife."

"Which was stolen from our uncle," Leo reiterated.

"Do you think I would sit down to take tea with a man I believed wasn't innocent?" Gray asked.

"I have no idea what you do."

Ellen rolled her eyes.

"Can I ask how you knew my aunt liked to wear orange? Did you meet her before she passed?" It had been bothering Gray, why Alex had said what he had. "And the treacle. Was that a guess?"

"Alex talks to people on the other side," Fred said from beside him.

"Side of where?" Gray asked.

"That have died and passed over," Fred said patiently.

"Should we be giving him all the family secrets?" Leo sighed.

Gray's eyes shot to Alex, who gave him a calm look back. He then glanced at Ellen. She saw visions. Was her brother gifted too? Gray felt an urge to flee. Get out of his chair and leave this house. Everything that was sane about his life had changed since he'd met Ellen Nightingale. Gray didn't like change.

"Your aunt passed from something to do with her lungs?" Alex said.

Gray nodded. She had died from tuberculosis.

"She loved orange and has been showing me a book with a dog on the cover. Also, she's insistent about the treacle. She has been trying to make contact for days. I just wasn't sure why. I understand now, as she was gifted as we are." He pointed from himself to Leo and then to Ellen.

"You too?" Gray rasped; his throat was thick as he stared at Leo.

"He denies it, but yes," Ellen said. "It is a lot to take in."

"I don't deny it. I'm just not like you two." Leo glared at his siblings.

"You keep telling yourself that," Ellen said, which had her brother's teeth snapping together.

Gray looked at Bram, who was smiling.

"Not me, unfortunately. Apparently, after some research into our family, it comes down from an uncle who everyone thought was eccentric. He and his three sisters were gifted. All have unfortunately passed now. But I found a diary in my family's attic. It talked about what they could do, and I wondered with this lot after living with them for a while. There was definitely something going on, so I asked and found out that I have very talented nieces and nephews."

He didn't know what to say about that.

"We will talk more later," Alex said to him. "Just you and me. There are a few of your relatives who would like to chat to you."

Nodding was the best Gray could manage. When the door burst open and in galloped Chester, he thought the madness was complete.

Chapter 21

Ellen was seated between her brothers at the table and across from the detective, who now was called Gray by her family. He'd been uncomfortable when they'd first sat down to eat, after she and Leo had argued over her leaving the house. Then Fred had spoken about what Alex could do, and he'd looked ready to flee.

But he'd relaxed as the three youngest Nightingales charmed him. She'd even heard him laugh at something Matilda said.

"He's a cold fish, and I don't want you wandering off with him again," Leo whispered in her ear. Of course, Alex leaned in, so he was listening too. "And I speak only from a place of love and concern, Ellen."

"Which warms my cold heart. But he is a detective, and one I doubt knows how to break the rules. He is rigid and proper and the complete opposite of us... well, when we're at home, that is. I was safe with him, Leo, which you would understand if you'd calmed down enough to rationally think about it."

Alex snorted. "Leo? Rational?"

"You can talk, you're entirely irrational," Leo muttered. "And it's because I worry about you that I may seem to behave irrationally."

"I know that, but you are being silly in this instance," Ellen added.

Leo exhaled. "All right, I'll concede if I must. That he is likely not a bad man."

"Who told you he wasn't? As clearly you've been digging up information about him?"

"Plummy."

"What did he say?"

"That our Detective Fletcher is highly respected. He's thorough and kind. He always has time to speak to anyone who wants his ear."

"That must have chafed on you, brother, seeing as you want to dislike him," Alex said.

"Shut up. What if those people, the Nicholsons, had known who you were and ridiculed you for your change in circumstance, Ellen?" Leo said.

"Then I would have coped, as you have taught me to. Now, one day, Leo, some woman will probably have you, and I will need to live on my wits alone, as you will not be at my side every second," Ellen said with a large dose of sarcasm. "So stop fussing."

"I'm not fussing, and I will never marry," Leo vowed.

Ellen did not comment on that, as she felt the same. Instead, she talked about what she'd seen earlier to her uncle.

"I had two visions while at the Nicholsons, Uncle Bram. One of George and his sister arguing, both were upset, and the second was of a man. He was..." How did she explain he was naked?

"She saw his back view," Gray added.

Ellen battled the flush of color filling her cheeks.

"You're blushing?" Alex smirked. "Care to share why?"

"He was turned away, so I only saw him from behind," she said, giving him a look.

"Ah, all of him from behind do you mean?"

She nodded.

"And the rest of him?" Leo asked. He was laughing now but trying to hide it. He was exhausting, one minute wanting to kill someone and the next smiling.

"Only the rear. I saw a mark on his forearm as he had his arm raised in the air," she gritted out. Her eyes shot to Fred and Matilda, but they were arguing around Detective Fletcher and paying her no attention.

Leo snorted, so she elbowed him. Lottie then held out her arms, so she took the little bundle of sweetness. They all loved this sweet girl.

"Aunty Ellen," Lottie said. She then reached up and kissed her with jam-coated lips.

"Thank you, darling, that was just what I needed."

"Continue with the description of the mark, Ellen," Uncle Bram said.

"It wasn't like the birthmark on Teddy's thigh. This was black, I think, a circle, but then I'm not totally sure. But it appeared familiar to me."

"A tattoo?" Leo asked. He then held out half of his coconut biscuit for Lottie, which she took with a smile.

"Say thank you," Ellen told her.

"Thank you," Lottie lisped.

"I think I've seen the tattoo before in one of your books, Uncle Bram."

"Ellen, he has hundreds of books," Alex said.

"The red book," Ellen added.

"Teddy. Go to my office and get that book, the one with the red binding and gold writing you love," Uncle Bram said.

"The Celtic one?" His uncle nodded, and he ran from the room.

"More treacle cake, Gray?" Ivy pointed to Alex, who reluctantly nudged the plate closer to the detective that he'd stationed before him on the table.

"No, thank you," he said.

"Have you shot anyone?"

The entire table stared at Matilda, who asked the question. She had a sweet round face and soft, pale skin and a thirst for knowledge that was hard to quench.

"That's entirely too bloodthirsty, sweetheart," Alex said.

She shrugged and looked at Gray.

"I try to never shoot people where it can be helped." The detective adjusted his necktie. Clearly, uncomfortable.

"Do you use handcuffs?" Matilda asked.

"If I need them."

"Have you chased many criminals through London?" Fred asked next, not to be outdone by her little sister.

"I have, yes." His eyes went from Fred to the adults around the table. All were now listening to the conversation taking place between Grayson, Fletcher, Fred, and Matilda.

"Have you been shot or stabbed?" Matilda asked.

"Both."

"Where on your body?" Fred asked.

"I was shot in my side, and stabbed in the forearm," Gray said quickly. He didn't want to continue this discussion, but he also didn't want to ignore the girls. Manners, Ellen thought, like the Nightingales, he'd been raised with them being ruthlessly adhered to.

"Ouch. I bet that hurt. Can you show us the scar?" Fred asked.

"No. I don't think that's appropriate."

They really should intervene, Ellen thought, and yet she knew that like her, the other adults were interested in learning more about Gray.

"Not the one on your side, silly, the one on your forearm," Matilda said.

"We have no issues with you removing your jacket." Alex waved his hand at Gray. "They're used to shirt sleeves. We're only wearing ours because we'd just returned home."

"I don't really think—"

"Are you frightened it will scare us?" Matilda asked. "Because I dissected a mouse the other day."

Gray looked at Ellen, and she nodded. "They are bloodthirsty these three. The mouse was also found dead first, Detective Fletcher. Have no fear they killed it."

His smile was strained.

"Girls, that is enough. Gray has no wish to show you. Perhaps you can respect his choices?" Aunt Ivy said.

Fred pulled up the sleeve of her dress. "I got this one when I fell out of the tree that Leo told me not to climb."

Ellen remembered that day. She'd come running at the screams and had seen the blood.

"Why is it you want to see my scar?" Gray looked at the little girls.

"We weren't allowed to ask a lot of questions once," Fred said softly, but Ellen and her brothers heard. "Now that we can, if one comes to us, we ask it."

Ellen gulped down the sudden sting of tears. She cuddled Lottie closer.

"I'll show you then, but don't blame me if you get upset and start shrieking," he teased them.

"We won't," they both said.

She then watched Gray take out his cuff link and roll up his sleeve, exposing a muscled forearm. The scar was about five inches long and ran from his wrist to halfway up his forearm.

"That's not an old scar," Alex said.

"No" was his only reply.

It was red and raised and must have caused him considerable pain. Ellen wondered how it had happened.

"I'm sorry, that must have hurt," Fred said. "Was the man who did this arrested?"

Gray nodded. "He was and is still in prison."

"Does it hurt?" she asked.

"Not as much as it used to."

He watched the detective's smile turn to surprise as Fred bent, kissed her fingers, and then tapped them on the scar.

"That will make it better. Aunt Ivy did that for me when we first came to live with her," she said.

Leo handed her his handkerchief as she sniffed. Ellen thought about the scar Gray had shown her sisters. Long and jagged, it must have caused him a great deal of agony. He'd also said he'd been shot. She felt a pain in her belly at the thought of him hurting.

"That was beautifully done, my darling," Aunt Ivy said.

Teddy chose that moment to reappear, but as Ellen was still watching Gray, she saw the deep breath he inhaled. He wasn't used to this. Being surrounded by all this love. Having people show an interest in him and ask questions.

In truth, she didn't know the life he lived but believed it was a solitary, controlled one, as hers had been.

"Pass the book here, Teddy," Uncle Bram said.

When he had, the young man went back to his seat, and his sister proceeded to tell him about Gray's scar.

Uncle Bram opened the book and laid it before him on the table. He then flicked through pages, clearly searching for something. Finding it, he handed it to Ellen. "Look through these. They are the ones that are circles or triangles. All old Celtic symbols."

She studied them with her brothers looking over her shoulder.

"That's it." Her finger jabbed at the page. "I'm sure that's what he had on his forearm. She lifted it and showed it to Gray.

"Triquetra," Gray said at the same time as Uncle Bram.

"What does it mean?" Alex asked.

"Unity, protecting an everlasting life, like many knots. Also, a symbol of strength," Uncle Bram said.

"It can also be associated with being a warrior," Gray added.

"Exactly," Uncle Bram agreed.

"Mr. Greedy has called," Mungo said, entering. He threw the detective a hard look. Gray ignored it.

"What does he want, Mungo?" Aunt Ivy asked.

"It seems an event has been called," Mungo said. "I advised him you had company. He said to bring Detective Fletcher with you. Apparently it will do him good to loosen up a bit." Mungo's tone suggested that was not possible.

Teddy, Matilda, and Fred shrieked, which had everyone else wincing.

"Go get your coats," Uncle Bram said. The children ran.

"Event?" Gray asked.

"Run now and don't look back," Alex answered him.

"Crabbett Close is a very social street." Ellen had no idea how to explain what was about to happen outside their front door.

"It's easier to just show him," Uncle Bram said.

"Show me what?" Gray looked around at the adults.

"Come, all will be revealed," Uncle Bram added.

"I need to leave. I have things to do, reports to write," Gray said, pushing back his chair to rise.

Leo got out of his chair and started clucking.

"Why are you clucking like a chicken?" Gray glared at him. And then her because she was giggling.

"If the chicken fits, detective," Leo said.

"You wanted to kill me when I returned your sister home not that long ago, and now you're clucking like a chicken. Noblemen." Gray shook his head.

"Which you are, if I may point out," Alex said.

"I have your coats, now hurry it along. I won't be put in the same team as that idiot Plummy," Mungo said from the doorway.

A scurry of movement had them all surging forward. Ellen put on her coat but forewent the bonnet. That would just get in the way.

"Will you be on my team, Mungo? You're always the fastest," Teddy said.

"We'll just have to see where Mr. Greedy puts us." Mungo placed a hand on the boy's shoulder.

Once, touching wasn't something they did easily. They lived their life by a strict code of social conduct. The children were seen at night, briefly, to be examined by their parents. The elder children of Lord and Lady Nightingale would then sit down to a cold and stilted meal while Teddy, Fred, and Matilda went back upstairs for theirs.

It wasn't until their life came tumbling down that they realized the true meaning of being part of a loving family. She would be forever grateful to her aunt and uncle for teaching them that.

Looking for Gray, she saw him at the rear of their group, pulling on his overcoat. Ellen wondered who loved him? Who was the person he turned to when he needed an ear or a shoulder? She had a feeling that there was no one.

Chapter 22

Gray wasn't sure what was going on but knew he didn't want to be a part of it. He had done enough things that he normally wouldn't with the Nightingale family. Including showing those young children his knife wound.

He could have scarred them. It wasn't like him to be rash. He blamed her. Ellen bloody Nightingale with her soft, alluring scent and sweet face. Then there were her brothers who, each in their own way, goaded him like his brothers once had, before they'd turned into uptight idiots.

His siblings hadn't always treated him like something stuck on the bottom of their shoes. Once, when they were young boys, they'd played together. Had fun. All that changed when their father decided it was time for Christopher and Henry to learn to become the young men they were meant to be.

"Come along, Gray, there is no point lollygagging. We shall be last chosen if that is the case."

"I was simply standing here waiting for your family to file out the door. I fail to see how that is lollygagging, Miss Fred."

He liked these children. They were loud and happy, and he knew that was a credit to the adults who now raised them. Having your father take his life and then being torn from everything you'd ever known was hard enough for adults but even harder on children, he thought.

"Come." Fred took his hand and tugged him toward the door they were now all surging through.

"Where exactly am I coming to?"

"To the Crabbett Close games."

"I beg your pardon?" He stepped through the door and into the late afternoon light. It was still warm, and the sky was softening as it settled over London. Tired buildings looked their best, and the city appeared different at this time of the day.

"It is nice that the sunshine is still out."

Gray looked at Matilda as she spoke. Surely she meant sun?

"Sunshine!" her siblings all shrieked. They then hopped in a line toward the gate.

He'd experienced a lot since he'd met this family, but that, to his mind, was simply madness. Perhaps that was it. They were all insane and hid it well... most often.

"Word of the week, Gray. When it is overheard, you repeat it and then follow what action was set at the beginning of the week," Fred said. "Matilda gave us sunshine."

"You didn't hop, Gray," Matilda added.

"I'm not a Nightingale, so I'm exempt," he said, thinking on his feet. That got her. She wasn't sure how to answer, and as he wasn't sure what to say about what he'd just witnessed, they followed the others out the gate. Fred was hopping and Gray walking.

"I'm still no closer to understanding what is going on," he said to anyone listening. He shot a look down the street.

He could make a run for it, and it was likely no one would chase him.

"Crabbett Close games, Gray," Teddy said loudly. "Are you hard of hearing?"

It wasn't said as an insult as it would have been if Leo asked, but with the innocence of a child who was simply asking. "No, I just don't know what Crabbett Close games are, Teddy. I'll add to that I'm not sure I want to."

"It's capital fun. You'll love it," Fred said. She tugged on his hand, and he found himself following her.

"Why are all these people gathered?" Gray asked as they approached the circle of grass in the middle of the close.

"Hurry it up back there," Alex called over his shoulder.

"What am I hurrying to?" *And why?* he added silently. The real problem here was that he didn't want to leave. This family welcomed him into their home. He'd eaten a meal, and they'd asked him to call them by their first name. All of it had warmed something that had been cold inside him for so long. Even while he thought the entire family was mad, he had enjoyed being part of it for a brief moment in time.

"If you truly wish to run, I'll create a distraction." The words were whispered in his ear.

He'd thought Ellen had been in front of him, but she'd doubled back when he wasn't looking. Her eyes held a spark of mischief. Cheeks flushed, she was smiling. The woman was beautiful, and he could only imagine what the men in society had thought of her when she graced ballrooms. They must have fallen over themselves to get her attention.

"We shall not think badly of you if you wish to leave, Detective Fletcher—"

"Gray," he said. "After all, your family set the informal guidelines, so we should at least adhere to them."

"And you don't like to be informal, do you?" Ellen asked him.

"I'm not always formal," he made himself say, sounding stuffy even to his own ears. "I just have no call to be otherwise. My job, my life, it is the way I live."

Why was it he couldn't shut his mouth today?

"Oooh, there is Nancy, and she has a bowl of sugarplums!" With this shriek, Fred released his hand. She, Teddy, and Matilda were then sprinting through the gate toward the gathering of people.

"We once lived our life without emotion," Ellen said as they walked over the grass. "It wasn't until I had joy, love, and fun in my life that I realized how much I was missing."

"I did not say I lived without emotion."

But he did. Gray mapped his days and liked them to run in the order he'd thought they should, with slight variations, of course. Nothing usually ran to a complete plan. Take today, it had turned into mayhem.

"I am glad then that you do," she said.

"Now, will you tell me what is going on here, Ellen?"

They had stopped behind the group that had gathered in the middle of the grass.

"Everyone present lives here in Crabbett Close," Ellen said. "Uncle Bram has owned this house for many years. He bought it before he married Aunty Ivy. When we were ready to come back to London, this was where we came. The residents are unlike any people I've ever known." She was smiling again.

"When we arrived, we were nervous, but Uncle Bram said Crabbett Close would be good for us. The residents were marvelous. They were welcoming and accepting immediately. Most have lived there for many years. Some are retired, others still work in varying positions, and they are very social. Over the years, many traditions have started. This is one of them."

"This?" Gray asked, looking about him at the people. Some wore cloaks, others shawls, a few in their shirtsleeves.

"The Crabbett Close games."

"I beg your pardon?" He shot her a look as she giggled. The sound was sweet.

"Just listen."

"I think I should go."

"Then do so if that is your wish," Alex said from his other side. "But in doing so, you will miss out on the opportunity to eat some truly superb taffy cake and drink mulled wine. Plus, you will laugh louder than you have in many years, is my guess."

"Do I look like I need to laugh, then?"

Both siblings nodded. Well, that told him. Gray clearly came across as uptight and formal as he was.

"Perhaps it may be best if he observes, anyway. It may be too much for him," Leo said, moving to stand beside his sister.

"I was raised with two brothers until I was nine. Not much would be too much. I also box regularly."

"Why only until you were nine?" Alex asked Gray.

"My brothers needed to learn to be lords. I didn't."

"Nobility can be real widgeons," Leo said. "Thankfully, that no longer affects us."

"Oh, I don't know," Ellen said. "You can be a widgeon still."

"Harsh but true," Alex said.

Before Leo could retaliate, Gray intervened. "That will do, children." Surprisingly, they fell silent. Bram was just in front of them and turned to nod at him. He wasn't sure what that was for but returned the gesture.

"Detective Fletcher!" Constable Plummy boomed. "We are honored here in Crabbett Close to have you take part in our games. I am, of course, bereft that my dear Miss Bud could not make it."

"I did not realize you were romantically involved, Plummy," Gray said.

The man's face flushed with color. "Well, we are not romantically involved, but I have hopes that will one day happen. In my position, I must ask permission for such a thing, but it's my wish that soon I will have to."

"Well, best of luck then," Gray said. The man's jaw dropped open with shock, and yet again he was presented with the fact that he was a cold, unfeeling man.

"Now, Mrs. Greedy will select the teams as she can remember all your names, unlike me," Mr. Greedy said, drawing their attention once more. "Are there any new people here?"

Gray looked over heads and saw a grizzled old man with a cane talking. With him was an equally grizzled old woman. He'd already met the Greedys, and they had shut the door in his face.

"We have a guest, Mr. Greedy," Ivy Nightingale called. "Detective Fletcher is here."

"Is he now."

There were a few murmurings after that, and Gray wondered if they would ask him to leave, which he thought would be a good thing.

"As he helped get Mr. Douglas's granddaughter back from that scoundrel Barney Forge with our very own Notorious Nightingales, we'll allow him to stay," Mr. Greedy said.

All heads then turned, and Gray was suddenly the object of several pairs of eyes. Most were friendly today, unlike when last he'd met them.

"Detective Fletcher is our friend and has just taken tea with us," Bram said.

Bramstone Nightingale had just told these people his family had accepted Gray, so they should too. It was humbling.

"Well then, he's welcome, and there will be a piece of taffy cake just for him at the Douglas home, I'm sure," Mr. Greedy called, and everyone agreed.

Gray received the nods of acceptance with discomfort but returned them. He was experiencing so many different emotions, and none of them were comfortable. Like everything that had changed in his life since Ellen had stormed into it, he blamed the Nightingales.

"My hero," Leo taunted.

"Why do they call you that? The Notorious Nightingales and do I want to know?"

"Likely not," Alex said.

"No idea," Ellen added.

"I have thoughts on the matter, considering what I found you all doing the other night. You're some kind of vigilante group, which doesn't sit well with me," Gray said.

"Haha," Ellen said, not sounding at all amused. "We would never take the law into our hands, which by the way, there are not enough people upholding to ensure it is safe on the streets of London."

"Vigilante," Leo scoffed. "As if we, fine, upstanding members of society, would do such a thing."

Gray studied the three Nightingales. Not one of them was looking at him.

"None of you are fine or upstanding, and we are going to discuss this further."

"Do you think my aunt and uncle would allow their nieces and nephews to romp into danger?" Alex added.

"What you did that night outside the Hope and Anchor was not called romping."

"Bramstone, Ivy, Teddy, Plummy, and Mungo," the man Mr. Greedy called, interrupting their conversation.

"What is he doing?"

"Organizing," Ellen said to Gray.

"Fred, Ellen, Bud, Mrs. Varney and Detective Fletcher—"

"Why was my name just called out?" Gray asked the woman at his side.

Ellen wore her coat but no bonnet or gloves. Her smile was genuine, as was the flash of excitement in her eyes.

"Take your places!" Mr. Greedy boomed.

"He has the loudest voice in the street, so it is always him who calls out instructions."

"For what?"

"You had your chance to run, Detective Fletcher. You didn't take it, so now you are an honorary member of Crabbett Close," Ellen said. "Come along." She took his hand and tugged. Her fingers felt small holding his, and he had the urge to close them inside his hand and never let them go.

Gray was fairly sure he'd follow this woman anywhere in that moment, and wasn't that a terrifying thought for another day.

The mass of bodies surged toward the gate and through. Looking down the street, he saw they had set lamps on tables outside houses he hadn't noticed before. The tables held glasses and plates.

"Ah, Ellen."

"What?" She'd been speaking to a lady beside her who was wearing a turban. It was tall and the color of mustard and almost too bright to look at.

"What's going on?"

Chapter 23

Ellen had told him to stay where she put him and then left.

Apparently, Gray was the first to start this absurd event, which he had no understanding of. The others had dispersed and wandered off along the road. He wasn't as yet sure where they'd gone or why.

Gray liked to know where he was going and what he would be doing at all times. His hands tingled at the uncertainty of the experience.

"There are five people in your team. You are number one," Leo said from beside him. Next to him was Alex. Beside them was Bram and two other men who seemed as large. In fact, all those standing on a line to his right were on the bigger side build wise, even the single woman who wore a fierce expression on her face.

"I would rather be number two," Gray muttered.

"Why?" Leo asked.

"Because then I'd be number two," Gray finished lamely.

"Don't tell me you're one of those people like Mr. Greedy who favors even numbers," Leo said.

"Of course he is." Alex laughed when color filled Gray's cheeks.

"What? No, I'm not." Gray just resisted tugging at his necktie.

"You are." Leo laughed. "Well, well, the contained Detective Fletcher is not quite so contained."

"I have no idea what you are talking about," he said, sounding stuffy. "Would someone care to explain what the hell is going on?" *And why have I not run for the hills?*

They intrigued him, he realized. It had been the first time he'd felt this little surge of excitement in… well, since he'd met Ellen Nightingale, if he were being honest.

"Run to the first table. Drink what is placed in front of you, and do what they say. Then eat the pickled whelk," Leo said.

"What? Absolutely not, I hate those." He shuddered at the memory of eating one once. It had made him want to empty the contents of his stomach.

"If you wish to become an honorary member of the Crabbett Close community, which I have no wish for you to do, as I don't trust you yet, then you must do this."

"I don't trust you either, Lord Seddon, and I'm not sure if I want to be an honorary member of this insanity."

"I wouldn't. He's a smokey bastard," Alex said, grinning like an idiot. Clearly, he was excited about something.

It was like Gray had stepped into some kind of weird scene from a play and hadn't realized it. Perhaps he was asleep and dreaming?

"Stay alert. You will collect Fred, and she won't tolerate anything less than your best," Bram called to him. "Focus now, Gray, this could have the residents respecting or loathing you."

"And I care because?"

"You'll come to realize how vital Crabbett Close can be

if you get this right. They can treat any ailment, cobble a horse, and balance your ledgers. Someone from this street could cater to any of your needs, plus aid you in any investigation. It pays to have them on side, and this is your chance," Bram said.

"All true," the bear of a man to his right said. "We don't trust anyone from Scotland Yard without a reason to."

"Mind, we could do with one of 'em in our pockets," another man said.

"Excuse me, but I will not fit in anyone's pocket," Gray said in his coldest tone. It only made everyone to the right of him laugh.

He was respected by people, usually. Clearly, that was not the case in Crabbett Close.

"You'll be on your mark!" The loud voice of Mr. Greedy boomed.

It worried Gray that he now knew exactly what he sounded like, even though he couldn't see the man.

"You'll get set. Go!" A loud clap had them surging forward, and as Gray did not like to be left behind in any situation, he moved. Soon, he was running to keep up with Leo and Alex. The other three were also level. The woman was a few paces in the lead. Extremely spritely, she reached the first set of tables laid out across the street.

"Hello there, dearie, remember me? I'm Miss Alvin. We live here at number 22 Crabbett Close." Her smile differed vastly from the disapproving scowl of a few days ago.

She was again wrapped in scarves and also a thick cloak. Mr. Alvin had a woolen cap pulled to his bushy gray eyebrows.

"Stop your jawing now, Pixie, and hand him his drink," her brother said.

A mug of something was thrust in his direction. As Leo had already downed his and Alex had started on his cake, he took it and sniffed. The pungent bite of alcohol nearly made him gag.

"It's a bit wiffy, and if you've a weak belly," Alex taunted, "I'm sure Tabitha could make you a nice cup of tea, Gray."

He threw it down and only just managed to stop from throwing it back up by gulping several times. "Gah," he managed to rasp.

"The Alvin's cousin's recipe," Leo said, smirking. "Gin, treacle, and the secret ingredient of mutton fat."

"Why?" Gray gasped.

"You simmer it for two hours. Keeps you healthy apparently," Alex said.

"Eat your whelks, Detective." Leo opened his mouth and dropped one inside. He then chewed, smiling at Gray.

He was competitive. It was a flaw he'd fought most of his life and had won, until today. Pinching his nose, Gray took the whelk handed to him by Mr. Alvin and swallowed. His insides rebelled. He retched, coughed, but held it down. By the time he was in control again, he was alone except for Fred.

"I knew I was going to lose being in your team," she muttered, grabbing his arm. "Hurry, they are putting distance on us."

She tugged, and he followed, and he was running again.

"Fred, is it absolutely necessary I do this?"

"Absolutely."

He found Ivy holding the still smiling Lottie. The little girl waved, and he found himself waving back. They made an enticing picture so he looked away.

"Do I… ah, are there more pickled whelks, Fred?" He had to ask.

"No. You get kippers here," she said, reaching the next table before him.

Leo was there drinking with his uncle, brother, and others. Plus the extras they'd collected at the last table.

"You decide what you want now as there are two of us. Then I take something, and we divide it up like that. But there will be tasks now too."

"Tasks?" Gray stared at the kippers, and his stomach gurgled. The cake looked good, but Fred grabbed it before he could, so that left the mug.

"Hello, and good evening, Detective Fletcher. It is wonderful of you to befriend our amazing Nightingales. I have never met such good people."

"It's all right, Mrs. Varney. I will not arrest anyone, and especially not your precious Nightingales," Gray said. She'd been holding a broom with both hands when last he'd met her.

"Well now, that's good to hear. We won't have to hurt you."

Gray's eyes shot to the woman. He'd say around sixty, she had a pink bonnet covered in flowers of every color he could think up and pink lips. With her was her daughter, who'd said hello to Leo earlier. Was that only a short while ago? He thought it felt like a lifetime.

"Watch yourself there," a woman he didn't know said from beside him. "She's got her eyes set on finding a husband, and any will do."

"Drink for pity's sake, Gray. I am not allowed to due to my age and the fact none of the adults in my family will let me. So, you need to drink that mug, not just warm the contents!" Fred demanded.

"No, we will not allow you to consume any of the alcohol on these tables, Frederica!" her uncle shouted.

Gray sniffed the contents. The smell was not as pungent but equally strong. He didn't gag this time as the firewater crept down his throat, but it was close.

"You'd think for a man from Scotland Yard, he'd be able to hold his liquor," Alex said.

"They're clearly not the men we think they are if they can't stomach a wee dram or two," someone said.

Gray thought the man had been introduced to him but couldn't remember the name. Mind you, his eyes were watering, so no one was very clear to him now. Gray drank little... if at all. He preferred tea.

"Run, Gray!"

Following Fred's lead, he did as she asked and lumbered down the street holding her hand. He was listing slightly now and didn't seem to be able to right himself. Those mugs had been filled to at least halfway, and he was feeling the effects. He noted Matilda had joined them and was holding his other hand.

"Hello," he said, looking down at her. "Where did you come from?"

"I'm on your team, Gray. Honestly, you need to focus. This always happens to the men who start the race."

"What happens?"

"You start stumbling and laughing manically. I never want to drink alcohol if it turns me into a fool," Fred said.

She wasn't wrong. Alcohol made fools of men, but not him. Gray was completely sober, he told himself as he stumbled slightly. He reached the next stand on the bend of Crabbett Close. The light was fading, and he noted candles and lamps were on the tables.

"Stay close now, girls, it's getting dark," Gray said.

"We're in Crabbett Close. Nothing happens to us here," Matilda said.

"Right. Silly me."

"But it was a nice sentiment, Detective Fletcher," a sweet voice said from beside him. Looking over his shoulder, he found the smiling eyes of Ellen.

She picked up the cake before he could reach it, and Matilda, the horrid substance on a plate.

"Jellied eel," Fred said. "She loves them."

"Dear Lord, why?" Gray shuddered as he watched the child eat it.

"You drink. I'll do the task," she said.

"You'll sing the last verse of *Home Sweet Home*, Miss Fred," Mr. Douglas said. Gray remembered that he was the grandfather of the girl that Barney Forge had abducted.

"Drink now, Gray," Ellen said while Fred sang on beside him.

Ellen looked lovely in the candlelight, her skin glowing. She was also laughing at him as he looked down at the mug Mr. Douglas was handing him.

"How is your granddaughter?" Gray asked, hoping to stall the moment he had to swallow whatever was in there.

"Very well, thanks to you and the Notorious Nightingales," the man said.

Beside him, Alex picked up his mug and raised it to Gray, which meant he had to toast him. They clinked their mugs.

"Drink up, Gray," Ellen said.

"I don't think I want to." He went for honesty.

"I suppose I could, but I'm not really meant to take part until the next table." She was laughing at him.

"There's another table?" He felt ill at the thought.

"Two actually."

He drank. It was thick as molasses and seemed to stick to the sides of his mouth.

"I love the molasses-laced whisky best," Leo was saying from beside Alex. He was actually licking his lips while Gray tried not to empty his stomach on his boots.

When he ran, this time it was with the little girls and their lovely big sister. Beside them now galloped Chester. Tongue hanging out, tail wagging.

"I bet he doesn't have to drink," Gray muttered.

"He's a dog, Gray. They are exempt," Fred said.

By the last table, he was having trouble focusing. His eyes felt squinty, and his legs didn't seem to belong to his body anymore.

"Come on. Nearly there," Ellen said from beside him in a chirpy voice.

"Wh-what's in that?" He pointed to the mug that a man with glasses and no hair held out before him.

"That's Mr. Peeky's famous spiced rum," Ellen said.

Exhaling slowly, he picked up the mug and threw the contents down his throat as Bram was doing beside him. It was smooth and tasted like the best rum he'd ever drunk.

"Thank God," Gray muttered. "And thank you, Mr. Peeky," he stammered out.

"Are you all right, Gray?" Bram asked.

He tried to focus on the man, who seemed to be clear-eyed and untouched by the quantity of alcohol he'd just consumed.

"It takes time to adjust, but you'll get there." He then clapped Gray on the shoulder, and he staggered but stayed upright.

"Right. Let's go." Ellen took his arm.

"Where? Did we win?" Gray asked.

"No. We came last," Matilda said. "Because you were too slow."

"Thash, that's hardly my fault," he said slowly. "It's my first time. Surely you weren't that good the firsh time?"

"Perhaps, but we don't like losing," Fred said as she glared up at him.

They were now back on the grass, and someone was playing a fiddle. He turned to look at Ellen, who was holding his arm, which Gray thought was to steady him. Squinting, he attempted to focus on her face.

"You have a very pretty fash," he said, and then his knees buckled, and he fell forward onto the ground.

Chapter 24

Ellen woke suddenly. Vivid and real, she wasn't sure if it was a vision or a dream. She'd been in George's bookshop, standing before a set of shelves, holding a book in her hands.

"B," she said to herself. The letter on the cover had been B, and the second word, Bestiary.

But that was all she could remember or had seen.

She didn't know what that signified, and yet she knew it was important. She would not have had the vision or dream, were it not. Looking out the window, Ellen saw dawn was creeping through the gap in the curtains.

She had to tell this information to Gray. Perhaps sending a note would get him here, seeing as he had not shown his face since the Crabbett Close games over a week ago and was clearly avoiding them.

Her uncle and Leo had caught Gray as he fell. Mungo and Alex had then taken him home, ensuring that the detective had been delivered into the hands of his staff safely.

Alex had told her that Gray woke briefly on the

carriage ride and smiled at him. He'd then said thank you, for what Alex had no idea, and then he'd fallen asleep once more.

Every barrier Gray had erected around himself had lowered that night. With the alcohol, he'd become different. He'd lost his inhibitions and laughed with her family and the residents of Crabbett Close, who had slowly warmed to him.

As the sun began to rise, Ellen lay there thinking about the man that was Detective Fletcher. Handsome and intelligent. He had seemed unruffled and always professional. Yet her family had unraveled him, as had the residents of Crabbett Close. Even Leo was warming to him.

She could be honest with herself here in the quiet of her room. She felt something for Grayson Fletcher. Something that Ellen knew could bloom into a great deal more.

Gray, like her, had turned his back on society. For different reasons, but still he had walked away from what he'd always known, and Ellen thought this gave them a common ground too. There was also the fact that when he touched her, she wanted to throw herself at him and never let go.

In short, Detective Fletcher made her feel emotions she'd no longer thought herself capable of feeling. It was terrifying and yet exciting at the same time.

Leaving her bed when the sun was high enough to ensure that tea would be made, Ellen washed and dressed. Leaving her room, she went in search of her aunt and uncle who would have risen early with Lottie.

She found them in the parlor, sitting beside each other in companionable silence, like they did most mornings while Lottie played.

"Hello, Aunty Ellen."

"Good morning, Lottie." She bent to kiss the little girl and then her aunt and uncle.

"Good morning, niece," Aunt Ivy said. "How did you sleep?"

"Well, but I had a vision or dream. I'm unsure what."

Uncle Bram waved her into the seat across from them. "Tell us about it."

He poured her a cup of tea while she talked, telling them everything she remembered.

"And you say you saw a B and the word 'Bestiary' on the cover?" he said.

She nodded. "I didn't see who had written it."

"And this book was in George's store and you believe important?"

"I was in his store holding it. I felt like I shouldn't have been and that George wanted no one to touch it," Ellen said. "Which makes absolutely no sense."

"Well, if it's an expensive and rare book, then it does, and a possible title with those initials is the *Blackstead Bestiary* written by Pierre Rosterman in the 1300s. It's highly sought after and worth a great deal."

"Yes," Aunt Ivy said. "I remember it was sold recently here in London to a private collector."

"Do you think that could have been George?" Ellen asked.

"There were many interested, and most would have paid a lot of money for it. I guess it depends if George had the funds or purchased it on behalf of someone," Aunt Ivy said.

"Do you think it is connected to his murder?"

"I don't think we can discount it, but we also don't know if it is this book or, for that matter, the original. George could have simply had a copy. But it is information we must pass on to Gray," Uncle Bram said.

"Perhaps you need to go back to the bookshop and have Gray meet you there. He has been avoiding us since the night Mungo and Alex took him home," Aunt Ivy said. "This could be a good reason for us to make contact with him because I feel this family is good for the uptight detective."

"I'm not sure he would feel that way," Ellen added.

"He will, niece. We just need to force ourselves on him like a new pair of shoes—eventually they fit well," Uncle Bram said.

"I should imagine he may have woken with a sore head and a healthy dose of embarrassment," Aunt Ivy said.

"Do we want him to fit into this household?" Ellen asked, curious as to what they would say.

"He is a good man, Ellen, and worthy of our company. From what I gather, he does not have many people who are close to him in his life, and that is sad."

"I am sure he is a good man, Uncle Bram. As I'm sure you would not have let him into our home for a meal if he were not," Ellen said.

"I always think you can tell the character of a man by the way he is with children," Aunt Ivy said.

Ellen wasn't sure why they were talking to her like this and was certain she didn't want to know.

"I will go to the markets this morning and select flowers for the house. When I return, I'll send word to the detective and tell him of my vision," Ellen said.

"Very well, but Mungo will drive you."

"I had thought to walk."

"And now you will drive," Uncle Bram said in that tone she knew well.

"Very well."

"And niece," Uncle Bram said as she reached the door.

"Yes?"

"Remember that not all men will treat you as your ex-fiancé did. Some will respect you and see you as their equal."

She nodded, unsure what to say to that. Did her aunt and uncle think that she felt something for Gray? Their words would suggest that as the case. But how had they known? She and the detective had barely spent time together.

AN HOUR LATER, Ellen was on her way to the market, still mulling over the conundrum that was Grayson Fletcher. Perhaps she would invite him for tea with the family again because while she did not understand yet what she felt for the man, or for that matter if she wanted to, she did think her uncle was right. Gray did not have many people close to him in his life, and her family were wonderful, if sometimes annoying, people.

Ellen loved the flower market and often did the ordering for the household. Her family allowed her this time and had since she'd first visited the place and declared she enjoyed it. Of course, there was usually Mungo waiting for her just outside the gate, but Ellen felt as if this was her little slice of independence. Something she'd never had living with her parents.

When the carriage stopped, she stepped down, received, and listened to the lecture from Mungo he delivered every time. If she had not returned at the exact time stipulated, he would come looking for her.

"Don't talk to anyone," Mungo snapped.

"Surely I must speak with the flower vendors?"

"Them yes, but no one else. Especially not men. I'm not sure what your aunt and uncle are about letting you go in there alone."

Ellen swallowed down the sigh, reminding herself that he cared about her and this was his way of showing it.

"I promise not to speak to any strange men, Mungo."

He gave her a hard look and then nodded.

"Get on with you then."

Minutes later she was wandering down the aisles of flowers, inhaling the scent of blooms and greenery. It was an unusual scent, almost earthy, and she loved it.

"Good day to you, Miss Nightingale."

"Hello, Miss Jolly."

And this of course was another reason why her family did not mind her coming here alone. A handful of the vendors were either related or friends with Crabbett Close residents. They kept an eye on her and would report anything back to her uncle they felt necessary.

Making several selections that she organized to have delivered to 11 Crabbett Close, Ellen chatted and admired what was on display.

It was as she neared the end of a row that she got another vision. Brief and over in seconds, she saw a forearm with the black tattoo on it she'd seen in Uncle Bram's book. Looking down the aisle, Ellen found a man. He was standing at the end, and his eyes were on her. A shiver of unease traversed her spine. The look he was giving her was not one of interest but intimidation.

"Don't stare at him, miss."

She turned to the woman who had spoken.

"Pardon?"

"He's one of them, Baddon Boys," she said, shooting the man a nervous glance. "They're a bad lot. They run in a gang and cause all kinds of trouble."

"I've never heard of them. Are they around here?"

The woman nodded. "Best to keep your distance from them, miss, if you don't mind me saying so."

"I will, and thank you for telling me. Could I ask a question?"

The woman nodded.

"Do these Baddon Boys have a tattoo at all?"

The flower seller's eyes widened, and Ellen knew why. She could feel him. The man was now behind her.

"Who wants to know?"

She turned on her heel at the hard words and came face to face with him.

"Pardon?" She put on her most haughty voice.

"You asked about tattoos. Why?"

Think, Ellen.

"Is this what you're looking for, love?" The man shoved up his sleeve and showed Ellen his forearm. It was the exact tattoo from both her visions.

"No indeed, a man helped me the other day when the wheel on my carriage broke. I saw that tattoo on his forearm and hoped to thank him. He walked away before I could do so." Ellen was quite proud of the answer she'd thought up. It sounded plausible, to her at least.

He frowned.

"Here are your flowers, miss," the woman said to her. Ellen turned back to grab them. "It's best to cut the stems before you put them in water. They last longer." The woman continued to chat, and she answered as best she could considering her head was full of questions.

"He's gone," the flower vendor then said. "You'd best leave. You don't want to run into him again. To my mind, he seemed awful interested in you. I saw the look he was giving you before he came over."

"I will, and thank you." Ellen walked back along the

row, thinking the woman was right. She needed to go, and she now had more information to share with Gray.

"Miss Nightingale? Ellen?"

She knew who that voice belonged to. Detective Fletcher was coming toward her. He wore his top hat and black coat, once again the immaculate gentleman, not the unraveled one from a week ago. Ellen smiled at the memory of him telling her she had a very pretty fash, which she guessed meant face.

"Why are you smiling?" he asked.

"Look around you, sir. What is there not to smile about?"

He did as she asked and frowned.

"I'm not sure you should be here if it makes you frown."

"I believe I owe you an apology, Ellen."

"I don't think so." She matched his solemn tone. "Detective Fletcher, I—"

"For passing out and being carried to a carriage and delivered home," he cut off her words before she could tell him about the man. "I have never been in such a situation before. Forgive me for my loss of control."

"Let me put you at ease, Detective Fletcher—"

"I thought we were using first names now?"

"Gray," Ellen added, taking pity on him. "Everyone has the experience you had the first time they participate in a night around Crabbett Close. Leo emptied the contents of his stomach into Mrs. Greedy's rosebush. She has yet to forgive him, but as they had the best blooms ever the following year, she is coming around. Alex slept in Mrs. Varney's front parlor and woke to Tabitha Varney standing over him in her night robe."

Gray was smiling now, and it made him look younger and devastatingly handsome. Ellen wondered if she would always react to his nearness. Her heart fluttered and she felt a ridiculous urge to sigh.

"I assure you, no apology is necessary."

"Do the women not drink? Other than the large lady who started with me," he added.

"Mavis Johns," Ellen added. "Something of a legend in Crabbett Close."

"Others have taken part, but it is always the biggest men and Mavis who start as they seem able to hold more alcohol than others. Although once Mrs. Greedy participated, and she outdrank everyone."

He barked out a laugh. "So I can return to Crabbett Close is that what you're saying?"

"I am, and you can."

"I could almost imagine I'd dreamed that entire evening. It was so unlike anything I've ever experienced or want to again."

"Surely it was not that bad."

"Worse." But he laughed. "Your brothers will make my life hell."

"They will, but that too shall pass."

"What has you here?" He looked around him. "Alone, Ellen?"

"You sound like my uncle. Mungo is outside waiting. Not that I need to offer an explanation for being at the flower markets."

"There are dangers and criminals everywhere, Ellen. It pays to remember that. I can't believe your brothers allowed this."

"Mungo is watching over me by standing on the seat of the carriage. If I do not return at the time he has stipulated, he will come in and find me. I also have my umbrella." She lifted her coat and showed it hooked to her skirts.

"Plus, there are relatives and friends of Crabbett Close residents dotted everywhere."

"My mind is at rest."

"What has you here, Gray?"

"I thought to find a woman whose son I need to question about a series of robberies. So far, I have been unable to locate her."

"Well, I will not keep you. But before I go, I need to tell you I have had two visions this morning."

He held out his arm to her. Ellen looked at it.

"I do not bite, Ellen."

She placed her fingers on it, and they started walking down the row of blooms.

"The roses are beautiful colors," he said.

"Aunt Ivy loves them." She stopped to order some to be delivered.

They walked on, and it was surprisingly comfortable to do so at his side, even though she was aware of this man more than anyone she'd met before.

"Grayson?"

The arm under her hand stiffened, then fell, leaving Ellen's to drop to her side. Shooting Gray a look, she saw the tension in his face as the muscles in his jaw bunched. Ellen then glanced at the man coming toward them and felt her stomach clench.

With him was a woman. Ellen knew both people well. She and Gray stopped, and horror had her feet suddenly feeling like they were stuck to the ground. This was her worst nightmare. Facing her past.

"It is you," the man, Lord Howe, said. He was now a few feet away, his eyes on Gray. "Why are you here at the flower market?" His eyes then turned to her, and she saw the flare of recognition. Their paths had crossed in society.

He'd danced with her and had even shown Ellen interest for a while.

Panic slithered its fingers through her. She felt herself preparing to flee, but a large hand settled on her waist, holding her in place. Gray was supporting her, and suddenly she felt stronger.

"What has you with my brother?" he demanded of Ellen.

This was Gray's brother. How had she not connected them? Lord Howe was the reason she hadn't thought of the man as a Fletcher. He carried his father, the Earl's other title as many elder sons did.

"I'm sure you meant to greet Miss Nightingale properly, brother?" Gray said in a hard voice.

Lord Howe's bow was insultingly shallow.

"I must offer you my congratulations for your upcoming nuptials, Christopher. I have not received my invitation, but I'm sure that will be rectified soon. Ramsey paid me a call, and he has his," Gray said, still in a tone that would shatter a diamond.

Lord Howe blustered, and his cheeks flushed with color. "Yes, of course. I wanted to personally deliver it to you."

"Ah, that must be it then," Gray said calmly. But Ellen felt the tension in the hand he held to her back. He was as unhappy to see these two as she was.

Christopher's hair was lighter, and his body slighter than Gray's, but the resemblance was there in the facial features of the brothers.

"And is this to be my sister-in-law, Christopher?" Gray asked.

"This is Lady Mary Smythe. Mary, this is my youngest brother, Grayson."

It was obvious to everyone that Lord Howe was reluctant to introduce his brother, which Ellen found sad. Her family might annoy her excessively, but they were never ashamed of her.

"We are here looking at flowers," Lord Howe said when a heavy silence settled over them.

"Really? That surprises me. I had no idea you were an expert on such things, Christopher."

"I'm not," Lord Howe gritted out. "Mary merely wished for me to accompany her."

"And you acquiesced to her request. What an accommodating fiancé you are, brother."

Gray was goading his brother. From the corner of her eye, she could see his jaw was clenched like he would rather be anywhere but here.

The woman at Lord Howe's side whispered something to him. Ellen knew who she was. Lady Mary Smythe, and once they'd been acquaintances. Not friends, as she'd not had any of those until she'd met Samantha and the twins. But they'd been in the same social circles and had looked down their noses at those that hadn't.

"Miss Nightingale, this is a surprise. I have not seen you since…" Lady Mary Smythe let her words fall away as she appeared to look contrite and failed. "Your father," the woman added. "Well, you know what I mean, I'm sure."

Until she'd seen the twins, Ellen had avoided anyone from her days in society. If she saw someone she recognized, she hid or fled. She did not go places they were, like her family did. The choice had been hers, and they'd respected that even while they'd tried to get her to join them when they went to the theatre or anywhere she'd once frequented.

"It really is sad what happened," Lady Mary added, not looking sad at all. She was excited to have a wonderful tidbit of gossip to share with her friends.

And this was the reason. She did not want people looking down their noses at her. Did not want to be ridiculed by those who had once been her equals. The wonderful burn of anger gave Ellen the strength she needed to speak.

"That my father killed himself, do you mean? Or that because he took his life, his children were cast from society and shunned, through no fault of their own?"

Lady Mary Smythe pressed a hand to her mouth in shock at her words. Ellen felt her anger drain away as swiftly as it had arrived. She could feel her hands starting to shake and hated herself for the weakness. She thought seriously about fleeing. The hand on her back moved in small circles, sliding warmth through her.

Ellen focused on it and the reassurance it was giving her and not the people from her past standing before her.

Chapter 25

Gray had learned to show no expression very early in his life. It stood him in good stead with his job, and now, when he wanted to punch the smug look from his brother's face.

Christopher's shock had soon vanished to return to the supercilious expression he often wore after seeing Gray. The eldest of three, their father had doted on him and ensured he'd turned out exactly like the tyrant who had sired him.

"Oh, surely that is unjust, Miss Nightingale," Lady Mary mewed. "It is not the fault of society that your father—"

"I'll stop you there, Lady Mary," Gray said, feeling the shivers start in Ellen's body. Her body was so rigid he was sure she'd shatter into pieces at his feet if he didn't get her away from here. Panic, he was sure, was telling her to run. "Some in society are a group of elitist vultures who prey on those they see as beneath them. They also like nothing more than for one of their own to fall from grace so they can turn on them."

He felt Ellen suck in a deep breath and release it slowly

at his words. Gray moved slightly, just a shift of his feet, and his body was now close to hers. He could feel her tremors. Ellen was fighting to hold back the panic. The brave, strong woman wasn't brave when faced with her past. Glancing at her briefly, he noted her pallor, but she was not looking down or away. Her eyes were facing forward, chin raised slightly.

Good girl.

"How dare you suggest we are elitist vultures!" Christopher thundered, now red in the face.

"I said some, Christopher. If you fall into the category, I did not put you there, but you did."

He hadn't seen his father or brothers for two years. Gray had attended a funeral. They had not spoken to him. Only his mother made the effort. He had to say, looking at the man before him, he didn't miss him.

There was a small pang for what they'd once shared many years ago. He saw the boy was long gone from the man before him. Had Gray ever been so pompous? Possibly, but his aunt and uncle and lack of a title coming his way had changed that.

Christopher had not been that lucky and was a product of their father.

"I don't believe we have anything further to say to each other, brother. I'll look forward to receiving my wedding invitation. Good day." He bowed. "I wish you every happiness for your life together."

"Oh, but I had wanted to speak with dear Miss Nightingale," Lady Mary tittered. "After all, I am not a vulture and wish only to chat, as it has been so long," she said with total insincerity.

In fact, what she wanted was to get information so she could share it with her friends. The thought of anyone gossiping about Ellen did not sit well with Gray.

"Good day." He walked, taking Ellen with him by pushing her in the back. Gray kept moving along the row and toward the flower entrance. Once they were through the gate, he said, "Where is your carriage, Ellen?"

She pointed down the road but did not speak. He saw Mungo sitting on a driver's seat. He nudged her on. They walked the short distance in silence.

"What's happened?" Mungo said when they arrived. He was frowning, eyes on Ellen. "Miss Ellen?"

"'Tis nothing." Her words had a tremor in them.

Gray opened the carriage and lifted Ellen inside. He then spoke to the driver.

"Take us to a tea shop, Mungo, please," he added. "Miss Ellen met some people she used to know, and it upset her."

The driver hissed something vile in his thick Scottish accent.

"Is there a tea shop?" Gray asked.

The man nodded.

"Drive us there."

Mungo studied him for long seconds and then nodded again. Gray climbed inside.

"What are you doing? I wish to go home," Ellen said when he sat in the seat across from her. She was crying, her eyes red, and cheeks stained with tears. The sight made him feel like going back into the flower market and finding his brother. He then wanted to bloody his nose and tell Lady Mary she was a very poor second best to Miss Ellen Nightingale in every way.

"Taking you out for tea. It seems you need a fortifying cup before you return to Crabbett Close and your family."

She sniffed.

"If you return looking as pathetic as you currently do,

you will be subjected to an inquisition, which I'm not sure you are up to," Gray said.

"I am not pathetic." There was no strength to her words. She wiped her gloved hand over her face, looking like a child. "But I have taken great pains since I left society never to see or interact with anyone from it."

"But you have seen them, surely? You could not get about London without doing so?"

Her eyes lowered.

"How have you avoided them?"

"I walk the other way or hide if I see someone that will recognize me. My family goes out to places. I choose not to."

Gray couldn't believe that this woman, who he thought a bloody Amazon who backed down from nothing or no one, had allowed members of society to force her into hiding.

"That's cowardly, Ellen. Which I never would have thought was a word I would use for you. You are worth ten of those people. People who mean little or nothing to you."

"I'm not a coward!" Her pretty blue eyes fired to life and shot sparks at him. "How dare you suggest such a thing!"

"If you are not a coward and have done nothing wrong, why does it matter to you what anyone thinks of you? Why avoid people when you know that the fault for what happened was your father's, not yours or your family's?"

Gray moved to sit next to her as another tear rolled down her cheek. He wiped it away with the pad of his thumb.

"By doing what you have, you've allowed yourself to feel small in your own eyes and in the eyes of your family.

You've allowed what happened to change you so much, Ellen, and for the better but not in this."

She glared at him, and Gray liked that scowl far better than the defenseless victim she'd been minutes before. That look had touched him deeply.

"Don't let those two empty-headed fools make you feel any less than the brave, fearless woman you are, Ellen Nightingale. You are strong. Don't let them weaken you."

Her eyes held his as the anger drained away. More tears fell.

"Thank you, your words humble me," she whispered. "I-it took me so long to find my rage and not feel shame after what happened. I was numb. Creditors were calling, and people I'd always known were turning from me or shutting their doors on us. I decided I never wanted to see or speak to someone from that time again."

"I'm sorry that happened to you and your family, Ellen. But none of it was your fault. And we both know that all members of society aren't bad. Look at your friends, the Sinclairs."

She sighed. "I never again wanted any part of that life and then today there they were. Your brother and Lady Mary. I was shocked and reacted accordingly."

"Tell me you weren't one of those silly, vapid women who fell all over themselves, so my brother acknowledged you?" he teased her.

"Actually, your brother made advances on me," she said in a husky voice. "I was considered quite a diamond of the first water, I'll have you know."

"I can imagine you were." Gray didn't like the flash of jealousy he felt thinking of Christopher anywhere near this woman.

"Thank you, Gray."

"For what?"

"Supporting me and then calling me a coward. For saying what you did. I may not have liked it, but you are right. My family has been trying to force me out of hiding but failed. Perhaps it is time that I no longer run the other way when my past is before me."

"If I'm honest, seeing my brother was not easy."

"You handled him brilliantly," she said. "But I could feel the tension between you. Is there no way——"

"No," he cut her off. "We are different people now."

She was close to him. His hand on her shoulder, comforting her. Ellen leaned toward him. Gray turned his head, and her mouth slightly touched his.

"Ellen," he whispered against her lips. His arms then went around her, and he pulled her gently into his body. This time it was he who kissed her. Soft yet insistent. She tasted of the sweetest dessert and yet there was a hint of spice too. Her lips were so plump, her body curvaceous against his.

He'd needed this and had been fooling himself to say otherwise. He wanted to feel her skin beneath his hands, caress her body.

The carriage jolted, and they fell apart. Her eyes were wide with surprise, and yet he saw no regret or fear. Only heat lingered in the blue depths.

"I'm not apologizing for that." Gray's words came out hoarse. His body was hard, and his skin felt tight. "Because I have wanted to kiss you since the first night I met you."

"You were angry with me that night," she whispered instead of slapping him, which would surely have been the right reaction. Yet what had he expected from this woman who could subdue a man with her umbrella and had visions? She was nothing that was normal and everything that was wonderful and exasperating.

Looking down into her lovely face, Gray felt something bloom inside him.

"I was angry because you were walking about alone on a foggy night after finding a body."

Her eyes held his, and he swore something passed between them again, but neither said a word about it. Thankfully, the carriage chose that moment to stop.

"I will not regret it either, Gray." She leaned in to kiss him. Their lips clung, and it took all his strength to pull away.

He didn't reply because he wasn't sure how. This woman was a dangerous combination of vulnerable and strong-willed. Sweet and fiery. He'd met no one like her or felt as he did in her company with anyone else. For now, he would take her to tea, and then when he was alone, he would think about what was growing inside him for Ellen Nightingale.

He opened the door and helped her down.

"We are to take tea at Miss Patty's Tea Shop, Mungo. I will bring you back something," Ellen said.

The Scotsman glared down at Gray. He gave him a look, and the man's brow rose. Gray stared at Ellen, who was glancing around her, and mouthed the word "upset."

Mungo mouthed back the word, "Who?"

Gray narrowed his eyes and then shook his head. He then silently said, "Later." It was all over in seconds and Ellen unaware of the exchange, but the Scotsman was not happy. However, he said nothing further.

"We shall return soon," Gray said. He then took Ellen's elbow and headed toward the lavender-fronted tea shop that had large gold letters above the window stating it was Miss Patty's Tea Shop.

"I've never been here," he said. "I don't go to tea shops."

"Good Lord, really? My family are regular visitors," Ellen said. The fear and sadness were no longer in her eyes, which made him feel a great deal better.

The place was busy, and he directed them to a table near the rear.

"Hello, Jane," Ellen said when a young girl came to take their order. "How is your brother?"

The girl smiled. "Much better thank you, Miss Nightingale. His leg is still in a splint, but we've hopes for not too much longer. Thank you again. You and your family saved our Eddie."

"No thanks needed. We're just glad he's healing."

"What was that about?" Gray asked Ellen after the girl had gone.

"We helped her brother. A carriage had run him over." She shrugged as if it was nothing important.

"I'm sure there is more to that story."

"I have nothing more to say on the matter," she said.

The Scotland Yard detective inside Gray wanted to know all the details about what happened. Yet he knew that if it involved the Nightingale family, it would be unorthodox, for a good cause, and likely dangerous. Looking at Ellen, he realized it was important to him she stayed safe.

"I'm sure I shouldn't want the details, as it will probably go against every principle I have," Gray said. He moved the small vase on the table before him into the middle.

"Surely not. We are not criminals, and we merely want to help people." Ellen nudged it a few inches to the left.

"Helping people while putting yourself in danger." He adjusted it. She moved it again.

"Cease." He grabbed her hand as she reached for the vase.

She laughed. "Is order important to you, then?"

"Very," he said.

"Bud said she watched you climb our front steps the day you came to call after George's murder. She said it was quite odd. You walked up the steps and then down the top one and back up."

"Did I?" He looked at her twinkling eyes but said nothing. Gray knew his need for even numbers and uniformity wasn't rational, but it was the only part of him that wasn't. He usually hid it from people. Again, not the Nightingales or their staff.

"We also could not work out who had straightened all the animal figures on the sideboard. Teddy was surprised to see them in the formation they were. Not one out of line."

"Is there a point you are trying to make, Ellen?"

"I don't think so."

Her smile was bright. The memory of the flower market had clearly receded.

"A few quirks do not make me as unusual as you Nightingales," he said.

"Very true." She did not take offense. "Have you heard of the Baddon Boys, Gray?"

"I have, and what do you know about that gang of ruffians?"

"I had a vision." She told him about what she'd seen and then again about the man at the flower market.

"You did what?" Gray demanded after she'd told him about the tattoo vision and the man who'd shown her his.

"I didn't ask him to see it. He just overheard me discussing the tattoo and then rolled up his sleeve for me to see his forearm. I came up with a very good excuse as to why I was looking for a man who had one, as I've just told you."

"Dear God, Ellen. This is not a game." The scone he'd just consumed suddenly felt like it weighed a great deal more in his stomach than it should have. The thought of this woman anywhere near trouble terrified him.

"I know it's not, but were it not for me, you would not have a lead on George's murder. Thus far, I have found out about the tattoo, the Baddon Boys, and the argument between George and his sister. Plus"—she held up her hand as Gray opened his mouth—"I had another vision this morning that woke me."

"What did you see? Tell me you haven't confronted anyone else?" He'd despised women who fell about the place having fits of vapors, but in that moment, he conceded they could be onto something.

"Did you know the Baddon Boys have tattoos on their forearms like the one I saw on that naked man, Detective Fletcher?" Her chin rose as she gave him a haughty look.

"You don't know that every one of the Baddon Boys has a tattoo." But Gray thought she could be right. Often gangs carried the same mark. If the flower seller was correct and the man who showed Ellen the tattoo was a member of the gang, it was likely the case all the members had the mark on their forearms.

"And now I'll tell you what I woke up to this morning, and you can apologize for your cutting words."

He sighed. "What did you see? And I'm not apologizing for stating that you shouldn't be throwing yourself recklessly into danger."

She picked up the last scone on the plate and took a large bite. Damn, he'd wanted that.

Chapter 26

Ellen walked into Nicholson's bookshop behind Gray. Mungo had gone home to tell her family where she was, and Ellen had every expectation of one of them appearing soon. Leo did not trust Gray, but he did now at least have an uneasy truce with him.

Ellen and Gray had taken tea together after he'd kissed her. And what a kiss. She'd literally melted in his arms and had definitely wanted more. Men had kissed her before. Brief and chaste, and she'd felt nothing. Gray's kiss had been different. But what had it meant to him?

He'd also been angry with her when she'd told him she'd had a small confrontation with that member of the Baddon Boys gang. In fact, it had infuriated him.

"I'm locking this door, so then no one can enter, and you can't walk out and find trouble," Gray said.

"Very amusing, but I will remind you again that everything I've given you has helped you with your case, so you should thank me."

"Perhaps I should just take you home and explain to your family what you've been up to?"

"I am not frightened of my brothers."

"No, I doubt there is much that frightens you," he muttered. "This entire case is getting more confusing by the day," Gray added. "Until you Nightingales entered the scene, I could work through things and let them reach their logical conclusion. I would then arrest the guilty person."

"Look at this as having consultants to assist you," Ellen said. She was now behind the counter, inspecting what lay beneath.

"Thank you, but I have no wish for consultants. I work alone," he said.

"So far, we have a dead person, poor George," Ellen said, ignoring what he'd just said. "We have the tattoos, which we know the Baddon Boys's gang have on their forearms." She rose from behind the counter.

"Think we know they have," Gray added. "I'm sure there are others about London who have that mark on them and are not part of the gang."

"Why were the Nicholson siblings arguing and Olivia crying? Further to that, why did I get a vision directly after of the naked man?"

"There are too many loose threads," Gray said.

Something had changed between Gray and Ellen after they'd confronted their past together. They were closer. He was not so formal, and they seemed comfortable with each other. However, there was also that hum of tension from the kiss too. She felt his eyes on her lingering.

Ellen had vowed not to fall in love with a man ever. She had a feeling Grayson Fletcher might test that.

"You say this book, according to your aunt and uncle, could have been extremely expensive if it was the only volume ever written of the *Blackstead Bestiary*?" Gray asked after. "If it is that book."

"Yes. I'm not sure what it's about, but Uncle Bram said it was very expensive and sought after by some."

"I know that a bestiary is a collection of descriptions about different animals, and birds, real or imaginary," Gray said. "But that's the limit to my knowledge."

"Would someone kill over something like that?" Ellen wondered. "And how does it all tie together? The tattoos, the Baddon Boys, and the Nicholsons, plus the book."

"If they are connected, but you're right. How," Gray said, "if someone wanted that book badly enough, would they kill or perhaps hire a person to do that," he added. "Which could be where the Baddon Boys come in."

"Do you mean they could have been hired to do the killing?"

"Yes. I have checked on this Michael Dunston, who Mr. Nicholson said was angry when he could not buy the shop and George got it. He now lives in Wales, so it couldn't be him who was the murderer."

"Drat. He was the perfect suspect," Ellen said.

"There is no such thing as a perfect suspect, Ellen, and sometimes the most obvious is not the guilty party."

"How annoying."

They walked around the shop examining shelves.

"We have been through here extensively but found no clues on who killed George Nicholson," Gray said. "Do you know where you were standing when you saw yourself holding the book?"

Ellen turned on her heel, searching. A knock on the door had them both looking. A man was bent and peering in through the glass. Before she could speak, Gray had opened it.

"What are you doing here, Ramsey?"

The man was tall like Gray. He wore black trousers and

a gray jacket. Under his arm, he held his hat. He was also very handsome. But Ellen did not feel her heart flutter like she experienced when Gray was nearby.

"I was riding past and saw you come in here with a lady on your heels. I felt it necessary to follow."

The man pushed Gray in the shoulder, and he stepped back, leaving room for him to enter.

"Good day. I don't believe we had time to become acquainted when we met briefly at Gray's house. I am Mr. Hellion." He bowed. "This idiot's cousin."

"Miss Nightingale." Gray waved a hand her way.

"You have a lot of family for a man who does not seem to want any," Ellen said.

Ramsey barked out a laugh. "He's always been uptight. Does he still do the even number thing and have a passion for uniformity?"

She nodded. "We just took tea, and he had to—"

"Yes, thank you, that will do," Gray said, shooting her a mock glare. "Why are you in this neighborhood, Ram?"

"Appleblossoms Bakers is the only one in London who has perfected apricotines."

"You've been back in London less than a month. How is it you know this?" Gray asked.

"Delores Fancy is Mother's maid. She told her about them, and as I am my mother's favorite son—"

"Only son," Gray interrupted.

"She, of course, informed me, and I had to test Delores's claim in saying they were the best. As it turns out, I am pleased to assure her they are." Ramsey Hellion slapped his hat against his thigh as he talked. "What has you both in here?" The man's eyes went from his cousin to Ellen, and she saw the speculation.

"Investigating," Gray said.

"Really? That's exciting. Can I assist you in any way?"

Gray pinched his nose. He didn't even want Ellen here but needed her. The man liked to work alone, that much she knew.

"Are you a detective, Ram?"

His cousin smiled. "No indeed, Gray, but I'm sure I could be a civilian aiding you in your investigations like Miss Nightingale. Because while I know we are making advancements, I doubt a woman in Scotland Yard is one of them."

"I would make an excellent detective," Ellen said.

"Oh, I'm sure you would, Miss Nightingale," Ramsey added.

"I'm Ellen," she added.

"Ramsey."

"If you two are quite finished," Gray gritted out.

"Quite," Ramsey said with a wide smile, and Ellen thought he had perfected the art of annoying his cousin over the years they'd spent together. Ellen found she liked Gray's cousin very much.

"Is there any chance at all that you will leave? This is a murder scene, Ramsey."

"And Ellen is helping you?"

"She is." Gray didn't offer more.

"Very well, I shall step next door and purchase some apricotines and sit on the doorstep like a forlorn child until you are finished being officious."

Ellen giggled as he headed back out the door, whistling.

"Don't encourage him."

"He seems like a very nice man," Ellen said.

"The best of men," Gray added. "Now, if we could focus?"

They walked over every inch of the lower floor and

then climbed to the next. It was in the storage room that Ellen saw the tall, narrow bookshelf. "This is where I was in my vision. I'm sure of it."

Gray looked around the room, and then moved to the bookshelf. It was full. Ellen joined him as he began removing books off the shelf and searching through them and behind.

"Oh my," she whispered as they started taking them from the bottom, and she saw the small box. The top had scuff marks and was clearly well used.

Once they had the shelf cleared, Gray wiggled the board, and it came out in his hands, then the next above it.

"Do you think George kept things in there like his precious books?"

"Money too perhaps." He tried to open the lid, but it was, of course, locked and made of very sturdy wood. He muttered something beneath his breath. There was a keyhole but no sign of a key.

"What?"

"Can you get my cousin from the steps outside the bookshop and bring him up here please, Ellen."

They were crouched beside each other, his face inches from hers.

"Why?"

"My father and his uncle both had many things they locked away in desk drawers and boxes. Ramsey perfected the art of being able to open them with these metal picks he got from a blacksmith."

"Right. Well, I'll collect him then."

"Are you laughing at me, madam?" His eyes were dark and fringed by long lashes that a woman would envy.

"Of course not."

"I don't believe you."

"Well, you do like control and things to go the way you like them to go, and when they don't, it irks you."

"Irks?" His mouth was inches from hers now.

"Annoys?" The word was breathless. "I don't think you should kiss me in here."

Chapter 27

"You're very likely right, but with you this close, it is hard."

She eased back.

"Get Ramsey, Ellen."

She rose, and then ran down the stairs.

"Slow down or you may fall!"

"I won't!" She jumped the last two and hurried to the door. Opening it, she found Ramsey on the bottom step, eating.

"Hello, Ellen."

"Can you come? Gray needs you."

"Which will annoy him excessively but I will enjoy." He rose and followed her up the stairs. "Well now, cousin, I believe you need my expertise?" Ramsey said when they entered the room Gray was in.

"I do, which I am uncomfortable with." Gray was still crouched before the box. "Do you carry your lock picks with you?"

"Of course, I never leave home without them. One never knows when I will be trussed in chains and locked in an underground cell."

"As if we would be that lucky," Gray muttered. "Get down here."

While they discussed the box, Ellen wandered around the room. She touched surfaces and searched for anything that might be a clue. Leaving the room, she walked into the next and found only a table and chairs. Then she went downstairs and looked around again inside the shop for anything that had been missed, hoping she'd get another vision.

When the door opened, she realized she had not relocked it after Ramsey entered.

"I'm sorry, but the bookshop is closed," Ellen told the couple who entered.

They were well-dressed. The man was perhaps slightly older, but she did not think they were that different in age to her and Leo.

"We are here to speak with Mr. Nicholson. I am Mr. Brownly, and this is my sister, Miss Brownly," the man said.

"Are you a friend of his?" Ellen wasn't about to tell just anyone of George's death, but she also didn't want to break it to a friend in a callous manner.

"George was a collector of books like me, and he often procured rare editions on my behalf when I found one I wanted."

She nodded, wondering what to do now.

"Good day," Gray said from the doorway. "How may we help you?"

"This is Mr. and Miss Brownly. George sometimes bought books on Mr. Brownly's behalf," Ellen said, relieved he was here.

"I am Detective Fletcher from Scotland Yard," Gray said. "I'm afraid to tell you that Mr. Nicholson has passed away."

Miss Brownly looked upset about that. Mr. Brownly frowned.

"How did it happen?" he asked.

"Someone murdered him in this bookshop," Gray said.

Ellen was surprised he'd given them that information.

"Dear Lord," Miss Brownly whispered. "Poor George."

"Can I ask why you are here today? Was it just a social call, or were you browsing?" Gray asked.

"Mr. Nicholson had secured a book I have been searching for, for some time," the man said.

Ellen watched his sister shoot him a shocked look and then the expression schooled into a calm facade.

"We have searched for many years, and finally, George located it. I gave him the money, and then he notified me he had the book in his possession. We were traveling to Bath, but obviously overjoyed. I only just received the missive today as I returned this morning. I rushed over immediately."

"Can I ask what the book was, Mr. Brownly?" Gray asked.

"It is very rare, so I doubt you have heard of it, Detective Fletcher. It is called the *Blackstead Bestiary*."

Not by a flicker of an eyelash did Ellen show she had heard the title before. But she felt it in her belly as it clenched. Just this morning she'd had a vision which she believed included that book and now someone else was mentioning it.

"May we look for it, Detective Fletcher?" Mr. Brownly asked.

"I'm afraid that is not possible," Gray said.

"I paid a great deal of money for it. I insist that if it is here, it is to be handed directly to me." Mr. Brownly was getting angry.

"And it will be if I can establish proof that it is yours, and if we find the book, of course," Gray said calmly.

Anger crackled in the air.

"Come, brother, let us go, and the detective can do his job, which will ensure that you get your book." Miss Brownly put her hand on his arm.

"It is not simply a book, Miranda," he snapped.

"The fault is not your sister's, Mr. Brownly," Ellen said. "It is of the man who murdered George."

He glared at her, as if she'd had no right to speak to him. Miss Brownly, however, gave her a small smile.

"If you could please bring proof of your exchange with Mr. Nicholson for the book you claim he purchased on your behalf to Scotland Yard, Mr. Brownly. As surely an intelligent man like yourself did not simply hand over the money without some kind of written proof?"

The man's cheeks were now red with rage. His sister looked nervous.

"Good day," Gray said, moving to the door. He then held it open. When they had left, he shut it behind them.

"And yet another player enters the fray. I don't suppose you had another vision that said Mr. Brownly is the killer, did you?" Gray asked her.

She shook her head. "I feel sorry for that man's sister. He seems like a domineering angry type."

"Agreed. I'm also wondering if Brownly was lying. That he came here to bargain with George Nicholson for something he knew he had and then changed tack when he realized George was dead."

"That's dastardly!" Ellen said.

"Dastardly? How dramatic of you, Miss Nightingale."

To Ellen's surprise, he wrapped an arm around her waist and pulled her close.

"One kiss would never be enough with you." His

mouth took hers slowly, and Ellen melted into him. Instinctively, her arms went around his neck, and she held on as his lips explored hers. Where one finished, another started. His hand roamed her back, stroking her through the layers of clothing, and she wanted to be closer to him. Wanted to explore this wonderful feeling that was coursing through her.

"I have it opened!"

Gray eased her back, his eyes holding hers. Heat simmered in the dark depths. Heat and need that matched what she felt. Her body hummed.

"Come along." He kissed her again briefly. "You can witness my cousin gloating. At least having your beauty beside me will ease the pain slightly."

She walked up the stairs in a daze before him, quite liking the idea that Gray thought she was beautiful. Loving even more that he'd lost his reserve and kissed her for the second time that day.

They entered the room to find Ramsey sitting before the now open box.

"What's inside?" Gray asked. "Because there is no chance you wouldn't have looked."

"Ledgers and a small brown leather book, which has notes in it."

Gray held out his hand, and Ramsey gave it to him.

"Would it help if I went through the ledgers?" Ellen asked.

Gray studied her for long seconds, a small smile teasing his lips as if he knew what his kiss had done to her.

"Very well. We are looking for anything connected to Brownly and the book *Blackstead Bestiary*. Or anything that says who killed George Nicholson."

"Right then," Ramsey said, picking out a book. "It

looks like we two are assistants to Detective Fletcher from Scotland Yard, Ellen."

The only sound Gray made was a loud, weighty sigh.

Silence settled around the room then as they read.

"This is a notation of clients that wanted George Nicholson to procure books for him. Brownly was definitely one. But under his name are dates and books George got for him that were paid for, and there is no mention of the *Blackstead Bestiary*. The amounts are staggering." Ellen spoke first.

"Do you think Brownly was lying or not?" Ramsey said. "And why?"

"So you overheard the entire conversation, even though I told you to stay in this room?" Gray said.

"Of course. I sat on the bottom step and took in every word, which just quietly I was very excited to overhear as I've never heard you in an official capacity. You are quite impressive when you are calling someone a liar and they don't realize it."

"Of course I live to serve you."

Ellen battled the flush of heat that wanted to fill her cheeks. Had he heard when Gray said one kiss would never be enough with her?

"I have excellent hearing," Ramsey said, further increasing her discomfort.

"There is an entry here two weeks ago. A sizeable sum of money," Ellen said quickly to change the subject. She held up the book for Gray to see. "It just says Olivia beside it. Olivia is George Nicholson's sister," she added for Ramsey's benefit.

"If she's his sister, surely he can give her money?" Ramsey said. "Although Gray is terribly tightfisted, I'd doubt he'd give me money if I asked."

"Because you have more than me," Gray drawled.

She enjoyed watching them together. Liked that Gray had a friend, his cousin, and they were reunited once more.

"How long has it been since you saw each other?" Ellen asked Ramsey.

"Years, and too many to count. But I am now back and just in time. Gray has no social life and refuses to reenter society, so something must be done."

"I will not be reentering society."

Ellen shuddered at the thought.

"I'm sorry for what happened to you and your family, Miss Nightingale." Ramsey's voice became serious as he looked at her.

"Ellen," she said. "And thank you, but I will not be reentering society either, so your cousin has my support in that."

"There are other places you can socialize, it does not have to be in society," Ramsey protested.

"Getting back to the ledgers," Gray said. "Clearly George was methodical, but it doesn't say why he gave her such a large sum of money, further to that is why did she not ask her parents? I believe they have a great deal more than George did."

"Because the money was for something she didn't want her parents to know about," Ellen said, looking at him.

"Exactly." Gray smiled at her. "So what was it? Was it the reason they were arguing?"

"When did you see them arguing, and who are they? You need to fill me in on the entirety of the case if I am to assist you," Ramsey said.

"Absolutely not," Gray said.

"Hello?"

"You were last to open that door," Ellen said when Gray shot her a look. "Up here, Alex."

The thud of feet had her brother arriving in the small room seconds later.

"Leo sent me so he did not yell at either of you."

"Too kind," Gray said. "Your sister is safe. This is my cousin Ramsey Hellion."

"Good Lord, what a wonderful name," Alex said.

"I've always liked it," Ramsey added.

"And how is your head, Gray?" Alex asked solicitously. The wicked look in his eyes, however, was another story.

"Head?" Ramsey asked.

"This is a murder investigation. I cannot have all this interference," Gray said. "You need to leave."

"What is wrong with his head?" Ramsey asked Alex.

"If you tell him, I will arrest you on trumped-up charges that will be believed because I never do such things," Gray growled as he glared at Alex.

"We live not far from here. Our street is odd, and we have events. Your cousin participated in one. It did not go well for him, as it never does for a first timer," Alex said, ignoring the threat of arrest. "He over imbibed, shall we say." Alex then mimicked a gesture with his hand of someone falling over.

"I'm respected at Scotland Yard. Even feared," Gray said wistfully.

"Right. Someone do a brief overview of what's happening with the case of George Nicholson's murder and why you're here," Alex said.

"I will tell you later," Ellen said quickly. She had no wish for Alex to know about her confrontation with the Baddon Boys.

"No indeed, I'm happy to explain all the details about what you did today to your brother, Ellen," Gray said, reading her mind.

"What did you do this time?"

"I did nothing." She glared at Gray.

And so, the story was told. Alex was furious and vowed to tell Leo. Gray looked smug and had her wanting to smack the expression from his handsome face.

"Come, you are going home and can tell the others what you have done. They will not be pleased."

Gray frowned at Alex's harsh tone. "There is no need, she was—"

"I'll sort this, Gray, say no more, and I'm sorry you've had to deal with Ellen. Good day to you both."

Alex took her arm and led Ellen from the room.

"You will spend the day in your room thinking about what you've done, sister!"

She looked at her brother, and he crossed his eyes.

"Alex, I won't have you yelling at her!" Gray called.

"Don't give her another thought, Gray," Alex called back. "I'll lock her in her room. She'll only be allowed broth!" He then opened the door and towed her outside.

"Right. That will appease him. Now what do you want from Appleblossoms?"

Ellen giggled.

"I wish you had not confronted that thug, Ellen, but after coming face to face with Lady Mary and Gray's snobbish elder brother, I think you deserve a treat."

"Can I have an apricotine? Ramsey had one, and it smelled divine."

"Do you know I don't think I've tried one of those, but it's time to rectify that."

Brothers could cause many emotions inside Ellen. But love was the strongest of all.

Chapter 28

"Miss Nightingale is lovely, Gray. I'm going to call on her," Ramsey said as they rode through London on a cool morning.

The surge of rage was swift, but he tamped it down. His cousin had always known how to annoy him and had clearly overheard some of his conversation about kissing with Ellen in the Nicholson book shop.

"It's a beautiful day for a ride," Ramsey added.

Gray grunted a reply.

It was early, but a favorite time of day for the cousins. Ramsey, for all his protestations that he did not greet the day until noon, was in fact false. He rode most mornings and was as cheery before the sun rose fully in the sky as he was as it sank.

"Do you ride often, Gray?"

"No."

"Why? You love to ride," Ramsey said from beside him. His horse was a big-boned gray who looked ready to take a bite out of anyone or anything that came too near. Luckily, he seemed to like Gray's bay mare.

"I work, Ram. It takes up a lot of my time."

"Or you don't have anyone to ride with because you dislike people and have no friends." His cousin tipped his hat to a man trotting by.

"I like people."

"Who do you like?" Ramsey asked. "No wait, let me guess. You're particularly fond of Miss Nightingale."

"No more than anyone who is aiding me in an investigation," Gray lied.

"You forget I have known you all my life. I can see a lie from ten feet, cousin, plus there is the kiss you shared."

"Shut up," Gray muttered.

He'd dreamt of her last night. The feel of her pressed to his body, his lips on hers. He'd never felt about a woman the way he did about Ellen Nightingale, and that terrified him. Terrified but at the same time excited him.

Gray had always believed he'd spend his life alone, working until he no longer could, but Ellen had changed that way of thinking. She made him believe in the future and that she would be part of it, but as that thought scared him too, he pushed it aside for now.

"It is all right to admire someone, Gray. Even love them."

He turned so fast he nearly fell off his horse. His heart pounded suddenly, and his hands were sweating inside his leather gloves.

"I don't love her," he wheezed out. Gray had not even allowed himself to acknowledge that yet, so why was Ramsey speaking that way?

"Right. Well, I must have got that wrong. But if that is the case it means I can call on her and ask if she would go driving with me."

"I will kill you if you do."

He felt Ramsey's eyes on the side of his face, but Gray kept his forward between his horse's ears.

"As you should if you care for her."

"I don't know what I feel, Ram." He went for honesty. "For so long I have just lived my life as I thought I wished. Solitary. I love what I do, and my needs are met. I want for nothing." Except now he thought that was no longer the truth.

"What of friendship and companionship? It is not healthy to live without that, Gray. You have turned into a bitter man. In fact, you are more like the men in your family you ran away from than you were before you left."

"I beg your pardon, that is absolutely not true." But even as he protested, Gray knew Ram had been right. He was a cold man. He'd shut himself away from people because the ones he had formed a bond with had hurt him, died, or left. Which made him sound as pathetic as he'd told Ellen she was.

"Absolutely is the truth."

"It just happened, Ram. It wasn't a deliberate choice but one I made because I felt it was for the best."

"But now I, your favorite cousin, am back, and that is going to change. I have great hopes for these wonderful Nightingales also if they change you."

"Her eldest brother would see me thrown into the fires of hell."

"That's eldest brothers for you. However, I may have been absent from society forever, but I did go to my father's club two nights ago. I was, of course, welcomed with open arms once they were exposed to my charm and wit. I then spent a wonderful night hearing all the latest gossip. Old and new."

"Christopher and Henry go to that club."

"They do, and Henry was there. He's not as bad as

Christopher, actually. I think you should reach out to him. He asked after you."

Gray stayed silent.

"Right, well, it's something to think about. Just as an aside, I believe Viscount Lester is a loathsome beast. What that man did to Ellen Nightingale is unforgivable."

"I agree. How anyone could walk away from her, no matter the circumstances, is beyond me."

"I do believe I'm about to weep after that touching statement."

Gray saw the two horses coming toward him, but it was the riders that had him biting back a curse.

"Alex!" Ramsey waved.

"Will you stop," Gray hissed. But it was too late. The Nightingale brothers were coming their way. He'd hoped to avoid a confrontation with Leo over Ellen and the Baddon Boys. It seemed it was now unavoidable.

"What? I thought you liked them?"

"We are not ten, Ramsey, and in need of making a spectacle of ourselves."

"I was waving. Hardly making a spectacle. Plus, it is important to keep on side with your future in-laws."

Before he could dispute that claim, the brothers were upon them.

"Good morning," Alex said. "Lovely day for a ride."

"Superb," Ramsey said with his usual enthusiasm.

"Lord Seddon, my cousin, Ramsey Hellion." Gray made the introductions.

"Hellion." Leo raised a hand in acknowledgement.

"We are heading to the park for a gallop," Ramsey said.

"Wonderful. We'll join you," Alex said. He then rode away with Gray's cousin, leaving the two men who really didn't like each other very much together.

"Look, I—"

"I believe I owe you—"

They both spoke at once.

"You first, my lord."

"Leo will do," he said. "My sister is important to me, Gray. She has been hurt many times, and I am very protective of her."

Gray wasn't sure where this was going, so he nodded and stayed silent.

"She's headstrong and cares little about her safety."

"You have taught her to protect herself, but yes, I can see she can be reckless."

"Even as I know you're correct, I want to roar at you for calling Ellen reckless." Leo sighed. "My aunt and uncle told me I am too severe on her and anyone who is not family and comes near her. Which apparently is you?"

Gray had a feeling this could be a trap, so he kept quiet.

"My point is, Gray, that I know you cannot be a bad man, and you have shown us that more than once. You stood in to look after my sister at the flower market, and I thank you for that."

"You're welcome."

"Good, I'm glad that's done with. Now, what's happening with George's murder?"

He was fairly sure he'd missed something in that entire exchange, but as it hadn't ended with Leo wanting to maim him, he left it alone.

"Has Ellen talked to you?"

"She has spoken about the tattoo and the Baddon Boys. It makes my blood run cold that one of them confronted her."

"And mine," Gray agreed. He then had perhaps the

first amicable discussion he'd ever had with the eldest Nightingale sibling.

"I've been giving the matter of Olivia and George Nicholson arguing some thought," Leo said.

"It seems everyone is now up to date on the case, even though that information should really not be common knowledge," Gray said.

"As I was saying, I've been mulling it over, and I have a theory. Would you like to hear it?"

"By all means, let's hear it," Gray said.

"I had a friend. His name was Linden Rothersham."

Gray knew the Rothershams were a well-to-do family who walked in society. He wondered if Leo had lost the friendship after his father had plunged the Nightingale family into ruin.

"He had a sister. He was unsure how they had met, but she became enamored with the man."

"Was he of noble birth?"

"He was a blacksmith and therefore totally unacceptable for a woman of my friend's sister's standing."

"How did they know about the blacksmith?"

"Lord Rothersham saw the man and his daughter together one day quite by chance. He was riding, and his horse threw a shoe. He walked into the blacksmith's shop and found her there. She was alone with a man."

"I see."

"The point I'm trying to make, Gray, is that perhaps Olivia Nicholson is doing something she shouldn't, and her brother found out. Perhaps the money was for that?"

"Is there nothing you Nightingales don't share?"

"No. We are very close now."

"But you weren't?"

Leo looked at Gray, and he saw pain in his eyes.

"No, I was a cold, arrogant bastard who completely

ignored my family when they needed me. I will never be that again, which can make me appear overprotective."

In that moment, Gray went from tolerating the man to respecting him. "I will never be a threat to your family, Leo."

"I'm not sure about that, but thank you just the same."

On those cryptic words, they rode into the park.

Chapter 29

"Why did I let you convince me this was a good idea?" Ellen asked as she tugged the hood of her cloak forward.

"We have been attending the theatre for months, but you have not. It is time, sister," Alex said.

She had once loved the theatre and had to admit to missing it, if only to herself.

"Why is it now time?"

"It just is," Leo said. "So be quiet."

Uncle Bram had informed her they were going and that Ellen would be joining them. She'd met some members of society and survived. Therefore, she would survive this.

Ellen had argued and cajoled, but her family had stood firm. So here she was, dressed as she hadn't in many years, going to the theatre.

"Lady Mary was not very nice," Ellen said.

"You made it through the encounter with Gray's help," Leo said. "And are here to tell the tale unscathed."

Gray had helped her, and she could still remember what his hand felt like, steady and reassuring on her back.

She almost wished he was here with her now and yet knew that was folly. Her family would keep her safe.

They were in the carriage. Leo and Alex were there, and she was wedged between them. Aunt Ivy and Uncle Bram sat across from them as they traveled to the theatre.

"Ellen, my love, you can handle this with ease," Uncle Bram said patiently. "You can drop a man to his knees with your umbrella and, very likely, your fists. You've done many reckless things to aid others and wandered about London unescorted and survived. Why do you care what a few people with small minds and a sheltered life think of you?"

"He is right," Alex said. "I see people who look through me, but I don't care, and do you know why, Ellen?"

She shook her head, eyes focused on her brother. He was dressed, as they all were, in their finest. Society clothes, Alex called them. They may no longer be part of it, but they could still look their best and carry it off.

"Because this life is better than the last one could ever have been. We just didn't realize that was a possibility," Leo answered for his brother.

She looked down at her hands. "After we saw his brother and Lady Mary Smythe, Gray called me a coward when I told him I had avoided anyone from our old life.

"Did he? Well, that's just another reason I like that man," Uncle Bram said.

"He called her a coward," Leo snapped.

"Leo, your sister is the strongest person I know," Aunt Ivy said. "But she is hiding, and that is not her. We were unsure how to make her face this, and now she has. Gray is right, she was being cowardly, sorry, darling." Aunt Ivy reached out to take her hand. "But it's true."

"I will never walk back into society," Ellen said.

"And you don't have to," Uncle Bram said. "But don't hide from it. None of what happened is your fault, just as not everyone in society is a shallow person."

"Tonight is a great way to start. Raise your chin up and show everyone you meet. You care nothing for what they think of you, Ellen," Uncle Bram said. "We are with you."

"Pity them, sister. They do not have what we do," Leo added.

She nodded as the nerves fluttered inside her belly. They'd done this, gone out to places their peers were. She hadn't. She'd fought to be strong when her world had collapsed, and she'd rebuilt it. This would be just another part of that.

Mungo dropped them off outside the theatre and told her to punch anyone who was rude to her.

"Mungo, she can't do that." Uncle Bram sighed.

The Scotsman grunted and rolled away in the carriage. Ellen walked between her brothers and behind her aunt and uncle, in through the door. She did not make eye contact when they reached the foyer and walked through the guests, but she felt the looks as eyes followed them.

"Uncle Bram has kept Father's box," Alex said. "You didn't ask where we would have to sit, so I just wanted you to know we will be there."

"Among them." She gulped down a breath at the thought of who would be to the left and right of her.

Leo held out his arm, and she placed her fingers on it.

"We are here," Leo whispered into her ear. "Right beside you, as we always will be, little sister."

The emotion those words created almost choked her.

"Did you think I was a coward, Leo?" Ellen nodded when someone smiled at her, and she tried to remember the person's name.

"No, but it is time, Ellen. No more hiding."

"Hello, Ellen."

"Duke." She curtseyed to the Duke of Raven and his duchess when they reached them. Lovely people who she liked. How had she put all of society in a chest that she'd shut and locked? These people were part of her old life, and she admired them very much.

"Look at you," Eden said. Sister to Dorrie and Somer, Eden was someone she'd always liked.

Her friends came from a loud, boisterous family as she did, and often they suffered insults from those that saw themselves as their betters. It had not deterred them from living their lives.

"You are stunning, and I'm so pleased to meet you again. The twins were beyond excited to have their fears now allayed over what had become of you, Ellen."

"I'm sorry to have worried them, Eden."

"That's done with now." The duchess hugged her. "But do not disappear again."

"I won't. You look lovely, Eden." Dressed in deep red, she was beautiful with her raven-colored hair and diamonds sparkling at her neck.

"I have wrinkles that weren't there a few months ago. It is most distressing, but then with my family, is it any wonder?"

"But still the most beautiful woman in any room, my sweet," James, her husband, said.

This was real love, she thought, like her aunt and uncle. Ellen would settle for nothing less. Gray slipped into her head. Could he love like that?

"Looking your usual handsome self, Bramstone."

"Thank you, Eden, I try."

"He's a rogue." Aunt Ivy smiled.

"These are good people of noble birth, niece," Uncle Bram whispered. "But don't look now, as we are not the only society members present who chose to leave or were forced from, their exalted ranks. Our friendly and easily inebriated detective is also present with a man I do not know."

Ellen followed her uncle's eyes and found Gray. He stood with Ramsey, his usual expressionless self. Immaculate in evening clothes, he appeared alone even surrounded by people. Eyes searching, checking who was nearby.

"That is his cousin, Mr. Hellion," Ellen said.

"Ah, I hear he is natured like Alex, or so Leo told me."

"Very much so."

Uncle Bram started chatting with the duke, and Ellen looked around her. This wasn't so bad. She had her family at her side, and while people were watching them, it didn't feel as horrid as she thought it would. Her eyes found Gray again.

"I think you like that man, sister dear," Alex whispered the words in her ear.

"I don't know Mr. Hellion very well, Alex. I have met him only briefly."

"You know I mean Gray."

"What?" She dragged her eyes from the cousins to look at her brother.

"Gray. I think you have feelings growing inside you for our uptight detective."

"I definitely do not," she said calmly. Instead of snapping, which was what she wanted to do. "Don't be ridiculous, Alex."

"Ah well, silly me, I must have gotten that all wrong."

"Absolutely wrong." Ellen had the urge to press her palm to her heart, since it was beating so hard. While she had acknowledged experiencing some emotions for Gray, she had no wish for her family to discuss the matter yet.

"No need to continue protesting, Ellen. I grasped the point."

She wanted to smack that grin from his face. Instead, she changed the conversation. What happened with her and Gray was between them.

"I've been thinking about that book, Alex," Ellen said. "If someone was aware it was in George's shop and they murdered him to get it, then how is it they knew to find it in the box?"

"You and Gray found the box," Alex said.

"True. But who, beside the seller of the book and that Mr. Brownly, knew it was in Nicholson's bookshop?"

"Do you think George told his family he had it?" Alex said. "I wish he'd pay me a visit and show me something that could help us find out who murdered him."

"Perhaps like Father, he won't?"

Alex shuddered. "I'm pleased Father hasn't. Gray's aunt, however. She's persistent."

"Do you think that's because she was like us?"

"Very likely, but I also believe she's trying to tell us something about him. I haven't grasped what as yet. It's still a bit hazy and confusing with the colors she always brings with her."

Ellen giggled.

"What?" Alex asked.

"Us. You and me talking like this. If some of them"— she nodded to the patrons before them—"knew what we were, they'd lock us in Bedlam."

"And yet we're saner than most of them, sister dear."

"I wonder what Gray found in the rest of those ledgers you told me were in the box?" Alex said.

"Gray is struggling with our interference and the knowledge that we know so much about the case. The man is a stickler for doing things correctly," Ellen added.

"But as we don't have secrets, he will just have to get used to it and our help," Alex said.

"Agreed."

As if mentioning his name summoned him to her side, Ellen found the big, disturbing detective with his cousin coming her way.

Gray introduced Ramsey to her family.

"Mr. Greedy told me to inform you there will be another event coming soon, Gray," Alex said. "With more pickled whelks."

Gray visibly shuddered.

"I must come next time to learn more about this event. Could I come as a guest of the Nightingales also?" Ramsey asked.

"But of course, I will send word," Alex said.

"Gray loves pickled whelks," Ramsey added. "Once, when we were children, I dared him to eat six, and he relieved his stomach of its contents for many hours after."

"I had reservations about introducing my cousin to you, Alex, as you are alike, which concerns me that you could become friends, and no one will be safe," Gray said.

Ellen laughed at that.

"Friends, what an interesting concept, don't you think, Alex?" Ramsey said.

"Extremely."

"What makes a good friend, do you believe?" Ramsey continued. "Someone who likes a good joke? Conversationalist? Happy and friendly?" he continued.

"Agreeable? Social?" Alex added when Ramsey stopped. "Handsome?"

"And this is what I was worried about," Gray said, but he was smiling.

"Gray?" the Duke of Raven asked. "It is you."

"James." Gray looked happy to see the duke.

"I wondered when you'd reappear," the peer said. "He helped me with some enquiries on a certain matter," he added, noting the surprised faces around him.

"It's good to see you again," Gray added.

"And now it is time for us to head to our seats," Alex said. "Where are you sitting, Gray?"

"We have seats—"

"That will never do," Aunt Ivy said, joining their conversation. "There is plenty of room in the box. Come along, you can join us."

"There really is no need, our seats are excellent," Gray said after introducing Ramsey to her aunt and uncle.

"There is every need. Now, let's go as the performance is about to start. We do not want to miss the beginning of the play." She then looped her arm through Gray's and started walking. They all fell in behind.

Followed by the duke and duchess, they walked up the stairs to their seats, and Ellen thought again this wasn't so bad. She was surrounded by people she liked, and maybe it had been wrong of her to hide from something she'd always loved.

Looking around when they reached the upstairs foyer, her eyes locked on the dark angry ones of her ex-fiancé, and every inch of the calm she'd just felt evaporated.

Chapter 30

Gray had spent the day at Scotland Yard going through the books he'd retrieved from George Nicholson's locked box. He reviewed what he knew and made more notes. He'd also tried and failed not to think about Ellen Nightingale and that kiss. The way she had little creases around her mouth when she smiled at him and how beautiful she was. But it wasn't just her looks that intrigued him. The woman was intelligent, feisty, and fun to be with.

He couldn't fight the fact anymore that she meant something to him. That he cared for her. He wasn't sure how it had happened in such a short time, but it had. As yet, he wasn't sure what to do with this recent knowledge. But like everything he did, he would analyze and think it through before taking action.

After a long day, he'd gone home ready for a drink, a meal, both in solitude, and then a full night's slumber that would reset his odd mood. Gray rarely let anything interrupt his ability to work on a case. Ellen did that, and he could not allow it to continue.

When he'd entered his home, he'd found his cousin

seated in his parlor. Shoes off and feet resting on the arm of his sofa as he lay full length along it. On his chest was a plate of food.

He'd then told Gray they were going to the theatre tonight. Gray hated the theatre. Ramsey had walked around the house one step behind him until he agreed. He'd done that often when they were younger. His cousin was incredibly tenacious when his mind was set.

"This is exciting," Ramsey said from beside him while they waited upstairs with other theatergoers to reach their seats, which as it turned out, were now in a private box. "Your Ellen's family are very nice people," Ramsey whispered to him. "Except for the glowering eldest brother, Lord Seddon."

"He's untrusting, and who can blame him? I'm no different, and she is not my anything."

But he wanted her to be his something, and that terrified Gray. When he'd seen her across the foyer looking nervous, hands clenched in front of her, he'd known that what he felt for that woman would not easily be pushed aside.

"If you say so."

"I do."

He found her a few feet in front of him. She wore gold beneath the deep blue cloak. Her hair shone as she passed beneath any light. Her eyes were on the move, head turning from side to side as she took everything in and looked for danger. She was uncomfortable in this setting, Gray could tell. Her head tilted slightly to answer her aunt, and his eyes went to the soft skin just under her ear. He wanted to place his lips there.

Christ. He turned away.

A woman to their left gave Gray and his cousin a flirtatious smile. Ramsey bowed and smiled back. Gray scowled.

"For pity's sake, man, it takes no time to smile," his cousin hissed.

"When you are raised, having manners rammed down your throat, you tend to rebel when you no longer have to adhere to them constantly," a deep voice said from behind him.

He looked over his shoulder into the eyes of Leo. Gray nodded, and Leo returned the gesture.

"What he said," Gray added to his cousin.

"If we are mannered alike, Ramsey, then these two could be identical twins in their sour demeanor," Alex said, pointing from Gray to Leo.

They continued to bicker as they moved through the opening and into the Nightingales' box. It was the perfect viewing position to see the performance that would take place below.

"Now, you sit there, Gray and Ramsey. Ellen, you can sit between the cousins. I will be next to Ramsey, and Bram next to me. Leo and Alex can take the row behind," Ivy said.

No one argued with her and definitely not him because he got to sit next to Ellen.

"Do you like the theatre?" Gray asked her when they were settled in their seats with all the eyes from the other boxes on them. How scandalous. Not only were the Nightingales here but also the long-lost Grayson Fletcher.

"I do," Ellen said, and something in her tone had him looking at her. Her face was pale, eyes wide.

"What's wrong?" Gray asked her.

"Nothing is wrong."

"Now that's a lie."

She pressed her lips together.

"Ellen, tell me what has happened?"

"It is not enough that I am here in a public setting with members of society?"

"If that's the reason, then of course." Her eyes went to his and away again.

Gray was sure she was lying.

Looking around them, he found a box directly across the theatre that held his family. Father, brothers, Lady Mary, and his mother. They were looking at him, so he nodded. His mother raised her hand, and his father said something, so she lowered it.

Gray smiled at her, remembering Mrs. Nicholson's words. She acknowledged his gesture with a nod.

"If only we could pick our family," Ellen whispered. "Life would be a great deal easier." She'd seen what had taken place.

"It would." Gray sat back in his seat and focused on the stage as the performance began. He enjoyed sitting there with the soft weight of Ellen's thigh against his and her scent filling the air. As the second act began, Gray realized he wasn't as tense as he normally would be seeing his family. Was it because he was with the Nightingales who were society outcasts also? *He wasn't alone anymore.*

That thought had heat blooming inside him.

Staring down to the mass of people below, he searched through them, for no other reason than he could and often did. It was part of who he had become as a detective. He was always searching for something or someone.

He focused on a well-dressed man standing beside a young lady. Gray realized it was Mr. Brownly. As he watched, the man bent to speak to his sister and then excused himself and made his way out of the theatre.

"Walk, Gray?"

"Pardon?" He looked at Ramsey.

"It's the end of the second act. Come, we shall find some food."

"I'll join you," Alex said, clearly hearing the word food.

"I'll be back shortly," Gray said. "I must speak to someone."

Ellen was chatting with her aunt now, so he excused himself and ran down the stairs. Once he reached the foyer, he wove his way through the crowds. He didn't see Mr. Brownly anywhere, so he headed outside.

He wanted to talk to the man. Gray needed to find out if he was guilty or just greedy and using the opportunity of George Nicholson's death to get the book.

It was dark, but lamps lit the front entrance. Making his way to the side, he carried on down the street, looking for Mr. Brownly. It would not be easy as there were lots of people and carriages about. He'd been walking for about five minutes when he saw a woman. It was her side profile, but something about her was familiar.

Gray watched as she slid into a narrow opening between two buildings.

Following, he kept to the shadows. Light from a street-lamp showed him a man was there, and the woman now concealed by his body.

He was about to leave, as surely it was just a liaison between a couple, likely a prostitute and client, when the man moved.

Not much shocked Gray these days, but seeing Olivia Nicholson did just that. He couldn't make out what they were saying, but by the man's gesture, it was a heated exchange.

Gray slipped back out of the narrow opening but stayed close enough in case she needed help. He waited in the shadows.

Why was she here with that man? Surely she hadn't

been attending the theatre as the Nicholson family was in mourning?

Minutes later, the couple came out. Olivia Nicholson, with her hand pressed to her mouth, the man's face a mask of despair. Without giving him another look, Olivia ran from him and down the road. The man just stood there watching her until she reached a hackney tucked in the shadows. Opening the door, she climbed inside.

Gray had learned to read people, and he knew when someone was distraught, and this man was that. Shoulders slumped, his eyes followed the hackney as it rolled away from them. He then turned and walked back to the theatre.

Gray followed and watched him go to the rear. He took something off the back of the cart and carried it into the theatre.

The game had suddenly changed again. Was Olivia Nicholson in fact involved in her brother's death? He struggled with that but also knew he could discount nothing in this business.

He returned to the front and through the foyer. Running up the stairs, he reached the top. Gray was so deep in thought he bumped into a man.

"Watch out!"

"Apologies." He retreated a step after nearly knocking him over. The man turned, and Gray bit back the curse.

"Grayson," his father said, and it was only a name, but the tone was dripping with disdain. With him was Viscount Lester. The man who had broken his engagement to Ellen when the late Lord Seddon took his life.

Had she seen Lester? Was that why he'd thought her upset?

Gray knew men like these two. Belief that they were the best society could offer. Arrogant snobs who valued titles and wealth above all other traits. They both had lineages of power and wealth at their backs.

"Father." He bowed.

"Why are you here?" his father demanded.

"I'm watching the play like you. However, unlike you, I am with friends and not my family."

"Well, leave. It's embarrassing that people are seeing my son. A detective!" He spat out the words.

"Your love warms me, father." He looked to Lester. "Why does it not surprise me to find you with a man such as this one?"

"I saw you with her. You bring shame down on your family," Lester snarled.

He controlled the surge of rage over this man acknowledging Ellen in such a disrespectful manner.

"Miss Nightingale and her family are worth ten of both of you. They are people who, through no fault of their own, were cast aside by society callously."

"She is—"

"I will stop you right there, my lord," Gray said in a hard voice. "I will not tolerate one word from you that is not dripping in compliments to Miss Nightingale or her family. They are my friends, and as such, I will not stand by and have them insulted by the likes of you."

"I would expect the man you've become to keep company with such people," his father shot back as he looked down his nose at Gray.

"Your son, do you mean?" Leo said the words, and Gray had not realized he was close until then. "An honorable man who earns an honest living, a concept I doubt either of you understand."

"How dare you speak to us in such a manner, Lord Seddon!" Viscount Lester roared.

"How dare I." Leo leaned into Lester, his face now

inches from the man's. "How dare you turn your back on my sister when she was at her most vulnerable."

"Back away now, Leo," Gray said, gripping his shoulder. He could not discount the man punching Lester. Not that he'd blame him, but the Nightingales did not need any more reason to become notorious.

Suddenly, he wanted no part of this. All his father cared about was that Gray behaved in a manner he saw fit, and Viscount Lester was someone who simply saw women for breeding purposes and to run his home. Status was everything to these men. They would never change.

"Let's go, Leo," he said. They walked away without bowing.

"Your father is a bastard," Leo said.

"Now wouldn't that be amusing if he was? But I take your meaning," Gray added. "Thank you for calling me honorable, Leo."

"Thank you for defending my family, Gray."

No more was said as they entered the box.

"Are you all right, Gray?" Ramsey said as he took his seat. The play had begun. "You were gone a while, and I sense tension in you."

"I'm well, Ram, I promise."

And Gray thought that actually he was. He'd always dreaded seeing any member of his family, and twice in the last few days, he'd met two of them, and he realized something as he'd looked at his father. His disdain could no longer hurt him. He'd found what he loved in life and did not need any member of his family to accept that or him. He also now had friends, even though he'd not been searching for them. Then there was the woman at his side who he felt a great deal more than friendship for.

"Ellen," he whispered in her ear.

"Yes?" She looked at him, their faces now close.

"I just saw my father with Viscount Lester."

"I'm sorry," she said. "That must have been hard."

"Surprisingly, it wasn't. Leo joined me, and between us, we set them straight about a few things."

"I'm glad." She smiled.

"Is Lester the reason you were upset? Did you see him?"

She nodded, and then annoyance flashed across her face. "I don't know why I reacted as I did. That man is a revolting snob."

"Perhaps with more exposure, you'll feel able to cope?"

"Perhaps."

"He wasn't worthy of you, Ellen."

"Thank you."

"You're welcome." He battled for about a minute with what he had seen outside on the street. Ellen had the image of Olivia Nicholson fighting with her brother. She'd also seen the tattoo on the man's arm in that room. Was the man she was with one of the Baddon Boys?

"I think we have another player in George Nicholson's murder," he said so only she could hear.

"Who?" She didn't turn to look at him anymore.

"I will call at Crabbett Close when I can and tell you everything."

She studied him for long seconds and then nodded. Ellen then faced forward once more to watch the play. Something shifted inside him as he stared at her side profile. An inevitability that he could no longer fight. Before he'd realized what he was doing, Gray leaned closer until his mouth was inches from her ear.

"I care about you, Miss Ellen Nightingale."

Her lips lifted. Gray faced forward, and then it was her turn to whisper in his ear.

"I care about you also, Detective Grayson Fletcher."

They then sat beside each other and watched the rest of the play, and Gray had never enjoyed a performance more. Having her near calmed him when he'd not known he'd needed calming. She cared about him as he did about her, and for now, that was enough.

He looked at his family's box and saw each of them. Henry and his mother had their eyes on him. He nodded again, and they nodded back.

More than enough, he thought, looking at Ellen.

Chapter 31

Ellen walked along Crabbett Close with Leo and Teddy. They were wrapped in coats and scarves as the day was one of those gray ones, and the sun had not shown itself.

The three siblings had been sent to collect a dozen apricotines with Bud's blessing, as she was busy making their evening meal and had no time to bake anything for their afternoon tea.

The entire family had congregated in the parlor where Mungo had lit the fire. There they'd stayed until they had played a robust game of Snap to see who would leave the house to collect their treats.

"Good day to you all!"

"Constable Plummy," Leo said by way of reply when they drew level with Mr. Peeky's house.

The officer was standing outside the door and looked to be holding it open.

"I daren't ask," Ellen whispered.

"What are you doing, Constable Plummy?" Teddy said. "The weather is foul. Shouldn't that door be closed?"

"Well now, I'm aiding a resident of Crabbett Close,

Master Theodore. Mr. Peeky's door is squeaky, and he's applied something to stop that on the other side. I am then going to open and shut it until the squeak has gone."

Leo coughed, and Ellen managed to hold her features in their current pleasant expression.

"Plummy, you're a right flapdoodle." Mrs. Greedy threw this at the constable as she shuffled past wrapped in an overcoat.

"Very kind of you to say so," Plummy said with a smile.

"Right then," Leo choked out. "We'll be off."

"Good day to you all, Nightingales!" Plummy called.

"Flapdoodle is not a compliment," Teddy muttered when they'd moved on.

"I'm not entirely sure if Plummy is very smart or exceedingly dimwitted," Ellen said. "Insults slide off him."

"He's kind to me, Fred, and Matilda. Just the other day, he brought us lemon drops."

"Did he? Well, I may need to revise my opinion of the man if he brings those," Leo said.

They trooped on, noting lamps and candles lit in windows to ward off the gray day.

"Oh, Lord Seddon. I wonder if I may take a moment of your time?" Tabitha Varney said from her doorway. "I have an urgent matter that needs attention, and I am not strong enough to fix it."

Teddy sighed. "Walking anywhere in this street takes a great deal longer than it should."

"Amen," Ellen said.

"I just need Lord Seddon."

"And yet we are here, so will help also," Ellen said when Leo gripped her fingers tight and squeezed.

"Oh well." Tabitha looked annoyed. "If you must."

"They're hardly likely to want to stand about in this

bleeding pea-souper now are they, Miss Varney," Nancy said from next door. "Here's a sugarplum to tide you over, Master Teddy." She walked out with a bowl and held it over her gate.

"Get me one," Leo said out the side of his mouth.

Ellen and Leo then headed into the house. Tabitha held the door open and accidentally brushed against Leo. He yelped and jumped back, landing on Ellen's foot.

"Ouch!"

"Sorry." He then grabbed Ellen and put her in front of him. His hands were on her shoulders. "Lead the way, Miss Varney."

Ellen made a few clucking noises but followed Tabitha. The urgent matter that needed attention was, in fact, a jar on a shelf she could not reach. A chair would have fixed that, and it was clear to everyone in the room she'd hastily come up with the problem.

Leo got the jar down, and instead of handing it to the woman, placed it on the sink. He then grabbed Ellen's hand.

"We must go. Our brother is waiting for us outside."

"I was just about to make tea." Tabitha pouted. "Surely a big, strong man such as yourself is in constant need of sustenance?"

"He's quite the weakling, actually. Alex is much stronger," Ellen said.

"A lot stronger," Leo reiterated. "He is far more charismatic than I too."

"Leo had his heart broken and has vowed to never love again. But Alex, his heart is just fine," Ellen said, finding a way to get her brother back for placing two spiders in her bed yesterday. Ellen did not like spiders. Her scream had roused the entire household at 11 Crabbett Close.

"Really? Heartbroken, you say?" She looked at Leo. He appeared forlorn and nodded.

"Well then." She waved them to the door. "Good day to you both."

They left the house and collected Teddy, who was now eating Leo's sugarplum and chatting with Nancy.

"Let's go, Teddy," Leo said.

"That was very well done of you, Ellen. I think you may have just transferred Tabitha Varney's affections to Alex from me. It was a brilliant move," Leo said.

"If it works, you will owe me a great deal. But I had to get him back for the spiders."

"You are a terrifying woman."

"Thank you."

Teddy was ahead of them, sucking on his sugarplum.

"Ellen, when we went to the theatre, I found Gray out in the foyer with his father and Viscount Lester," Leo said.

"You didn't tell me that."

"I'm telling you now."

It had been three days since they'd said they cared about each other. Gray had still not called to tell her who the other person he suspected in George Nicholson's murder was either. The truth was she missed him. Now that she'd admitted to caring it seemed to have opened something inside her, and he was constantly in her thoughts.

"What did he say to you?"

The elder Nightingale siblings had started some enquiries about the Baddon Boys, themselves.

While out last night looking for Mr. Greedy's cousin, Cedric, who had drunk too much and not returned home, they'd asked a few subtle questions, as they'd searched for him. The responses they'd received had been chilling.

The gang wrought fear in the areas of London they

termed as theirs. Every crime that was possible to commit, they had committed. Most often they got away with it too.

Did Gray deal with men like that all the time? The thought was a terrifying one for Ellen.

"I heard him defending us. Saying we were his friends. He then told his father and Lester that they were not to utter your name unless it was to compliment you."

Warmth filled her chest. Gray had defended her.

"You sound like you respect him, Leo."

"He is easier to tolerate than I thought" was all her brother would concede.

"How is it London can be fine one day and this the next?" Teddy said. "I loathe this weather."

"Me too, little brother," Ellen said. A vision of men sprinting toward them filled her head suddenly. Panic sliced through her. "Run!"

"What?" Leo demanded. But it was too late. The attack came so fast they didn't see it. A hand grabbed her from behind.

"Teddy, run!" Leo roared as two men grabbed him.

Ellen's umbrella was hooked in its loop, but Leo had his cane.

"Run, Teddy!" Ellen cried when her little brother hesitated. "Go to the bakery!"

She heard his footsteps running away from them. Ellen then stopped struggling, and the hands holding her relaxed. She kicked back with her foot, and her attacker grunted. The seconds gave her time to free her umbrella. She spun. There were three men. Shooting Leo a look, she saw he had four on him.

"Run, sister!"

"Help!" Ellen screamed as loud as she could, and then they were on her.

She swung and lashed out with her umbrella, also using

her hands and feet. She got in jabs and blows as she heard fists connecting behind her.

Leo!

"She's a fiery bitch!" These words were followed with a punch to her jaw that had her stumbling back. Tripping, Ellen fell to the ground. Then boots lashed out and kicked her, and pain shot through her. A face appeared above Ellen, bending until it was inches from hers.

"Stop investigating what doesn't concern you, or next time we'll come for someone you love, and we'll kill them. You and that detective mind your business or pay the price."

More kicks came, and all Ellen could do was hold her hands over her face.

"No!" she heard the roar, and then suddenly Alex was there with Uncle Bram and others. They were safe.

Leo? Ellen tried to find him, but there was so much pain, and then there was darkness.

Chapter 32

"A Mr. Hellion is here to speak with you, Detective Fletcher."

Happy for the reprieve, even if it was his nosey cousin, Gray said, "Show him in, Harry."

While he waited for Ramsey to arrive, Gray thought about what he'd learned. Mr. Brownly was not the fine, upstanding gentleman he appeared. He'd looked into the man and had come up with a few things that raised his suspicions.

There was also the matter of why Miss Olivia Nicholson was in that alley with that man and why her brother had given her a large sum of money two weeks before he died.

"Gray."

He looked up as Ramsey appeared in his doorway. The expression on his face had him rising from his seat. His cousin never looked that way. He was rarely serious.

"What has happened?"

"I went to Appleblossoms Bakery, Gray. Ellen and Leo, they were set upon outside the store this morning."

"What?" He grabbed his coat and shoved his arms through the sleeves as panic gripped him. *Not Ellen.* Please, not her.

"Her brother ran into the bakery screaming."

"Theodore," Gray gritted out as he grabbed his hat and sprinted for the door. "Move, Ram. I have to get to her."

"Her family and the shopkeepers arrived, but the men had gone. Ellen, according to Mrs. Appleblossom, was on the ground, as was her brother."

She had to be okay.

He ran through the building and was soon outside.

"I have my carriage. Come," Ramsey said.

It only took them minutes to reach it and seconds to be on their way. It felt like forever.

"What else do you know?" Gray rasped.

"Mr. Appleblossom's cart was there. They loaded them onto that and drove them home. I have no more information."

"She will be all right, as will Leo," Gray said slowly. Surely he'd know if they weren't.

"You love her?"

He made himself look at his cousin. Gray then nodded.

"She will be all right."

He ran Ramsey's words repeatedly through his head, telling himself they were the truth. His brave, spirited Ellen had to be all right. There was no other option.

The trip was not a long one, but the carriage seemed to crawl through London until finally they had turned into Crabbett Close. He had the door opened and was outside before it had stopped.

Running up the steps, he entered to utter chaos inside the Nightingale home.

"I have liniment," Mrs. Greedy was saying.

"I've made a batch of me tonic," Mr. Peeky said. "It needs time to cure but needs must."

Mungo saw him and walked through what looked to be all the residents from Crabbett Close to reach Gray.

"How are they?" Gray said instead of "how is she?"

"Leo is better than Ellen. The bastards kicked her on the ground. Leo couldn't reach her as he had four on him and Ellen three. Poor Master Teddy hasn't stopped crying. He was with them."

Gray wanted to roar. Wanted to hit something hard. He struggled to rein in his rage and focus.

"Where is she?"

"Upstairs. All the family is with them."

"Mungo, this is Ramsey, my cousin. He can help you with this." Gray waved a hand at the residents.

"Go," Ram said when he looked at him. "Mr. Mungo and I will have this under control in no time. Whatever this is."

He didn't ask permission, but no one stopped him. He walked through the worried residents and took the steps up two at a time. Walking the hall, he found a door open and only Lottie in there with who he guessed was a nanny.

"Where are they?" he asked.

"Hello, Gray." Lottie gave him a shy wave.

"They are on the next floor, sir," the woman said.

He left and ran to the next floor. He found her uncle pacing the hallway. Fists clenched, head lowered.

"Bram?"

His head shot up, and those eyes were what he would expect the molten fires of hell to look like.

"Are they—"

"Both will survive. They took a beating but will recover."

"Thank God." Relief had his knees buckling. Gray braced a hand on the wall to steady himself.

"I'm going to kill someone, Gray."

"As you should want to, Bram. But I'd rather you waited and took me with you."

Their eyes locked, and the older man exhaled slowly.

"These children are ours, Ivy and mine. When they hurt, we hurt."

He'd never seen the patriarch of this family looking as he did in that moment. Utter devastation was written on his face.

"Do you know how long it took Ivy and me to reach them when we had news of my brother's death?"

Gray shook his head.

"Two weeks, and in that time, some of society had made it clear that my nieces and nephews were tainted and no longer fit company. Creditors had called. We found the doors locked, no staff in the town house except for Bud and two nannies. Leo had faced everyone with Alex at his side. They'd visited lawyers and done what they could. Pale faced, wide eyed. They were terrified of what would happen next when Ivy and I arrived."

Gray saw the memories in the man's eyes and could only imagine the hell he'd found his nieces and nephews going through.

"We took them away. All of them. Just loaded them into carriages and left London. They came because we would not allow them to do otherwise. They were distant, fighting the anger and shame. Especially the older three. It took us six months to reach them. Six months to break through what my brother had turned them into. I won't allow them to suffer anymore, Gray."

"We won't let it happen again," Gray vowed. Understanding passed between them. This man knew he cared for Ellen.

"Can I see her?"

"The doctor left her and is now attending to Leo. She doesn't look good, Gray."

"I don't care. I need to see her, Bram."

"I know you do. Come."

He followed Ellen's uncle down the hall and then into a room. Bud and Fred were in there. His eyes went to the bed.

She lay in a white nightdress with her eyes closed against a mound of pillows. Her blond curls were loose and tangled. There was bruising under her right eye, and her cheek was red and swollen. Rage consumed him as he took an inventory of all her injuries.

The others moved back as he made his way closer, and Bram went to the opposite side of the bed where Chester sat with his chin on the mattress.

Almost as if she felt him, her eyes opened, the blue depths filled with pain.

"She's bruised all over," Fred said, coming to stand at his side. Her little face was pinched with worry.

"It will be all right, Fred." He ran a hand down her back. "Ellen is safe."

"Make it all right, Gray," she whispered. "Make those people that hurt Leo and Ellen pay."

"Fred," Ellen whispered as if speaking hurt her. "I'm not going anywhere."

"Come here, sweetheart," Bram said. The little girl ran around the bed and into his arms.

Gray looked at Ellen again. He couldn't find the words to say what was inside him. He wanted to touch her. Kiss her hurts and run a hand over her hair. Needed to hold her but wasn't sure he could let her go if he did.

"We will visit your brother," Bud said. "Then I think they both need a nice cup of tea and cake. Will you help me prepare the tray, Miss Fred?"

The little girl nodded and left with the housekeeper, and Gray kept his eyes on Ellen. His anger was an inferno as he studied every inch of her abused face.

"Tell Gray what they said, love," Bram urged Ellen. "Tell him everything, and I will check on Leo too."

That Bram was leaving them alone and Ellen in his custody to watch over humbled Gray.

"Ellen," her name was torn from him when her uncle had left.

"I'm all right."

"Liar." He rose and bent over her, pressing his lips to her hair, the only place he hoped she was not hurting.

"It's all right, Gray." Her hand patted his shoulder.

"No. It's far from that," he said, falling back into his seat. "Tell me who did this to you?" Gently, Gray picked up her hand, noting the bruises on the knuckles. His rage grew even more. He kissed the abused skin softly and then cradled her fingers in his.

Her eyes were tired and wounded. His Amazon was hurting.

"Leo, Teddy, and I were going to Appleblossoms to get some apricotines for afternoon tea, and suddenly I saw them in my head. Men running at us. I felt the panic and told Teddy to run."

"Not you?"

"I couldn't leave Leo."

"Ellen, there were too many of them. You both should have run." His words came out harsh. "Even the indomitable Notorious Nightingales must retreat now and again."

"We couldn't. They crept up on us and had me from behind before I knew it. It was the same for Leo."

"Okay. It's all right now," Gray soothed. "Tell me the rest."

"When I fell, one of them bent over me and said, 'Stop investigating what doesn't concern you, or next time we'll come for someone you love, and we'll kill them. You and that detective mind your business or pay the price.'"

Gray frowned. "Surely the only investigating you've done with me was in the bookshop. Then you had that confrontation with that man who was part of the Baddon Boys at the flower markets."

She dropped her eyes.

"Tell me," he demanded.

"Leo, Alex, and I had to search for Mr. Greedy's cousin, Cedric, last night."

"You went out after dark again?" The rage he'd just pushed down inside him surged to life once more.

"It was not late," she dismissed his words. "We asked some questions about the Baddon Boys, but—"

"You did what?" It came out as a roar.

"Subtle questions," she added.

"This is not a game, madam. That gang deals with corrupt people. Noblemen, and politicians. Christ, Ellen, you could have been killed. They have made people disappear, never to be found again!"

"Yes, it was not a terribly sound notion in hindsight, but at the time it was a matter of simply conversing as we asked after Cedric. We had no idea that word would get back to these Baddon Boys."

She tried to move, and the breath hissed from her throat as clearly, she was in pain.

"God's blood," Gray muttered. "I don't want you hurt. I-I need you to promise me you will take no more risks,

Ellen." He felt irrational at the thought of her out at night, where anyone could hurt her.

"I can't promise to stop protecting those who need it. Those I care for."

"You are not serious. You've just proven how unsafe it is out there for you."

"We've been helping people for months, Gray. People who have no one else to turn to." Her eyes begged him to understand, but all he could see were the bruises someone had inflicted on her.

"No more. I demand that you promise me you will never again take such risks. Never again go out at night with your brothers. Never—"

"I will not be controlled by a man." The words were a whisper, but Gray heard them. "I am no longer a victim."

"I am the man who cares about you. Damn you, they could have killed you! I want you safe, not to control you." Rage was making him roar at her.

She didn't back down. Didn't look away from him, just lay there against those pillows, pale and hurting. Gray was consumed with anger and had no outlet.

"Our parents dictated my every move for years. I could not walk out the door without being told in which direction and what to wear. I will never allow a person to do that to me again." The words were not spoken in her usual proud tone. These were subdued, almost as if speaking them hurt her.

Someone had punched her. Pushed her to the ground and kicked her. The woman he loved, and she wouldn't promise him to stop taking risks. Gray knew in his bones he could not live with that knowledge. Not live knowing someone could hurt her again when she walked recklessly into danger.

"This is who I am," she whispered.

"And you can never change? You will continue to walk into danger with your family?" Gray growled out the question.

"If people need our support, then yes."

"That's what the police and Scotland Yard are for!" he barked.

"There are not enough of you to go around," she snapped back and then winced as she moved. "People are hurt constantly because there is no one to help them. They have loved ones going missing or they are threatened."

"And it is the job of you and your brothers to keep them safe, is it?" He looked at her. The beautiful woman who he knew held his heart. The woman who would not change who she was to accommodate his love.

"We help where we can," she said. The fire that she'd shown him briefly had ebbed away. She now lay back even more exhausted after their fiery exchange.

"And you will not stop if I ask you to?" Her silence was the confirmation he needed. "I will leave you then."

"Gray, try to understand." She reached for his hand, but he stepped back from her.

"I do. You will not change what you do, and I cannot stand by and watch you be hurt again." He turned and walked from the room.

Chapter 33

Ellen's body healed slowly. Her ribs still hurt, but her bruises were fading. She had spent days in bed reading or staring at her ceiling rose because her family had forbidden her from leaving her room.

Leo had crept in or she to his when no one was looking, and they kept each other company. Neither of them had spoken much. It was just enough that they were together.

Ellen tried not to think about Gray. He'd walked away from her because she had not given him the assurance that she would stop taking risks. But she couldn't, even for him.

She'd never loved a man before, but she had given her heart to Grayson Fletcher, because with his departure from her life, he'd left her with a deep, aching pain.

Ramsey had visited her, but as Matilda and Teddy had been with her at the time, neither of them had mentioned Gray, and for that she was grateful. Everything to do with that man felt raw inside her.

"Hello, is this where you are hiding?"

Leo limped out and sat beside her in the other chair.

She was enjoying a brief break of fresh air… well, as fresh as you could get in London. The sky was still overcast, but the cool breeze was wonderful after days inside.

"How are you feeling today?" he asked her.

"I want no more of Mr. Peeky's tonic."

Her brother snorted.

"I don't want any more of that chest rub from Miss Alvin. I'm sure it's burned my skin," Leo said.

"Are you better now, Leo?"

"Much." He held out a hand, and she took it.

"I was so scared for you, Leo."

"As I was for you when I saw those three men set upon you." He closed his eyes.

"I'm well."

"The day I learned what our father had done, Ellen, I realized that suddenly I was head of the family. That I had to pick up the pieces of our lives after he'd destroyed it. I was scared. You, the little ones, you were all so sad, and you needed me to be strong. I wasn't sure I had that strength inside me."

"Oh, Leo, that was never your job alone."

"It was, but I had you and Alex at my side, and with your help, I've grown and changed from the selfish man I once was."

"You have. Arrogant and opinionated but no longer selfish."

He snorted.

"Knowing my sister was fighting for her life and I could not reach her was the most terrifying moment I have ever experienced, Ellen."

She burst into loud, noisy tears, possibly long overdue, as she had not wept since Gray had left. Leo pulled out his handkerchief and handed it to her.

"You're my little sister. I should protect you, and I had already failed in that, and I was about to fail again."

"No! You have never failed me," Ellen said.

"Ellen, my sweet, I never considered how you felt about marrying that vile old man."

"You could not go against Father. I understood that."

"Perhaps, but I should have tried."

They sat in silence for a while.

"And now I need to ask you a question, Ellen, and you have to be honest with me."

"I'm always honest with you."

"Now we both know that for a lie," he teased.

She snuffled out a laugh.

"Ellen, do you love Gray?"

Exhausted and heartsick, she told him the truth.

"Yes. But it matters not how I feel because he told me I must stop going out with you and Alex to help others. He demanded that I promise to do so because he cannot live with the woman he cares for plunging recklessly into danger."

"And you said no?"

"Of course I said no. I will never again allow a man to dictate to me what I must or must not do. You cannot expect different from me, Leo."

Her brother sighed. "Ellen, could you not have just said you'd try? Gray is a man who likes control and order. You wrestle that from his grasp, and he's not sure how to function. He is a protector, our detective, which he will instinctively want to do if he cares deeply for someone. You."

"I like who I am now, Leo. I don't want to change what I have become."

"I understand that, and loath as I am to admit that man is good enough for you, I now think he is, and trust me, that confession did not come easy."

"I'm scared to change any of what we have," she whispered. "I don't want to lose this and who I am. I'm happy."

"I know, but we cannot stay the same forever. One of us was bound to find someone who would love them, and sister dear, it looks like that is you. It will take time to adjust together, Ellen, but is it not worth at least trying if you love Gray?"

"He didn't want to try," Ellen said. "And what do you know about working things out?"

"He had just found out thugs had hurt you and rushed over here not knowing what he would find. Gray walked into your room and there you were lying on your bed bruised and hurting. Surely, he is allowed a moment of panic-induced rage. Love does not make us sane people, sister."

"What do you know of love, Leo?"

"Absolutely nothing but what Uncle Bram and Aunt Ivy have taught us."

"I fear our differences are irreconcilable," Ellen said.

"Don't be pathetic, of course they're not. The man is knee-deep in love with you. Fight for him, Ellen, and then be my strong, domineering sister and show him how he cannot live without you just as you are."

One minute she was looking at Leo's smiling face and the next she was back with the naked man. But this time he was turning, and she saw his identity.

"Ellen!"

Leo was shaking her when the vision faded.

"It's Brownly," she whispered. "He is the naked man. The one with the tattoo on his forearm."

"Brownly, the man who came to the bookshop saying he'd bought the *Blackstead Bestiary*?"

"Yes. He has the tattoo, Leo. Don't you see? It connects him to everything."

"Are you sure?"

She nodded. "He came to get the book, but if he's one of them, perhaps he knew George was dead, or did he send someone to kill George, and they couldn't find the book... I don't know. But we must tell Gray!"

"Take a steadying breath now, sister. You are not yet back to full health. We will inform Gray, but I must have your word. You will do as I say and take no risks?"

"I promise, Leo."

"Good girl, I almost believe you mean that. I'm sure your besotted detective would have."

They walked slowly back inside.

"I've been looking for you two!" Alex ran down the stairs.

"Well, you didn't look far. We've been seated outside for at least thirty minutes," Leo said.

"Do not speak to me in that voice." Alex pointed a finger at him. "You could have both died."

"When Gray's Aunt Tilda showed me your watch, Leo, and Ellen's Lottie necklace, I knew you were in danger. Uncle Bram and I left the house at a run, and when we reached you, we didn't know..." His words fell away as he exhaled slowly.

"I'm sorry, brother." Leo gripped his shoulder, and Ellen took his hand.

"We are all right, Alex."

"I keep reminding myself of that."

"Now what is it you wanted us for because we need to go at once and find Gray, Ellen has had a vision," Leo said.

"I think Gray is in danger," Alex said. "His Aunt Tilda showed me a grave, and it had his name on it."

"What? No!" It was a cry torn from Ellen.

"It doesn't mean death, just the prospect of it," Alex added quickly.

"You couldn't have said that first?" Leo glared at Alex.

Gray couldn't die, she wouldn't allow it. Her chest was burning, and she felt nauseous as the thought of the man she loved hurting or worse.

"Bud, get Ellen's cloak and bonnet, please. We are going out," Leo said.

"You're not going anywhere." Mungo appeared to stand beside the housekeeper. "Your aunt and uncle are gone from home with Lottie. They will not wish you to leave without their knowledge while you are both hurting."

"We have to, Mungo. Gray is in danger," Ellen said.

Panic made it hard to speak. What if he was hurt? What if... no, she would not think of that. She had to get to him. She'd pushed him away, but Leo was right, she should have tried to talk to him.

"Very well, but you'll do nothing without me, and we leave word for Bram," Mungo demanded. They all nodded, but like her, she knew her brothers would have their fingers crossed.

They would do what was needed to find Gray and keep him alive.

Ten minutes later, she was in the carriage with her umbrella and her brothers, heading toward his home and praying she was not too late. Praying the man she loved was there so she could tell him she wanted a life with him.

Wanted the chance to try.

Chapter 34

Gray was like a man possessed. He'd been out every night since Ellen and Leo's attack to find who had done it, but so far, he had nothing. But he would find who was responsible because he would not stop until he did.

He'd spent several hours at Scotland Yard reading through files and asking questions of his colleagues about the Baddon Boys, learning nothing new.

He had to find the men who had hurt Ellen. That was the only thought driving him. That and the need to find George Nicholson's killer, because he was convinced that Ellen's attack and the murder were related.

Leaving Scotland Yard, Gray's empty stomach had forced him to get nourishment, so he'd gone to Miss Patty's Tea Shop for the second time in three days. This was where he'd sat and talked with Ellen the day she'd been upset. When he'd kissed her. He felt closer to her but not close enough.

Gray didn't need people, but he needed her. Life without seeing Ellen Nightingale lay before him, barren and endless.

Pulling the small diamond pin from his pocket, Gray rubbed his thumb across the gem. He shouldn't have taken it, but he'd known it was hers when he'd found it outside her bedroom door.

"Why are you here, Gray?"

He was so preoccupied he hadn't seen his cousin approaching. "I'm taking tea, Ramsey. It's what you do in these places."

"You look like hell." His cousin pulled out a chair and sat across from him. He then picked up a scone from the plate before him.

"Talk to her, Gray. You love her, and she loves you."

He'd been too hard on Ellen, Gray knew that now. Fear had made him do it. He had to go back to Crabbett Close and speak to her.

"I'd just come to that realization actually."

Ramsey smiled. "So, it is love, then?"

Gray nodded. "I need your help, Ram."

"Really? Well, now as it happens, I have the day free. Do tell, cousin? I am all ears. Do you want me to plan your wooing of Ellen?"

"No. I have that covered. This is to do with the Nicholson case."

He'd thought long and hard about how to approach Olivia Nicholson again because after seeing her with that man, he knew he needed to. Gray just wasn't sure how to get her alone, or to ensure he didn't terrify her into silence.

"I have to interview George Nicholson's sister again. I want you to come with me because women like you—"

"And you frighten them," Ramsey cut him off. "Plus, you can't bring Ellen along."

"Even if she wanted to help me, which she likely doesn't. She's still injured." His hand curled into a fist.

"You will find who did this to Leo and Ellen, Gray. I have faith in your abilities as a detective to see this done."

"I will," he vowed. "But now we have an interview to attend. You are my assistant."

Ramsey beamed. "Wonderful."

"Idiot. Let's go."

As the hackney took them toward the Nicholsons', Gray wondered how Ellen was for perhaps the hundredth time that day. Were her injuries healing?

"I'm not sure what happened between you and the beautiful Miss Nightingale. However, as neither of you will mention the other, my guess is you became scared of your feelings for her and ran."

"I told her I couldn't watch her repeatedly plunging into danger." Gray told his cousin the truth.

"But she is expected to cope with you doing that?" Ramsey asked him.

He hadn't thought of it that way.

"Don't be a fool, Gray. She's not like the pampered daughter of society she once was anymore. She's strong and spirited, and I'm sure if you use some of that intellect your colleagues say you have, I doubt you'd want her any other way."

He wouldn't.

"She's fine, if you're interested. I saw her yesterday. We did not discuss you, as two of her delightful younger siblings were there. So, I regaled them with stories that had them laughing, and we ate a rather superb treacle cake."

"You visited Ellen?" Gray asked, trying not to shout at his cousin. "Is she all right?"

"Still sore, and the bruises are changing color, but she is well, as is Leo."

"Why did you see her?"

"Because you may be an idiot, but I am not, and I

knew you'd want to know she was well." Ramsey was rarely stern, but he was that now. "She is your match, Gray. The one woman who can stand up to you and be your equal. Don't ruin this because of rigid morals."

"It is not wrong to want her safe."

"And she will be with you. But without you, she has to rely only on her family. Surely having her at your side will ease your fears more than not having her there?"

Gray dropped his face into his hands.

"You have always avoided emotions because you find them messy, cousin. You were raised without them, like Ellen. But unlike you, she has learned to express what she feels. That house in Crabbett Close is full of love and happiness, and that could be yours. Don't turn your back on all that."

"I had decided to go and see her. I love her very much, Ram."

"Then ensure you do not mess things up. Change is good, cousin. Embrace it and cast aside your moral compass."

"Are you finished?" Gray glared at Ramsey.

"Absolutely not. But for now, tell me about this Olivia Nicholson and why you need my charm and wit to speak with her."

"I'm having serious doubts."

"Surely not."

Twenty minutes later, they were once again inside the Nicholson town house.

"I can't imagine what it's like to lose your son," Ramsey said as they were ushered inside to a parlor.

"Hell," Gray whispered.

As luck would have it, only Olivia and her mother were there. Both were still pale and exhausted and clearly grieving.

"Mrs. Nicholson, Miss Nicholson. I'm sorry to intrude, but I have more questions," Gray said. "This is Mr. Bigglesbottom, another of my assistants," he said, pointing to Ramsey. His cousin did not even flinch at the alias. Instead, he bowed soberly before the women.

"Please accept my deepest sympathies for your loss," he said.

Both women found a small smile.

"Detective Fletcher, do you have news?"

"We are closing in, Mrs. Nicholson, but as yet, no arrest has been made," Gray said.

"Mrs. Nicholson," Ramsey said before Gray could speak again. "I wonder if you would tell me about that exquisite painting you have in your front entrance?"

"Oh well, of course." Mrs. Nicholson looked almost excited at the prospect of showing off her artwork. "It's my husband's pride and joy."

"I am looking at purchasing a painting, as I have recently moved into new premises," Ramsey said as he ushered the older woman out the door. "Clearly, you and Mr. Nicholson have excellent taste."

Gray would remember to thank his cousin later.

"Miss Nicholson, I will get straight to the point, as I have no wish for your mother to hear what we discuss."

"I don't understand," Olivia Nicholson said in a tremulous voice.

"I went to the theatre a week ago, and I saw you with a man. You were hidden down a narrow lane. I had been searching for someone else and found you."

What little color there was left in her face drained away.

"I am not here to judge you or cause you trouble, Miss Nicholson, but I am investigating your brother's murder, and I must follow every lead I get."

"Surely you do not think that I... I would never harm my brother, and neither would Benjamin," she said in a terrified voice.

"Benjamin? Is he the man you were with?"

She nodded, tears falling down her cheeks. Gray pulled out the clean handkerchief he always carried and handed it to her.

"I have it from a reliable source that you and your brother have recently argued, Miss Nicholson," he said gently. "Can you tell me why?"

"Pl-please understand I did not want this to happen."

He nodded, and she began her story.

"We met by chance, Benjamin and I, but it did not take long before we both fell in love." She pressed her face into the handkerchief as she shuddered out a breath.

Gray felt sorry for the woman, but he had to know if she or this Benjamin were in any way responsible for George Nicholson's death. Ellen had visions about the argument between the siblings and the naked tattooed man.

"My parents will not approve because Benjamin has no work, but he tries and finds what he can. He is the very best of men but has no family—"

"I am not here to judge him or you," Gray said again. "Will you tell me why your brother gave you a large sum of money not long before his death, Miss Nicholson?"

She pressed a hand to her mouth briefly, and Gray noticed it was trembling. Damn Ellen for making him feel. He had the urge to pat her shoulder or squeeze her fingers. Thankfully, she inhaled deeply and composed herself, so he did neither.

"I could always talk to my brother, but when I told him about Benjamin, we had a terrible argument, and I left in tears. Two days later, a note came telling me he wanted to speak with me at the bookshop. I called, and he said he wanted to meet Benjamin."

She was now torturing his handkerchief with her fingers.

"I took him to the bookshop. He and George spent two hours conversing. Afterward, he gave me the money and told me he would employ Benjamin in the bookshop, but he needed new clothes and a place to l-live." She sobbed, and it was a heartbreaking sound.

"G-George wanted to m-make Benjamin presentable, so m-my parents accepted him," she whispered.

"And then he was murdered, and now you don't know what to do because you've lost two men you loved?"

She nodded, the tears falling faster. "When you saw me with Benjamin, I was saying goodbye. I h-had slipped out of the house without my parents realizing it. I could not do this to them. Tell them I wanted to marry a man they did not see as suitable when they were grieving for George."

"If I may offer some advice to you, Miss Nicholson?"

Her eyes looked at him. Tired and infinitely sad.

"You must tell your parents the truth. Dress your Benjamin well and bring him for tea. Your parents loved your brother, and I'm sure respected him. If he liked Benjamin, then that is in his favor. Do this for George and for yourself."

"D-Do you think so?"

"I'm sure of it," Gray said. "The bookshop is still there. Perhaps one day you could run it on your brother's behalf with your future husband?"

They left after that, and Gray was unsure if she would heed his words or if the Nicholsons would allow her to be with her Benjamin, but he hoped it all worked out for Olivia Nicholson.

"Well?" Ramsey asked as they rolled away from the house.

"She's in no way involved in her brother's death."

"Good and bad news, then. Where are we going now?"

"I'm going to speak with Mr. Brownly again. Something does not sit well with that man. I've heard stories where his name came up alongside some seedy characters and yet nothing has ever stuck. I'm going to see if I can't get something out of him."

He dropped Ramsey at his home and then directed the carriage to the Brownly residence. As he arrived in the street, he watched a carriage roll by and inside was Mr. Brownly.

"Follow that carriage," Gray said on impulse to the driver of the hackney. He then sat back and contemplated how he was going to approach Ellen and tell her he'd been a fool and wanted them to have a future together. Ramsey had said be honest and tell her he was scared. Which, of course, he'd denied, but it was the truth.

He'd loved and lost his aunt and uncle and his brothers. While they still lived, they were no longer who they'd once been. If he gave himself to Ellen, she could hurt him too.

But to not have her in his life would be worse.

He put Ellen from his head as the hackney rolled to a stop in Whitechapel. He needed to concentrate because they were now in the heart of where the Baddon Boys gang carried out their criminal enterprises. Gray's suspicion was strengthening.

He'd felt something was off with Brownly, and this might just prove it.

Climbing from the hackney, Gray followed from a distance after Brownly had left his carriage. The man walked toward two brick buildings. He then waited for a large iron gate to open, and entered. It swung shut with a loud clang behind him.

Gray had done a lot of research on the Baddon Boys, and he knew this was their headquarters. He'd even driven past here to see what it looked like and survey the surrounding area.

Moving closer, he could see no one around, so he pushed the gate to check it was indeed locked. It didn't move. The place would be hard to penetrate, he thought, as he walked around the perimeter to the side of the building. There was a door, and he tested the handle.

"Unless you've a right to be here, you better have a good reason."

Gray turned and found the two men before him. One, he noted, had scratches down his cheek.

"I see Miss Nightingale left her mark."

The man's eyes widened, telling him what he needed to know.

Gray swung a fist and connected with his jaw. He didn't see the one coming from his right and dropped like a stone into darkness.

Chapter 35

Ellen and her brothers had not found Gray at his home. He'd left for work several hours earlier, the butler said. They'd traveled to Scotland Yard next.

Alex had gone inside while she and Leo waited in the carriage to see if he was there. Twenty minutes later, he'd returned.

"Well?" she demanded.

"Some hatched-faced man left me sitting in a hard chair for too long. He then returned to inform me in a snooty tone that Detective Fletcher was not in the building," Alex said.

Ellen's heart sank. *Where was Gray?* She knew he was in danger. Knew he needed their help.

"I asked where Gray had gone and when he left, and the man said he could not disclose that information. I was close to telling him he needed to work on his manners, as they were below acceptable standards."

"There is a standard?" Leo asked. He then winced as he moved to find a more comfortable position. His body was still bruised and sore like Ellen's.

"Of course there is," Alex snapped. "Without manners, what are we?"

"Indeed," Leo muttered.

"Is he with Ramsey, do you think?" Ellen asked. "We need to find him."

"I know that we do, sister, and we will," Alex said.

The carriage door opened, and Uncle Bram filled the space.

"Hello, family. I'm glad I found you." He stepped inside the carriage. "Have you located Gray?"

"No, and I fear for him, Uncle Bram. Mr. Brownly is the naked man I saw with the tattoo, and Gray's aunt showed Alex a grave with his name on it." She tried to force down the panic.

"All right, love. Take a breath now." Uncle Bram sat beside her. He then put an arm around her and held her close. "We will find your man, my sweet."

"Where does Ramsey live?" Leo asked.

"I know." Alex rose and gave Mungo the address through the door above him. They were moving in seconds.

"Now, I am going to be your stern uncle," he said, looking from her to Leo. "We will find Gray, but neither of you will do anything to strain your injuries," Uncle Bram said. "I mean it."

She and Leo nodded.

Her body hurt, and her jaw was sore from the fist she'd taken there, but none of that mattered. All she could think about was Gray and her belief something was very wrong.

"Why can't I see anything else?" Ellen asked.

"Even Aunt Tilda is quiet, which is odd, because the woman has been in and out my head since Gray entered our lives," Alex added.

"You will see when you need to," Uncle Bram said in his steady way.

When Mungo pulled the carriage to a stop, Uncle Bram got out first and then helped Ellen down.

"I heard that hiss," he said. "I am not pleased you and your brother have left your beds, niece, even as I understand why."

The door opened as they were about to knock on it, and there stood Ramsey, as usual, immaculately dressed.

"Nightingales, how lovely. But should you two be out of bed?" He shot Leo and Ellen a look.

"It's Gray, Ramsey. He is in trouble. I feel it," Ellen said.

"Feel it?"

"It's too hard to explain, and I'm not sure you'd believe it anyway. But what we need from you is something of his," Alex said.

"I was with him earlier. We took tea at Miss Patty's Tea Shop."

Gray rarely went out for tea. He'd told her that, but he had today with his cousin. Was she the reason he'd gone there?

"You're really worried about him, aren't you?" Ramsey looked at each of them. They all nodded.

"Very well. I will return soon." He disappeared back into the house, leaving the door open, which told them they could enter.

It was nice, not subdued like Gray's place. This had more color.

"This is my cousin's." Ramsey returned with a top hat. "He left it here once, and I liked it, so I kept it. He never remembers where he leaves things."

Alex immediately took it and put it on.

"My cousin and I have large heads," Ramsey added as it lowered past Alex's ears.

Ellen and Leo touched the brim.

"It's best not to ask," Uncle Bram said. "I assure you they are quite harmless, Ramsey."

"Ellen," Leo said. "I just had an image of your diamond pin Teddy gave you for your last birthday. Have you lost it?"

"I was wearing it the day we... the day we went to purchase apricotines."

"So, it could be lost?" Leo persisted, and she nodded.

"Are you like Aunt Tilda?" Ramsey asked.

Alex nodded, and the hat tilted forward over his eyes.

"Aunt Tilda is still flashing orange at me, but the name Mary... No wait, St. Mary's."

"Whitechapel," Leo said. "Your pin is there, I'm sure of it."

"The Baddon Boys have their headquarters there. They have a large brick warehouse."

"How do you know that's where they're located?" Leo asked.

"Because when I found out it was the Baddon Boys who may have hurt you, I wanted the location where to find them." Uncle Bram's words were cold as ice.

"I forget sometimes what a mean bastard you can be," Leo said. "But you will not be taking them on alone, Uncle."

She felt the vision slide into her head. Ellen reached out to brace herself on Alex's shoulder, and then she saw him. Gray was bound, hand and foot. Blood ran from his nose.

"No!"

Chapter 36

"Easy, Ellen. What did you see, sweetheart?" Uncle Bram's arms came around her.

"It's Gray. Someone has hurt him. He's in a small room, locked in there," she added, remembering the key she saw.

"Not for long, he's not," Ramsey said in a tone that rivaled her uncle. "Lead the way, Nightingales. I have only recently reconnected with my cousin, and I want to keep him around. Besides, I'm sure there is a wedding in my future."

Her wedding to Gray. Ellen knew he was talking about that, but she couldn't let herself think that far ahead. She had to focus on getting him back first.

They got back into the carriage. Uncle Bram climbed up beside Mungo onto the driver's seat, and the carriage was moving.

"Is he all right up there?" Ramsey said, pointing to where their uncle sat.

"They are friends and have spent years traveling the

world in far worse circumstances than he currently is in," Alex said.

"Ellen, look at me," Leo said to her.

All she could see was Gray. Bound and hurting. Her brother grabbed her chin and turned it until their eyes met.

"Be strong and find your anger. Gray needs that now. We will get him back. That is my vow to you."

She nodded.

"We can't just walk in there, they would likely outnumber us," Alex said.

"We need something to flush them all out," Ramsey said.

While they debated, Ellen thought about Gray. She did what Leo had said and let the anger consume her. No one hurt the man she loved and got away with it. She and Gray were going to spend their life together, even though he didn't know it yet. They would get their chance to talk, and when that happened, she would tell him what was in her heart.

She would get that chance.

"He told me he loved you."

"Pardon?" She looked at Ramsey.

"My cousin said he loved you and that he was coming to see you, Ellen. Coming to talk and my guess is to apologize."

"He is not the only one who needs to apologize, Ramsey. We both have things to say to each other." Ellen looked at her hands. "I need to find him so we can."

"And you will." He squeezed her hands.

When the carriage stopped, they got out. Ellen looked around her. Dark had fallen, and wisps of fog were begging to close in around them. Buildings closed in on them, rising high on either side. In the distance, she heard a faint hum of voices.

"Hold the horses, Bram," Mungo said. He then disappeared, and Ellen did not know where to.

"Where has he gone?" Alex asked.

"I should imagine finding someone to look after his horses as Mungo will come with us," Uncle Bram said. "And here he is now."

Mungo did indeed have four young boys with him when he returned.

"I've promised them money, so someone hand some over," the Scotsman said.

Money was handed over with the promise of more when they returned to the boys.

"This way." Uncle Bram pointed to the right.

They walked in the shadows, trying not to be seen, Leo swinging his cane and Ellen holding her umbrella. She knew Alex had his sticks.

"If this is where the Baddon Boys are located, surely they will have men out here monitoring things," Leo said.

"Someone is coming," Ellen said.

"I would dispute that, Warwick. That apple and blackberry was good but not as good as the pear." The voice came from in front of them. "It was worth the visit to Whitechapel just to taste that pastry."

"Cambridge?" Ellen stepped out of the shadows as four men approached.

"Ellen?" Cambridge Sinclair stopped before them. With him were his brothers Devonshire and Warwick Sinclair, plus their brother-in-law Mr. Huntington. "What has you and your family here?"

"Good God, what happened to your faces?" Dev asked.

"Better yet, why are you out here in the dark?"

Warwick asked. "I have a feeling it's not a social occasion you are about to attend."

"Bramstone?" Dev asked. "What's going on?"

"We could use your help," Uncle Bram said. "But it could be dangerous."

"Excellent. Danger is my middle name," Cambridge said.

"No, it's not. Harold is," Warwick added.

"Anyway," Mr. Huntington said. "How can we help?"

"The man whose house you invaded the other day, Detective Fletcher? He is in trouble, and we believe hurt inside the Baddon Boys' headquarters," Ellen explained.

"Is he now," Dev said. "Well then, shall we get him back?"

They moved down the street with the Sinclair brothers and Mr. Huntington, and Ellen felt a great deal better having their support.

"Are you well, Ellen?" Dev asked. He walked at her side.

"I am. We, Leo and I, got set upon."

"We believe they were Baddon Boys," Uncle Bram said.

"A cowardly action to attack anyone but a woman even more so," Mr. Huntington said. "My wife will have something to help you heal completely."

Ellen knew Essie was a healer, as her twin sisters often talked about her.

"Thank you."

"There. See that brick building? That is their headquarters," Uncle Bram said.

Ellen looked at it and felt Gray. He was close.

"Aunt Tilda is dancing in my head, which tells me he's there," Alex said.

Dev walked across the road with Warwick and around

the side of the building. When he returned, he said, "He's in there and alive. Down on the lower level of the building at the rear."

Ellen felt almost light-headed with relief. She had always known there was something special about the Sinclair and Raven families, but like her own gifts, she'd never asked why.

"How did you—"

"Like us, it's best not to ask," Uncle Bram interrupted Ramsey.

"We need some reason to get them outside. Getting in there would be near-impossible," Warwick said. "There are at least twenty-five men inside."

"We need a distraction," Ramsey said. She saw the questions he was holding back.

"I suggest a drunken fight," Mungo, who had been quiet until now, spoke. "Make it loud and then we could throw bottles at those." He pointed to the windows immediately beyond the wall behind which housed the Baddon Boys' headquarters.

"That's worked for us before," Cambridge said. "We'll draw them out, and you get them with Warwick and Dev."

It sounded risky to Ellen, but what other option was there?

"Wait. Those men gathered around that fire we passed about ten minutes ago. I'm sure we could induce them to join us," Cambridge said.

Mungo grunted his agreement, and Cambridge took off at a run with Alex and Ramsey.

"Ellen?"

"Yes, Dev."

"Do you love that man in there?" He pointed to the building.

"I do."

"Excellent, you're a perfect match."

"How do you know that?"

"I'm sure there are a great many things I don't know about your family, as I'm sure there are about mine" was all he said. Ellen agreed.

They did not have long to wait before they heard the noise of men approaching. Loud and singing.

"Good Lord, are they all drunk?" Leo asked.

"They were, so I can't imagine that's changed, and Cam is incredibly persuasive and can get people to do most things," Warwick said.

"Right then," Uncle Bram said. "We create a disturbance and lure them outside. If that can be achieved. I'm sure not all will leave Gray, but some."

"I'm going in," Ellen said.

"Ellen, you are still injured, as is Leo," Uncle Bram said.

"We're going in," Leo said.

He sighed.

"Warwick and I will go with Ellen and Leo," Dev said.

"I should go," Uncle Bram added.

"Trust me to care for your family, Bramstone," Dev said.

The two men shared a look, and then Bram nodded.

The men arrived, a large group of them. Two held pieces of wood like torches, fire blazing at the ends.

"Can I punch you, Max? I've always wanted to," Cambridge said.

Then men spilled onto the street, singing and shouting. One tripped and landed on another.

"Well now, no punch required," Mr. Huntington said. "They've started the fight for us."

"Hardly seems fair," Cambridge said.

Dev, Warwick, Leo, and Ellen moved to stand beside

the building, near to the gate. She hoped this worked. Hoped they were not seen.

"That has to hurt," Warwick whispered as Max got Cambridge in a headlock. "My brother-in-law could squeeze the life out of a person with those arms."

The commotion grew as more punches were thrown. Mungo was there and Uncle Bram, yelling at the top of their voices.

"They're coming," Dev whispered.

The gates were opened, and men ran through the opening and across the road.

"I count eighteen, which leaves seven inside, including Detective Fletcher," Warwick said. "Let's go."

Ellen had her umbrella now gripped firmly between her hands, and Leo held his cane.

We're coming, Gray.

Chapter 37

His ribs ached, and his nose throbbed. The two men had grabbed him, with a third soon joining them. He'd fought them back, but there were too many, and a punch had knocked him to the ground. When he woke, he was in a small, cold room bound hand and foot. How long he'd been here, he had no idea. But one thing he knew was that Brownly was one of the Baddon Boys or an associate.

Gray sat on the floor in the dark as the room had no furniture or light and waited for what they'd do to him next. He was sure he'd end up missing, never to be found again. But he couldn't allow that to happen. Gray had too much to live for now.

He loved Ellen, and he needed to tell her that. Then there was Ramsey who had come back into his life. He felt desperation surge through him. He had to find a way to escape.

The sound of a key turning in the door's lock was almost a relief. Sitting here with his thoughts was hell. He'd rather fight with everything he had inside him than wait to die.

He didn't want to die.

The door opened, and lamplight showed him a dark head but little else.

"Detective Fletcher, it is Devonshire Sinclair. We have come to get you out."

While he was grappling with that information, a figure slipped past him and ran at him.

"Gray!"

"Ellen?" She wrapped her arms around his waist. "Why are you here?" he rasped. Even as he longed to see her, burying his face in her sweet-smelling hair, the fear of what could happen to her had him saying, "It's too dangerous." The thought of these thugs getting their hands on her again terrified him. "Get out! Run now."

"I will, but you're coming with me," she said, cupping his face.

"It's exceedingly dangerous, Gray." Leo appeared. "Which is why we must leave."

Another man dropped before him.

"I'm Warwickshire Sinclair. Allow me to release your bonds."

"I-I don't understand? How are you here? Take her out."

"We can explain more later. Right now, we need to all leave here," Leo said.

"Get her out, Leo. Please." Gray wasn't above begging.

"Not without you," she said.

His hands were freed, and he couldn't help it. He had to hold her.

"You shouldn't have come. You're hurting—"

"Perhaps we could save this until we have you both safely back in the carriage?" Devonshire Sinclair said from the door.

Gray released her but took her hand, needing her

anchored to his side. They left the room and started back the way they'd come. Fear had him pushing Ellen behind him, so she was wedged between him and Warwickshire Sinclair.

They nearly made it to the gate out when a voice from behind stopped them.

"Halt!"

They turned, and Gray tried to force Ellen behind him again, but she refused to go.

"Stay," he hissed. She wrestled free of his grip and stood at his side with her umbrella braced before her like a bloody baton. Christ, he loved this woman.

"You murdered George Nicholson," Gray said.

The man held a pistol pointed his way.

"Will you take us all out, then?" Devonshire Sinclair asked.

Gray's pistol had been taken off him before they threw him in that room.

"Ellen?" Leo said.

"Middle," she said, which had him shooting her a look. Her hair was loose, she wore her blue cloak, and the bruises on her face were different shades of plum now. She'd never looked more beautiful to Gray. He needed to keep her safe. Had to get her out of here.

"Right," Warwickshire Sinclair said.

"Left," Leo said.

"Be quiet!" Brownly looked nervous, but he recovered. "My intention was to scare you Nightingales off. It seems I underestimated you and should have had them kill you both."

"You realize there are two lords before you, not to mention a detective from Scotland Yard," Devonshire Sinclair said. "How is it you will make us all disappear?"

"We'll find a way," Brownly said, but he looked scared.

"There are many more of us," Leo said.

His eyes shot to the door that led outside.

Gray didn't see Ellen move, but seconds later, the gun was flying through the air as her umbrella caught Brownly's hand. She then jabbed him hard in the stomach, and he dropped to his knees, moaning. Leo's cane took a man down, and Warwickshire Sinclair's fist the other.

"Excellent," Devonshire Sinclair said. "I knew there was a reason my twin sisters were your friend, Ellen. It seems you have the same spirit as they. I never even had to throw a punch."

"I want him," Gray said, reaching for Brownly, who was writhing on the floor gasping for air.

"Allow me," Warwickshire said, hauling the man to his feet. He then shoved him at Gray.

Using Brownly's pistol, which he pointed at his spine, he nudged the man forward. They walked outside to a mass of bodies. Some were laughing, others cheering, and only a few were still fighting.

They culled their men out of the melee of bodies with little effort as they'd been watching for them.

"Let him go!"

"Come near us, and I'll shoot him," Gray said as one of the Baddon Boys approached. He held the pistol at Brownly's forehead.

They all backed down the road with what guns they had raised.

"Many thanks," Uncle Bram said when the Sinclairs and Mr. Huntingdon said their carriage was near. "I did not find who harmed my family, but it is enough to capture this murderer, as it was a good man he killed."

"We are glad to have helped," Cambridge said. "It certainly livened up what had been until then a mediocre evening."

"That's exceedingly harsh, considering you were with us," Devonshire said, pointing to Mr. Huntington, who merely shook his head. "We shall see you soon," he added.

"Thank you," Gray said. "I am indebted to you all."

"I'm sure we will have need for a detective from Scotland Yard at some stage, knowing our family," Lord Sinclair said.

They raised their hands and walked away, soon disappearing into the dark.

"Will they be all right?" Gray asked.

"Let me go, Fletcher, you have nothing on me," Brownly said.

"You're not serious. You had me kidnapped, and I'm charging you for the murder of George Nicholson."

"You can't prove anything!"

Gray watched Ellen dig into Alex's pocket and pull out his handkerchief. She then stuffed it in Brownly's mouth. He couldn't help it. Gray smiled.

The boys were paid and Brownly forced to the floor in the carriage. It was a tight squeeze. But they made it work to Scotland Yard.

Gray sat with Ellen at his side but could say little to her surrounded by her family and Brownly.

"He has a tattoo," Ellen whispered in his ear. "Brownly is the naked man, Gray."

He looked at her, and she nodded.

He leaned in close and whispered in her ear, "I love you."

Her smile was blinding, and for now, that was enough. When they stopped at the Watch House, he got out and took his prisoner and cousin with him.

"I will talk to you tomorrow," he said to the woman standing in the carriage doorway. "I love you."

"I love you too," Alex called.

"I don't," Leo added.

Gray then stood there grinning like an idiot as Ellen rolled away from him in her family's carriage.

"Wipe that smile from your face, it's sickening," Ramsey said. He then nudged Brownly, who was glaring daggers at them, but as he still had the handkerchief in his mouth Ellen had put there, he could only utter a few garbled, indiscernible words.

"Now, cousin, what is it I will need to do in there?" Ramsey said as he reached the building. "Hold the prisoner. Vouch for his villainous activities. Explain my heroic actions tonight?"

"Nothing. They know who I am in here, so I will explain the situation, see Brownly put behind bars for the night, and then we are leaving because I'm unsure how much longer I can stand."

Every ache and abused muscle in his body was throbbing now that Ellen had left him. He no longer had to worry about her, therefore he could feel pain.

Love is a strange thing.

Ramsey huffed out a breath of disappointment.

Twenty minutes later, he walked out and found his cousin asleep in the small waiting area.

"Ram, wake up." He nudged his foot. "I want to go home, and you need to make that happen."

His cousin groaned but was soon standing.

"Come along then, Detective Fletcher, I will, in my duty as your assistant," he said in a voice loud enough to carry to all corners of the building, "see you safely home."

Gray grunted but said nothing. Even talking hurt now. But he could still find a smile as Ramsey climbed into a hackney. Because Ellen loved him, and that was a wonderful thing.

Chapter 38

Ellen knocked on Gray's front door the day after they'd found him in that room.

"I've not even had my morning meal," Alex muttered from beside her.

"I saw you drink tea and eat a fruit bun."

"Nowhere near enough food for a man such as I, and why did you have to come?" he asked the large dog sitting at his feet patiently waiting to be let inside.

"He likes Gray," Ellen said. *And he's not the only one.*

She looked her brother up and down. "You appear healthy enough and not in imminent danger of fainting."

He made a tsking sound. "One hopes when you and Gray come to your senses, we, your family, are not called to leave their homes as dawn breaks just to bring your lovelorn self to his doorstep," Alex snapped.

Looking to the sky, she saw the sun was above them. Ellen said, "It is well past dawn, as you very well know. Stop being dramatic. And I am worried for Gray. He was hurting a great deal more than he let on last night."

"As are you still, sister dear." He reached around her and pounded on the door again.

"Stop that infernal banging." These words were followed by Ramsey now standing in the open doorway, glaring. "What are you two doing here?"

"My lovesick sister dragged me to this doorstep, Ramsey, so she could assure herself Gray was, in fact, well and not about to die."

"Alex!"

"What? I'm hungry, and you are being dramatic."

"Come in, Alex. As it happens, I purchased some apricotines from Appleblossoms Bakery not thirty minutes ago. We'll sit with our tea and eat them while Ellen and Gray fumble around with apologies and declarations of love," Ramsey said.

Ellen rolled her eyes and entered the house.

"Second floor, third door on the right. He is sitting in a small parlor writing notes on last night because he was too exhausted to do it before he slept. I have forbidden him from leaving the house again."

"Again?"

"He left the house before I could stop him for a brief visit somewhere, but is returned now."

"Is he well, Ramsey?" Ellen asked.

"Like you, bruised and hurting but well, Ellen." He smiled. "Off you go, and I will have tea ready when you both come down."

Ellen walked up the stairs and along to stand outside the third door. Exhaling slowly, she knocked.

"For pity's sake, Ram. I am the same as I was when you saw me five minutes ago," a voice from inside called. "I have said I will not leave the house again. Go away and let me finish."

She opened the door and walked inside.

He was seated at his desk writing.

"What is so important?" He turned and saw her. "Ellen." Her name sounded torn from him.

"I needed to see you."

He met her in two strides, his hands cupped her face, and his eyes ran over her. "I don't know how I existed without you in my life, Ellen."

"I am the same. It's an odd thing, don't you think, that after a short amount of time we have become so important to each other." Ellen never wanted to leave Gray again because she had a feeling that a life without him would be no life at all.

"Very odd but wonderful."

"Are you well, Gray?"

"I am now." His lips touched hers briefly. "How are you here?"

"Alex brought me. He's downstairs eating apricotines with Ramsey."

They stared at each other for long seconds.

"Do you need to sit, Ellen?"

"I threw my umbrella at Brownly last night. I'm sure I can stand here with you."

"I'm sorry," he whispered against her lips. "For speaking as I did. For ordering you to stop walking into danger."

"We try not to walk into danger every time we leave the house, Gray."

He snorted and then kissed her again. "These feelings inside me are new, and I didn't know how to deal with them."

"It is no different for me," Ellen said. She traced the tip of her finger over the bridge of his bruised nose. "I'm sorry you're hurting."

"I can't feel anything."

"I love you, Gray."

"I love you too."

"But you should know that I don't follow orders very well."

He barked out a laugh. "I knew that already, love. But I'm sure we can come to a compromise."

He pulled her into his arms, holding her close. Ellen thought this was perhaps her new favorite place to be.

"Where did you go this morning, Gray? Ramsey told me you left the house."

"I visited the Nicholsons after the news reached me that Brownly will be charged alongside the man who actually did the killing, for George's murder. They had a right to know their son was murdered through greed."

"Brownly—"

"Wanted the *Blackstead Bestiary* at any cost. When George wouldn't give it to him, he sent one of the Baddon Boys to retrieve it. There was a scuffle when George returned home to find the man inside his bookshop. He was shot dead, and the man fled," Gray said.

"But Brownly did not get the book?" Ellen asked.

"He did. He had two men return the night he found us in George's shop. There was yet another locked box, but this one was under floorboards in the room off the shop downstairs."

"How did we miss it?"

"Clearly I was blinded by your beauty." Gray kissed her again.

"I'm glad the Nicholsons have some closure now," Ellen said when she could think straight.

"They do, and there is more."

He told her about his talk with Olivia Nicholson, and Benjamin the man she loved.

"He was there this morning," Gray added. "It seems

the Nicholsons are coming to terms with the fact their daughter is in love. Olivia was the one who showed me out when it was time to leave. She thanked me for what I said to her the day I called. Her father is allowing Benjamin and Olivia to run the bookshop on a trial process and if that works, they will talk about making it permanent," Gray said.

"Oh, Gray. That's wonderful. I'm so pleased you spoke with her, and convinced her to introduce Benjamin to her parents," Ellen said hugging him close.

"Now." He released her and backed away. "I want to talk to your uncle and brothers, but here and now, I can't wait." He eased back from her and started to lower himself to the ground.

"Don't you dare get down on your knees with all the injuries I know you have!" Ellen cried. "Yes, I will marry you."

"I haven't even asked yet." He was smiling but had straightened.

She giggled and then was laughing. Ellen felt lighter inside than she had in a long time. So, this was love.

"You've had enough time alone in there with my sister. Get out here now, Fletcher!" A loud thump on the door followed these words. "All our family has arrived."

"With me unfortunately comes them," Ellen said.

"I can hardly wait," he drawled. "Come along, my love, or all the apricotines will be gone."

They were all in his parlor, and Gray's butler was in his element, running about the place serving tea and food.

"You both look happier," Uncle Bram said. He came to stand before them with Lottie in his arms. She held out her arms for Gray to take her, which surprised Ellen.

He took the little girl, holding her against his shoulder.

"I want to marry your niece," he then said. "As this family is unconventional, I may as well ask all of you."

"No!" Leo roared.

"Yes" came from Ramsey and the rest of the Nightingales.

"Oh, very well." Leo got to his feet and shook Gray's hand. "Hurt her and there will be nowhere you can hide."

"A missive has arrived for you, sir," the butler said, handing out a piece of paper to Gray.

Ellen watched as he read it, hoping it was not bad news.

"Brownly's house has just been searched and the *Blackstead Bestiary* found. They have arrested him for being an accomplice in the murder of George Nicholson," Gray said.

"Excellent," Uncle Bram said. "We have more to celebrate, it seems."

"Thank you," Gray said to Ellen, when her family were all seated drinking tea and eating. He'd put Lottie down, and she was now being chased around the room by Teddy, shrieking loudly. It left his hands free to hold Ellen's.

"For what?"

"For seeing something in me you could love. For helping me find George Nicholson's murderer and coming to rescue me last night. Lastly, for being the most wonderful, infuriating woman I have ever known."

She leaned to kiss him. "You are very welcome, and thank you for being my uptight, handsome detective, who I will love until the day I draw my last breath."

Chapter 39

The wedding of Miss Ellen Nightingale to Mr. Grayson Fletcher was a great deal less grand than his eldest brother's would be. It took place a month after the day they'd arrested Brownly.

Ellen had declared she would like the ceremony outside in the small park in the middle of Crabbett Close. While unorthodox, Gray thought it a grand idea, so the locals along with Ramsey and the Nightingales got to work.

Gray now stood at the end of the aisle, beside his cousin, Leo, and Alex, as it was pathetic, according to all of them, that he only had one friend to call upon.

Ellen wanted a handful of people they loved and had befriended and no fuss to witness their vows. Clearly, she didn't know her neighbors in Crabbett Close very well.

"I wonder where the pews came from?" Ramsey said from his position beside Gray. Before them were five wooden pews to the left and five to the right. Seated on those were people, friends and family.

"There is a church somewhere that will have its congregations standing this Sunday," Alex said.

Ivy, Mungo, and the Nightingale household staff sat in the front pew. Behind them were the entire Sinclair and Raven family taking up the rest of the rows. All who he'd recently been introduced to, and found he liked very much.

The residents of Crabbett Close were seated on the left and the right to make it seem like Gray actually had more than four people there for him.

Not that he cared. The only important person in his life was about to walk down that strip of red-and-gold patterned carpet.

"My fear is that was stolen right out of a prosperous household," Gray said.

"You are not on duty today, Detective Fletcher, and look at that carpet closely."

He did. "My God, Ram, that's from your house."

"So you need not worry about theft... although I can't vouch for—"

"Cease." Gray raised a hand. "I do not want to know."

"That's probably best," Leo added.

The residents all sat in their seats, twittering with excitement like hens roosting. Some wore hats festooned with ribbons, others bonnets with new satin ribbons. Men were in their Sunday best.

Flowers were everywhere he looked. Standing on poles, tied to the edges of chairs with ribbons. Two huge urns stood on either side at the beginning of the aisle.

"I believe those were borrowed from the Alvins' mother," Alex said, nodding to the urns.

"They're close to ninety. How do they have a mother alive?" Gray asked.

"It's a mystery," Alex said.

Luckily, London had put on a fine, cloudless day for his nuptials, or they'd have taken the entire event inside 11 Crabbett Close.

"It's a beautiful day to sit in the sun, eat, and celebrate love," Ramsey said.

"Mr. Peeky has supplied plenty of his rum for the occasion," Leo said with an evil grin for Gray.

"I have a question," Gray said. "As I will soon be married to a Nightingale, that will mean I am one of you, right?"

"I guess so," Leo admitted reluctantly.

"Yes, exactly," Alex said, and Gray felt warm all over at the thought of being part of this large, wonderful family.

"So I may bring a guest to the next Crabbett Close event?"

Alex's smile grew as he glanced from Gray to Ramsey. "But of course you can."

"Excellent. You'll love it, Ram."

"You just want me to make a fool of myself, but as that never happens… good Lord." Ramsey's mouth fell open as he looked to the end of the aisle. "I invited them, but I never thought they'd come."

Gray turned and found his youngest brother and mother walking down Ramsey's carpet, looking shocked at what was before them. He felt the sudden burn of tears behind his eyes. Teddy was leading them to the front pew, where they then sat.

Gray moved to stand before them. "Thank you for coming. I realize this is—"

"Perfect," his mother said. "Congratulations, Grayson, I am glad you are happy."

He leaned down to kiss her cheek. "Thank you, Mother, I am."

He then held out his hand to his brother, and Henry took it.

"Congratulations, Grayson. Ramsey reminded us that

blood is important, and I'm sorry it took me so long to realize that."

"You are here, and that means more than I can ever say. Thank you."

He made his way back to Leo, Alex, and Ramsey.

"You're not going to weep, are you, because the ceremony is about to start, and if Ellen finds you crying, she'd think we did it," Ramsey said.

"Thank you for speaking with my family, Ram."

"Your father and eldest brother weren't receptive, but I'm glad your mother and Henry are here, cousin."

He hugged him and then Leo and Alex, because he felt he needed to.

"Right then. Here comes the love of your life, and you better make her happy, or we'll kill you," Leo said.

He saw Fred, Matilda, and Lottie first. They looked sweet in matching dresses and held baskets. Lottie was throwing petals at people, and the other two were scattering them on Ramsey's carpet runner.

The twins, Dorset and Somerset, and the Duke of Raven's sister, Samantha, came next. But it was the woman who appeared behind them that had the breath lodging in his throat.

Ellen wore cream silk and lace with a simple circlet of flowers on her head. They'd styled her blond curls with a few ringlets around her face and the rest were piled high on her head. She held her uncle's arm.

"For the love of God, man, breathe. It would not do for the groom to pass out before the wedding," Ramsey said.

It whooshed out of his mouth as she started walking toward him down Ramsey's carpet runner.

"She's stunning. I may nudge you out of the way and take your place," Ramsey said.

"You'd die trying." Gray felt the smile fill his face. She was going to be his. His love, his soul mate. His life.

She reached his side, and from that moment, everything was a blur. He was happy, and he hadn't even realized he wasn't before. But the feeling of joy filled him and never left as the day progressed.

After the service, they moved out to the street, where tables were set up and a trestle that held a banquet of food fit for a queen. To Gray's surprise, his mother and brother stayed and sat down with the Nightingales.

"If I may have your attention." Bram rose, tapping his glass until everyone fell silent.

Gray sat beside his wife. *His wife.* Her soft weight rested against him as she turned to look at her uncle, and he put his arm on the back of her chair, pulling her closer.

His wife.

"Thank you all for coming to celebrate the union of Gray and Ellen. My niece is to Ivy and me our daughter, as the others are our children. The man who eventually captured her heart was going to be strong, determined, and someone we would be proud to welcome into our family. Gray is that and more. I'm not sure he is ready for us, but we are ready to embrace him."

Everyone laughed, and Gray swallowed down more tears.

"Hardship often has us changing direction, but it also has us finding what we never knew we needed. To my family, I raise my glass and acknowledge your strength and courage. Your aunt and I love you all very much. Now, before I start crying, I would ask you all to stand with me and celebrate the newly married couple.

"To Gray and Ellen, we wish you every happiness!"

They ate and then danced in the streets.

"I thought my family was odd," Gray heard the Duke

of Raven say as he danced by with his duchess. "But I think these Nightingales and Crabbett Close residents run a close second. I find I like them all very much."

"Do you think we should start street parties like this one?" Cambridge Sinclair asked.

Not surprisingly, every member of his family ignored him.

Chapter 40

"Come here, Mrs. Fletcher," Gray said when they reached the front door of the home they would share, having slipped away from the wedding reception.

He'd left Ramsey deep in conversation with Nancy over the recipes for sugarplums, and Alex had been attempting to hide from Tabitha Varney.

Grabbing Ellen's wrist, he tugged her close, then swung her up into his arms. She opened the door, and he walked inside before closing it with the heel of his boot.

"Where are your staff?"

"I gave them the night off because I wanted to be alone with you, Mrs. Fletcher." Gray was sure he'd never tire of calling her that.

He walked to the stairs and up.

"Put me down!" Ellen gasped.

"No." Reaching his room, he juggled her in his arms, then opened the door. His staff had lit candles, and a tray was on a cabinet full of food and glasses of champagne. The bedcovers were drawn down.

"Oh, this is lovely."

"What can I say, I'm a romantic," Gray said, lowering her down his body.

She giggled as she walked around the room, examining every inch.

Ellen still wore her wedding dress as she said if she was only wearing it for one day, she wanted to make the most of it. Gray stood where he was and watched her.

Everything about this woman touched something inside him. Her movements were graceful, her smile infectious. He'd found his eyes on her constantly today. She'd talked to everyone in the same friendly manner. His mother or Mrs. Greedy, it didn't matter to Ellen.

"I like your home, Gray."

"Your home." He grabbed her as she passed. "Don't be nervous, my love."

"I'm not…" She exhaled. "Maybe I am a bit."

He kissed her. Easing her into it, taking her mouth on a slow, sensual journey until all the starch left her spine and she was slumped against him. Gray didn't stop, he just kept kissing her. He stroked her back and arms, getting her used to his touch.

"I want you very much, Ellen, but I would never force or frighten you."

"I know. Teach me, Gray." Her hands rested on his chest. "Show what can be between a husband and wife."

He shrugged out of his jacket and let it fall to the floor. He then pulled her closer.

"You do whatever feels comfortable, love."

"Can I touch you?" She trapped her lip between her teeth.

"I hope you will."

She slowly undid the buttons of his waistcoat and pushed it from his shoulders. Next, she worked his necktie and shirt buttons free. Spreading the sides open, she studied his chest. One hand then trailed over his skin, and he bit back a moan.

"Will you let me touch you too?" Gray asked.

She stepped back and turned for him to undo her buttons. He'd been working buttons through openings most of his life, but right then it was almost beyond him, but he managed. And with every inch he uncovered, the soft fabric of her chemise was exposed. The pale skin of the back of her neck drove his passions higher. His body was hard with the need to make her his.

When she turned to face him again, he pulled her close. Kissing her, taking her mouth on another sensual journey. Gray stroked his hand down her back over the swells of her bottom and then back up, teasing each knuckle of her spine. She shivered against him.

"Remove your chemise for me, love? Let me see you."

Ellen didn't hesitate at his words. Stepping back, she grabbed the hem and pulled it off her body.

"You're exquisite," Gray whispered, devouring what she had exposed with his eyes. He'd known Ellen was beautiful, but candlelight only enhanced that. She was a vision of lush curves and pale satin skin. Needing to touch her, he stroked the rise of her breast.

"Look at me, Ellen," Gray whispered. She lifted her eyes to his. "I love you so very much."

"I love you too."

"But I don't think you realize what you have given me, my sweet."

"What have I given you?" she whispered, her blue eyes full of love, and it humbled him that it was for Gray.

"When I first saw you that foggy London night, I thought my eyes were playing tricks on me. It was not possible you were that beautiful or spirited. Surely, I was imagining things. But you were so much more."

His fingers skimmed over her ribs.

"You have taught me to feel, my sweet. Taught me I was merely existing before you entered my life."

"Don't cry." He brushed the tear that trailed down her cheek.

"Happy tears," she said. "I too had locked away my heart and felt no one would ever have the key to release it. I was wrong."

"Ellen," he whispered her name reverently, and then no more words were needed.

Both were breathless in seconds as their kisses grew fiercer. Slowly they moved backward as one until Ellen's thighs hit the bed. She touched the waistband of his trousers, running a finger around his stomach.

"Will you take these off, Gray?"

"Are you sure?"

She nodded, and her eyes trailed over him. His chest was wide and muscled, sprinkled with hair. She leaned forward and placed a kiss above his heart, and he shuddered. Straightening, he pushed his trousers down his thighs, exposing his desire for her. Ellen's pulse quickened at the thought of what they were about to do.

"Let me be your maid." His fingers were in her hair, releasing the circlet of flowers and removing the pins. Then he was running his hands through her locks. With a gentle tug, her head fell back, and he was kissing her once more. Ellen lost the ability to think. She could only feel. His hands were on her body, tracing each curve of her breasts. His fingers stroked her nipples, sending ripples of pleasure through her.

She felt his hot breath on her neck and then lower, until he was licking the peak of one nipple.

"Just feel, love," he whispered as his hand moved lower to stroke the soft curls and then lower still. She tensed as one long finger touched the tight bud between her thighs. Desire spiked through her.

"Oh my."

"Oh my, indeed," he gritted out. The tension spiraled higher as he eased a finger inside her. Adding another, he then stroked in and out as his thumb rubbed the sensitive nub. Ellen came apart with a fierce shudder.

"Christ, you are beautiful," he whispered against her lips as he eased her back onto the bed. "And I want to be inside you very much, sweetheart."

"Yes," she whispered. "I want that too."

He climbed over her, bracing himself on his arms, and then Ellen felt the head of his erection pressing against her entrance.

"There will be some pain."

"I know." She arched up to kiss him. "Make me yours, Gray."

"Always. As I am yours."

He slid inside her slowly, and slick muscles clenched as he stroked forward. There was discomfort but also wonder. She was his now.

"Ellen," he rasped her name.

She felt his hands cup her face and stared up into his eyes as he breached the barrier of her innocence. Ellen's gasp had him stilling.

"Ssh, it will ease," he soothed.

The feeling was unusual, and she felt stretched, but there was also pleasure that she was now joined to Gray, her husband. His lips brushed hers.

"Has the pain eased?"

"Yes."

He withdrew, and the silken glide of his flesh inside Ellen stirred her body to life once more. Gray gritted his jaw as he slid back inside her. His rhythm grew faster, and tension climbed inside them both.

She felt the delicious tingles build to an almost excruciating peak, and then she was flying once more. Gray's hoarse cry met Ellen's as he threw back his head, and they soared together.

He lay on his side and pulled her back to his front. Her head pillowed on his arm. Ellen could feel the thud of his heart.

"Sleep now, my beautiful wife, and know I love you, Mrs. Fletcher."

"As I love you, Mr. Fletcher."

Ellen fell asleep smiling.

THE END

Sinclair & Raven Series

From USA Today Bestseller Wendy Vella comes an exciting Regency series about legend, love and destiny, with a hint of magic.

SENSING DANGER

He will fight his destiny

Legend says the Sinclairs heightened senses are a result of a long ago pact between them and the powerful Raven family. To Honor and Protect is their creed, but the current Duke of Raven doesn't make their task easy.

Arrogant and aloof, James, Duke of Raven, is determined to forge his own path and to hell with folk tales that his ancestors created. But when the breathtaking Eden Sinclair saves his life by risking her own, their past resurfaces, and with it comes the uncomfortable realization that they are linked by more than history.

Fate has determined she will protect him.

Eden is forced to see the man behind the cool, haughty façade when she must use her special abilities to keep him safe. His suspicion of her soon turns into something else, something far more dangerous. Eden is torn between duty and self-protection. Does she have the strength to fight fate, in order to protect her own heart?

BOOKS IN THE SINCLAIR & RAVEN SERIES

Sensing Danger
Seeing Danger
Touched By Danger
Scent of Danger
Vision Of Danger
Tempting Danger
Seductive Danger
Guarding Danger
Courting Danger
Defending Danger
Detecting Danger

Langley Sisters Series

Be swept away by the romance, intrigue, unconventional heroines, and dashing heroes, by USA Today Bestselling Author Wendy Vella's regency romance series.
The Langley Sisters Series

LADY IN DISGUISE

Will her secret bring her ruin or love?

Desperate and penniless, Miss Olivia Langley is out of options. To ensure her family's survival she and her sister decide to take a drastic step - they don masks and take to the road as highwaymen. Disaster strikes when, inside the first carriage they rob, they find the one man Olivia had hoped never to see again. Five years ago Lord William Ryder had broken Livvy's heart. Now he has returned and she has a bad feeling that if anyone can succeed at unmasking her deepest secrets, it will be him.

Can a rake reform?

Will knew his return would be greeted with both joy and resentment, but after five years of hard living he was ready to come home and take his place in society. He had never forgotten Olivia no matter how hard he'd tried, and whilst he hadn't imagined she would welcome him with open arms, the hostility and anger she displays are at odds with the woman he once knew. Will is horrified to find she's living a dangerous lie and refuses his help. But now that he's back, Will is determined to do whatever it takes to protect her, and finally claim her for his own.

BOOKS IN THE LANGLEY SISTERS SERIES
Lady In Disguise
Lady In Demand
Lady In Distress
The Lady Plays Her Ace
The Lady Seals Her Fate
The Lady's Dangerous Love
The Lady's Forbidden Love

Regency Rakes Series

Welcome to Regency England — a world of charming gentlemen, elegant ladies, and sizzling passion! Enjoy this stunning read from USA Today Bestselling author Wendy Vella.

DUCHESS BY CHANCE

He believes she betrayed him!

Daniel, Duke of Stratton, learns of his betrothal to Miss Berengaria Evangeline Winchcomb minutes before his father's death. Having gambled his fortune away, all the late Duke had left to sell was his son. To save his family's honor Daniel agrees to the marriage, but society's favorite bachelor is no longer a charming easygoing man— his father's betrayal has left him angry and with a thirst for revenge.

Has she replaced one tyrant for another?

Eva learns she is to wed the Duke of Stratton on the way to the church. Inside she feels a flicker of hope that at last she is to leave her horrid family— however that flicker is short-lived as she faces the cold unyielding man who is now her husband. Has she escaped one tyrant to be forced into marriage with another?

Is there any hope for Daniel and Eva's marriage despite coming from two completely different worlds?

BOOKS IN THE REGENCY RAKES SERIES
Duchess By Chance
Rescued By A Viscount
Tempting Miss Allender

About the Author

Wendy Vella is a bestselling author of historical and contemporary romances
such as the Langley Sisters and Sinclair and Raven series, with over two million copies of her books sold worldwide. Born and raised in a rural area in the North Island of New Zealand,
she shares her life with one adorable husband, two delightful adult children and their partners, four delicious grandchildren

Find me on www.wendyvella.com

Wendy also writes contemporary small-town romance under the name Lani Blake

Made in the USA
Coppell, TX
29 August 2023

20940990R00194